## Also by Cassandra Page

*Lucid Dreaming*

### The Isla's Inheritance trilogy
*Isla's Inheritance*
*Isla's Oath*
*Melpomene's Daughter*

# ISLA'S INHERITANCE

BOOK ONE

## CASSANDRA PAGE

www.cassandrapage.com

First published in the United States of America 2014 by Turquoise Morning Press

This edition published in Australia 2015 by Cassandra Page

The right of Cassandra Page to be identified as the author of this work has
been asserted by her under the *Copyright Amendment (Moral Rights) Act 2000.*

This is a work of fiction. Names, characters, businesses, places, events and
incidents are either the products of the author's imagination or used in a
fictitious manner. Any resemblance to actual persons living or dead, or actual
events, is purely coincidental.

Cassandra Page
www.cassandrapage.com

Cataloguing-in-Publication data available from
the National Library of Australia www.nla.gov.au

ISBN: 978-0-9944459-3-3

Formatting and cover design by KILA Designs
www.kiladesigns.com.au
Cover images: ©Shutterstock

*To my son, Nathaniel, who makes me laugh every day.*
*This is why Mummy wanted you to have long naps.*

# CHAPTER ONE

"Nice veil," the ghost commented as I entered the room. He was sprawled on a vinyl beanbag, a pair of black-and-white Chucks peeking out from under the hem of his sheet.

The ghost's voice sounded familiar, with the faintest hint of an English accent, but I couldn't place it.

"Thanks. Nice sheet, Casper." The living room was overflowing with weathered lounges and an abundance of beanbags. It was also overflowing with people, but, miraculously, one of the two-seater sofas was empty. I sat with a sigh. My boots were cute, but they weren't designed for dancing marathons.

"Don't you recognise me, Isla?" The ghost sounded hurt.

"Ah, no." That was a little unfair. All I could see of him was his eyes, which were brown, like those of most other people. Including me.

Although his were a lovely milk chocolate brown.

"It's me. Dominic."

1

*"Dommie?"* I sat up straight.

"If you must," he said, his voice dry.

"I didn't know you were back!" Dominic had been a year above me at school, in the same year as my oldest cousin, Ryan. I'd had such a crush on him when I was in year eight; the memory of my terrible love poetry made me squirm with embarrassment.

"I got back a few days ago. Been catching up with the folks," Dominic said.

"How was your grand backpacking adventure?"

"Grand," he said, a laugh in his voice. "Anyway, that's the reason for the lack of effort." He indicated his Halloween costume with a wave of his sheet.

"It could have been embarrassing. I almost wore the same thing." Uncomfortable in the short skirt Sarah had chosen for me, part of me wished I had.

"That would've been awkward. Lucky for me you decided to come as a ... goth bride?" He eyed the cheap veil that fluffed around my head.

"Close." I grinned. "I'm the Bride of Dracula. It was Sarah's idea. She got to be Dracula. We tried wearing plastic fangs as well, but those things are so uncomfortable." Plus when we tried to talk we'd spat everywhere. Ugh.

"Sarah's here too? Where is she?"

"Where do you think?" I nodded towards the other room, where a band was playing. Sarah, my other cousin, was drawn to live music like a moth to a streetlight, no matter how dreadful or, in this case, obnoxiously loud. "She'll find us when she's ready."

*"Fascist!"* a female goth sitting on the other couch shrieked, her voice cutting across our conversation.

*"Communist!"* the male goth beside her screeched back.

"Oh dear," I murmured as the girl fled, tears threatening her kohl. Her boyfriend appeared equally upset as he stormed out in the other direction, bat earrings trembling.

Conversation stopped for a moment. A ballerina and pirate emerged from their heated embrace and stared around.

"Well. That was rude." A wart-nosed witch scowled, adjusting the wire rim of her pointy hat. "I'm Emma, by the way." She gave me a little wave.

"Isla. And this is Dominic."

"We met briefly. So. You guys want to do something more exciting?" Her gesture took in the over-furnished room. The pirate and ballerina hadn't returned to their make-out session, although the ballerina seemed a little put out about it, one pink lip protruding in a pout.

"Like what?" Dominic asked.

"I don't drink," I added. Sarah and I were seventeen, although my birthday was next week and hers was in December.

"Nothing like *that*," Emma said, rolling her eyes. "Something more Halloween-y. I brought the fixings for an ouija board with me. Let's have a séance."

"No thanks," I said … at the same time Dominic said, "Sure!" He looked up. "Why not?"

"It's not really my thing."

"Scared? Don't worry, I'll protect you," Dominic assured me, reaching from beneath the sheet to take my hand.

His fingers were warm, and my resistance thawed. I hadn't seen him in almost a year; it would be churlish of me not to go along with them. Wouldn't it?

The sudden flutter of my heart in the back of my throat had nothing to do with it.

I took my hand away but smiled. "Well, okay. But don't

expect me to, you know, believe any of it or anything."

"Oh no, I wouldn't dare."

"Maybe we'll surprise you." Emma hefted a black shopping bag hand-painted with a Jack-o'-lantern design. She turned to the couple on the couch. "Did you guys want to join in?"

"Arr, we can, to be sure," the pirate enthused. The ballerina's pout grew fiercer; I worried she might trip over it if she stood up too quickly.

"Cool. Let's see if we can find somewhere quieter."

I waved to Sarah from the lounge room doorway and pointed upstairs to let her know where I was going. She waved back but kept dancing. If she was hot in the pantsuit and top hat, you couldn't tell.

Her Dracula costume was a lot more conservative than my Bride of Dracula costume. I sighed.

"What's the matter?" Dominic asked as we climbed the stairs. He held his ghost sheet up around his knees like an old-fashioned noblewoman so he wouldn't trip.

"Nothing." I tugged at the hemline of my skirt, concerned I was flashing people down the bottom of the stairs. It wouldn't go any lower.

The first room we tried was occupied—furtive movements from the bed sent us scurrying—but the second was empty. It was probably meant to be a bedroom, but the tenants had converted it to a small, cluttered games room. A low table surrounded by cushions was in the centre, a stack of board games underneath it. A folded ping-pong table leaned against the wall next to a hanging dartboard. A single bare bulb cast a dusty yellow light.

"This will do nicely." Emma sat on a cushion along one of the broad edges of the table.

"Do you mind if I de-sheet?" Dominic asked of no one in particular. "It's fine for swanning around and going 'ooh' in, but I can't see."

"Be my guest," Emma nodded, hat teetering.

Dominic's medium-brown hair was longer on top than I remembered, though still short at the sides. The longer hair was flattened by the sheet. I suppressed a smirk. "Nice to finally see you."

"Nice to see you, too." He waggled his eyebrows.

The pirate and ballerina arrived a few minutes later, each bearing a full glass of beer. "We needed a refill," the former said, plopping himself down at one end of the table. Then he remembered his pirate accent. "I be Kurt and this be me wench, Tamara."

His girlfriend sat opposite him, arms folded, leaving the long edge opposite Emma for Dominic and me. I sat, trying not to kick the battered Monopoly box under the table or flash my underwear at Emma. "So, how does this work?"

"First I have to draw up the board," Emma pulled a spiral-bound sketchbook and felt pen from her bag. She tore a blank page from the back of the book with a popping sound.

"I thought you said you had one?"

"No, I said I had the fixings for one." She started writing on the paper in a neat hand, the tip of the pen squeaking, audible over the muffled din from downstairs. "I can't afford one of those expensive wooden things. And I've always thought it would be better to have a board I didn't mind getting rid of. You know, in case something went wrong."

Tamara put her glass down on the table, her eyes widening. From the look on her face, she was regretting not sitting next to Kurt the Pirate. "What do you mean, wrong?"

"Don't worry, nothing ever has. I'm very careful."

"So what are you drawing?" Dominic asked, trying to read the paper upside down.

"We do the alphabet, numbers, some basic punctuation, and the most common words a spirit would want to use. 'Yes', 'No', that sort of thing. And a starting place."

"What sort of things could go wrong? Hypothetically?" Tamara wasn't letting Emma's comment go, whereas being a sceptic made me supremely confident in the face of the "supernatural".

"The books I've read talk about evil spirits, but I've only ever dealt with spirit guides."

"How new age," I murmured. Dominic patted my knee, and I caught my breath.

"No, it really works." Emma glanced up. "Wait and see."

"I don't think I want to wait and see," Tamara said.

"You could always sit and watch," Kurt pointed out. It sounded reasonable, but there was a challenge in his voice. "You don't have to join in."

Tamara straightened her shoulders and scowled.

By now, Emma had drawn the board in a neat hand. Letters from A to Z were in rows across the middle with the numbers 0 through 9 beneath them. Below were several words in boxes: SPACE, HELLO, GOODBYE. A full stop, exclamation mark—in case of punctuation emergencies, I supposed—and a question mark were down the side. YES and NO she wrote in two corners each, at diagonals to one another. Finally, she drew a pentagram in the top centre.

"Isn't that evil?" Dominic asked.

"That's a common misconception," Emma said, ignoring

Tamara's nervous laugh. The witch removed a couple of fat white candles and a small, cloth-wrapped bundle from her bag. "No, it's a symbol of protection from evil. That's why you see it in all the movies where people are summoning demons and stuff. It's to protect them."

"It never works."

"Not in the movies, no. That's Hollywood for you." Emma unwrapped her bundle and placed the contents on the table with a clatter. A plain scotch glass sat there, upside down.

"We're going to do shots before we start?" I raised an eyebrow.

"That's our focus point. Where we put our fingers."

Kurt snickered; Tamara gave him a dark look.

Standing, Emma put one of the candles on top of a short bookcase and the other on the windowsill. She rummaged around in her bag for a moment before pulling a face. "Anyone got matches?"

"Yarr!" Kurt the Pirate offered her a black lighter.

Once the candles were lit, Emma closed the door to the hall and turned off the overhead light. Darkness swam in and, for a few seconds, I couldn't see anything except the tiny flames. When my eyes adjusted the room seemed larger somehow, filled with deep shadows that trembled and danced in time with the flickering candle flames. The dartboard resembled a shadowy face. Emma swept around the table and resumed her seat. I glanced at Dominic, who remained perched on his cushion, eyes bright with curiosity.

He was good-looking—the candlelight leant his straight nose and perfectly formed lips an air of mystery—but not so good-looking I didn't wonder what I was doing there.

It was quieter with the door closed, but I felt the music throb through the floorboards and my thin cushion. If we were there too long I was going to get a numb butt.

"Okay." Emma rolled up her sleeves so they wouldn't trail on the table. She slid the upturned scotch glass across the paper until the pentagram was centred within it. "Everyone put a finger on top of the glass." We did. "Ready?" Without waiting for a response, Emma tilted her face towards the ceiling. "Is anyone there?"

Nothing happened.

"Is anyone there?" Emma asked again. She didn't seem worried. I glanced at Dominic, whose face had fallen.

"Is anyone there?"

The glass began to inch along the surface of the paper, picking up speed as it slid towards the YES. Tamara gasped, going white under the makeup. She looked like a porcelain doll. Or a ghost. Emma smiled, enjoying her moment. The guys watched with wide eyes.

"Welcome." Emma smiled. "What's your name?"

I studied the glass in its nest of fingers as it spelled out D-A-N-I-E-L. My eyes narrowed, searching for the whitening around the fingertips that would indicate someone was pushing the glass. Was that why Emma had turned off the light—to hide the tells?

"Hello, Daniel." Emma's smile broadened. "Daniel's my spirit guide," she added in an aside to the rest of us as the glass slid across to HELLO.

I watched with a frown as the others asked questions of "Daniel": where he was born, how he'd died, that sort of thing. I didn't pay much attention, too busy trying to see how the trick was being performed. It was a normal scotch glass and, if anyone was pushing it, they were being discreet. Emma was good.

Finally, she looked around the table at us. "Daniel can act as our intermediary to the afterlife, protecting us from evil spirits. Do any of you have relatives who've passed over that you'd like to contact? A grandparent or anything?"

"My grandpop's dead, but he was an old bastard." Kurt laughed. "I don't want to talk to him. Besides, your Daniel won't let him through if he don't like evil spirits."

Tamara shook her head, but Dominic turned to me. "Isn't your mother dead?" he asked softly.

"Yes." I looked away. I'd never known my mother. She'd died giving birth to me. But I didn't like the idea of turning her into a parlour trick.

Dominic saw my hesitation and winced, sheepish. Emma brightened, though. "What was her name?" she asked.

"Melanie," I said reluctantly. "Melanie Blackman."

"Hey, we don't have to do this if you don't want to," Dominic said.

"It's all right," I said. It wasn't real. It didn't matter.

"Melanie Blackman, are you there?" Three times Emma repeated the call, and, as before, the glass didn't move until the third time.

No.

"No?" Emma looked surprised—which was itself surprising, given she was the one moving the glass. "Melanie Blackman, are you there?"

The glass circled away from the word and back again, rattling across the paper.

No.

Obviously that wasn't meant to happen. "Daniel, are you there?"

There was a long delay while I imagined a sheet-covered ghost handing over the receiver of a telephone. YES.

"Why isn't Melanie Blackman there?"

It wasn't real. It didn't matter. But I still held my breath as I watched the glass spell out the reply.

S-H-E [SPACE] I-S [SPACE] N-O-T [SPACE] D-E-A-D.

There was a long pause. Then I stood, jerking my hand away from the glass.

"This is stupid."

I heard Emma, flustered, dismissing Daniel as I fled down into the hubbub of the party.

Dominic found me on the front lawn, taking deep breaths of the cool spring air as I tried to slow my racing heart. Tears pricked my eyes, but I blinked them away, avoiding eye contact with anyone.

The party hosts had only made a token effort to decorate. A rubber bat hung over the front door like deranged mistletoe, and Christmas fairy lights blinked cheerfully in the ground-floor windows and throughout the lower branches of the towering eucalypt on the front lawn, casting strange shadows on the grass. The night smelled of the sweet wisteria flowers engulfing a trellis on the neighbour's lawn.

"I'm sorry," Dominic said, hesitating a few feet away. He'd left his ghost sheet upstairs. "I shouldn't have mentioned your mother. It was stupid. And rude."

I glanced at him sideways, embarrassed I'd let Emma's game upset me, and even more embarrassed that anyone else had *seen* me let it upset me. I was the sensible, calm one in my family, like my dad. It was my cousins who were given to emotional displays and make believe. They were the artists. "Don't worry about it," I mumbled. I could feel my cheeks burning.

He stepped closer and hugged me. I hesitated before sliding my trapped arms around his midsection. He smelled delicious, of aftershave and soap. I hadn't hugged many men other than Dad. It was sort of nice. Dominic was taller than me—most people were—and his arms went easily around my shoulders.

I stepped back first and leaned against the tree. "I feel like a bit of an idiot, to be honest," I confessed, gazing up at the Christmas lights. Blink. Blink. "It's not like it was real."

"You don't think so?"

"Of course not. Ghosts aren't real. And my mother died when I was born. So if ghosts *were* real, she'd have been able to contact me." I realised I was attempting to make a rational argument based on superstition and closed my mouth before something even stupider fell out.

Dominic joined me against the smooth grey trunk, his shoulder touching mine as he gazed up at the lights. "I believe in ghosts."

I gaped.

"I do," he said. "When I was a kid, some mates and I used to play in the yard of an abandoned house where an old lady had died. We saw some pretty strange stuff there."

"I'm sure it all had a rational explanation though."

"Well, sure, if you want to be all Sherlock about it." He grinned.

"What I don't understand is why, if Emma was going to make something up, she'd make up something so hurtful and bizarre," I admitted after a moment. "It's not like she knows me, to have a grudge or anything."

"That does seem odd. I mean, it's easily disproved,

right? That your mum's not alive, I mean?"

"Yeah."

We fell silent for a few moments as three Disney princesses rustled up the footpath to the house. They were holding each other's arms and giggling.

Once they disappeared through the door—there was a brief blast of music and laughter—Dominic said, "It must be hard, not knowing your mother."

"Yeah," I said again, softly.

"Crap, I'm being rude again. Sorry."

"No, it's okay. It's not like I'm not used to her being gone. It was always just me and Dad."

"I thought you lived with Sarah and Ryan? And their mum?"

"I do now. But I lived with Dad till I was twelve. He has a place out in the bush, a small farm. Sheep, mostly, but chickens too. And a bad-tempered goat." A smile tugged my lips. "I moved to Canberra for school. Dad's hoping I'll get the grades to go to uni."

There was a lull inside the house; someone spoke into a microphone, distorted by bad wiring and distance, and another song began.

"It's funny," Dominic said, regarding me with a thoughtful expression.

"What is?"

"Well, Sarah's got red hair, and Ryan does too, under the dye. You can tell from the eyebrows. And they're both tall. You don't look much like them." He brushed a lock of my dark hair away from my face.

My breath caught at the gesture, sliding out of me in a sigh when his hand dropped away. I swallowed before speaking. "I know." When I was younger I was teased at school about how I must be adopted. Dad and Aunt Elizabeth were both tall with red hair, though Dad's was going strawberry blond, the colour fading with age. My aunt's probably was too, but her hairdresser was helping her with that. "Those genes run strongly in the rest of my family—apparently the rellies in England are almost all ginger too, and tall. Mum must have been a brunette shortarse like me."

"You don't know?"

I shook my head. I'd never even seen a photo of her.

"What about her family?"

"Never met them. Dad left England after I was born. He told me once he couldn't bear to stay in the place where he'd lost her." I stared at my hands. "He doesn't talk about her much."

"That doesn't seem fair," Dominic said.

"It's okay. I don't want to hurt him." But Dominic's words reflected what was in my heart. Life wasn't fair, after all. And what good would dragging up the past do?

"Hey." Dominic's fingers were warm under my chin, tipping my face up to his. "I'm sorry."

"Stop apologising!" I told him. Or started to tell him … only my sentence was cut short because suddenly he was kissing me. His hands cupped my hair through the cheap veil, drawing me into him. His lips were warm and tasted sweetly of soft drink, melting me to my toes. When I didn't pull away, he wrapped his arms around me; my head whirled.

I heard the screen door to the house slam and another brief burst of music, followed by footsteps on the grass. "Isla, are you—oops."

My face burned and I stepped to the side, out of Dominic's

arms. "Hi, Sarah."

Her top hat was askew, strands of hair hanging down around her freckled face. "Um. I heard about the séance thing and came to see if you were all right. But you clearly are." Her eyes sparkled. "I'll go."

"Is everyone talking about me storming off?" The embarrassment was back.

"Well, not *everyone*..."

"Oh." I didn't want to walk back into the house. I could easily imagine the stares and sniggers of the other girls. I didn't have Sarah's blithe self-confidence. "I might head off. I'm pretty tired."

"Okay. I'll get my stuff." Sarah didn't hesitate, even though I knew she'd be disappointed to leave. I loved her so much for that, even as I wished I had my own car so I didn't have to drag her away.

"I can give you a ride home," Dominic volunteered before she darted off.

She turned back, clearly delighted, and not because she wouldn't have to leave. The matchmaking minx. "You sure?"

"Yeah. I'll just get my sheet from upstairs and we can go. You okay with that, Isla?"

"Sure." I tried not to gush, but as soon as he was inside, Sarah gushed for me.

"Oh my god." She gave me a hug and pulled me into a little dance. "First kiss, first kiss!" she crowed.

"Shh, Sarah. Not so loud!"

"Why not?"

"Because it's not true?"

"Pecks on the playground don't count. This is great news!"

"But not that I'm seventeen and had never properly kissed a guy before," I hissed. "That's humiliating!"

"Pfft," Sarah said, but lowered her voice when I continued to glare. "You should invite him in when you get home." She waggled her eyebrows.

"*Sarah!* I've had enough firsts for one day, thank you very much."

She laughed.

# CHAPTER TWO

*T*wenty minutes later, Dominic pulled his sedan onto the verge in front of my house, putting on the handbrake but leaving the engine running. I was both disappointed and relieved—he wasn't expecting me to invite him in. The house was dark, the driveway empty; Aunt Elizabeth wasn't home. The only sign of life was Hamish, Sarah's black, rough-coated terrier, who poked his head between the curtains, watching the car.

"Thanks for the lift." I undid my seatbelt. "And for leaving early. Sorry I dragged you away."

"I don't mind. Given that I dragged you into the séance, it was the least I could do."

There was an awkward silence. I took a deep breath.

"Would you—"

"Mind if I—" Dominic said at the same time. We both laughed. "You first."

"No, you."

"Mind if I give you a call some time?" he asked. "We

could go out for coffee."

"I like coffee." I was sure I was blushing again and was glad the only light source was the headlights. I wasn't good at this dating business. If that's what we were doing. I wasn't very good at pre-dating either.

I'd say I also wasn't good at post-dating, but I hadn't yet had an opportunity to prove it.

"What's your number?"

I recited my mobile number and he programmed it into his phone, reading it back to be sure he had it right.

"That's it." I grabbed my purse and fished out my house keys. "Thanks again for the ride."

"You're welcome." He grinned. "I hope the evening wasn't too ghoulish."

I laughed, shaking my head, and slid out, closing the door behind me. Dominic leaned over to wave through the window, his lips quirked in a smile. I waved back and began to pick my way to the front door across the grass. It crunched under my boots.

Hamish barked, his high-pitched yapping distorted by the window as he danced on his back legs, scratching the glass.

And someone ran at me from the bushes bordering the neighbour's property.

I leapt sideways as the figure approached, sniffing as though he had a cold. He was about my height, with a strange face and long ears partly obscured by a hoodie. I tripped and fell backwards onto the grass. Pain shot up my arms.

"Hey!" Dominic jumped from his car. A brief scuffle ensued, and the hooded figure darted away, disappearing into the bushes.

"Are you okay?" Dominic's hand warmed my fingers, helping me to my feet. My palm stung in his grip.

"I ... I think so." My heart raced. "Who was that?"

"I don't know. A kid in a Halloween mask, I think. He had pointed ears and a wrinkly face. Like an alien. But not green."

"Bastard." My laugh shook as I examined my wrists. Bits of grass were embedded into my palms, and the makings of a bruise blossomed beneath the surface. I felt like an idiot. Again. That was the theme for the evening. "Thanks for coming to my rescue."

"My pleasure," he said, handing me my purse and keys. "Shall I see you to your door, ma'am?" he asked with a little bow.

"Yes. Please."

He stuck by my side as I walked up the half-dozen stairs to the door. The porch light turned on with a soft click, the keys jangling as I opened the lock with a trembling hand. Hamish poked his head out and gave Dominic's shoe a sniff before staring at the bushes, ears pricked.

"Thanks." I looked up at Dominic, feeling like a broken record.

"You're welcome," he said. My heart lurched as he brushed a soft kiss across my lips. Disappointment stirred my insides as he stepped back. "I'll call you."

I stepped into the hall and locked the door, unable to stop myself from turning and watching Dominic through the window. He hurried back across the lawn to his still-idling car. He was tall, lean and neatly dressed, even though under his sheet he could've gotten away with scruffy clothes. I caught my gaze straying to the seat of his jeans—they hugged his butt in a way that made my stomach flutter with butterflies—as he rounded the back of his car. Laughing softly at myself, I flicked on the hall light.

Hamish trotted at my heels as I walked to the bathroom, turning on all the lights as I went. I wasn't scared of the dark, but adrenalin pumped through my veins as though driven by a steam engine. It made me feel better to be able to see everything around me—even though I knew, if there was a stranger in the house, Hamish would have alerted me. Loudly.

Putting my purse and keys on the basin, I washed my hands, rinsing off the grass and bits of dirt clinging to my palms. The skin was dimpled from the impact. I splashed water on my face and winced as I brushed the hairspray from my hair. Satisfied with the lack of makeup and with my hair sticking on end, I went to bed.

Once I was curled under the covers, wearing an oversized *Big Bang Theory* T-shirt and satin boxer shorts, with my childhood teddy bear, Mister Monkey, nestled into the corner of the bed, I realised I had forgotten to brush my teeth. But I decided not to get up. My lips still tasted sweetly, of soft drink and Dominic, and I didn't want to lose the sensation.

I smiled in the dark, drifting off to sleep.

I was dreaming.

I didn't often know when I was dreaming, but there was something vivid about this dream; it lacked the hazy and disjointed feeling of my usual nocturnal ramblings. Although it was typically surreal.

I stood in the middle of a huge hall, wearing a ball gown of black silk; like the distant ceiling above, the fabric was flecked with starlight. A questing touch revealed the stars to be hard stones, like diamonds, except they sparkled with their own inner light. The skirt was full and wide, and whispered against the floor as I moved. My hands were sheathed to the elbow in gloves of the same silken material.

The other figure in the room—he wasn't there a moment ago, was he?—was a man dressed in a thousand shades of brown, a motley made of what appeared to be sackcloth. His face was a scarecrow mask, and he had long pointed ears.

The sackcloth jester was speaking, but I couldn't hear what he was saying. He paused, waiting for me to respond. I shrugged at him. "I can't hear you." My voice echoed.

He frowned, the sackcloth forehead furrowing, and gestured for me to turn around.

Behind me stood a full-length oval mirror, mounted on a stand. The frame was carved in hand-chased silver. That *definitely* wasn't there a moment ago.

My reflection was astonishing. It was as though someone had taken my photo and altered it in a number of small ways that, cumulatively, made me look quite different. Awake, I wouldn't have chosen to wear a dress with such a low neckline. The black fur stole around my shoulders did nothing to cover my cleavage, which was never so prominent in real life. Dream-me must be wearing an excellent bra.

My hair, worn loose and woven with more of the starlight stones on silver chains, wasn't brown but black as midnight, framing a face never so dainty in real life. My eyes were deep ebony, my lips blood-red. If it weren't for the colour of the gown, I'd look like Snow White.

When my gaze locked with that of my reflection, it began to move independently. I gasped, taking a step back as the reflection's eyes narrowed to stare at me so intently I thought it might reach through the glass and lock its gloved fingers around my throat. Its lips curled, and when it spoke I heard the word flatly through the glass.

"*You!*"

The mirror shattered, and I fell...

I awoke with the creepy-crawly sense I was being watched. The sight of a human perched on the end of my bed made my pulse jump in my throat, but then the figure shifted and I realised with a trembling sigh that it was Sarah, dressed in lime green pyjamas. Not some crazy reflection made of broken glass.

Sarah leaned forward. "You okay? Did I scare you?"

"What did you expect, waking me up like that?" I grumbled, running my hands over my face to brush away the cobwebs of sleep.

"Sorry," she said, her tone unrepentant.

"I had the weirdest dream. It was me ... but not me. Prettier. Except I don't think she liked me very much."

Sarah blinked. I opened my mouth to explain further and closed it again. The details of the dream were already starting to fade ... although the expression on my reflection's face stayed with me, as clear as Sarah's perplexed scrunch of her forehead.

I glanced at the clock. It was just after seven am. "Why

are you waking me?"

"I had to know. What happened with Dominic?"

"Nothing. Well, not like you mean." I sat up, rubbing my eyes before explaining our encounter with my mask-wearing attacker.

"And he rushed to defend you? How romantic." Sarah clutched her hands to her chest and sighed, fluttering her eyelashes.

"Oh, shut up. He thinks I'm an idiot, the way I fell on my butt."

"Guys dig the whole damsel in distress thing," she contradicted me. "It makes them feel all macho."

"Well, it made me feel like an idiot." I stretched. "And sore. If I could get my hands on the... I wonder what he wanted?"

"Given the mask, I'd guess to freak you out. Or maybe he was taking advantage of Halloween to wear a mask and steal people's purses." Her eyes widened. "He didn't steal your purse, did he?"

"No. Just my dignity."

"Shame. I was hoping you'd tell me Dominic stole your virtue."

She squawked when Mister Monkey hit her in the face.

Sundays were quiet in the Kent household. Aunt Elizabeth pottered away in the garden. She had an amazing green thumb, and, although neither her children nor I had inherited the talent, we could still appreciate the blooming roses in the back yard and the cool shade under the trees. Ryan was sequestered in the shed he'd converted, with his mother's grudging permission, into a studio where he could paint undisturbed by "you women", as he referred to the rest of us, tongue only partly in cheek.

Sarah and I had a maths test looming. I was studious by nature—I got reasonable grades because of hard work, not natural talent—but even Sarah was intimidated into studying for the exam. We spread our textbooks out on the kitchen table and tapped away on our calculators.

When the house phone rang, I scrambled to answer it, thoughts of Dominic filling my head before I realised he had my mobile number, not the home one.

"Hello?" I tried not to sound too disappointed, but it didn't work.

"I'm glad to talk to you too, pumpkin," my father laughed on the other end of the line.

"Oh. Hi, Dad. Sorry, I was expecting someone else."

"A boy?"

"Maybe."

"Why don't you call him?"

"I didn't get his number," I muttered. At the table, Sarah rolled her eyes. We'd already had that conversation. She wanted me to email him; I didn't want to look needy.

"Well, I'm sure he'll ring soon enough. Have you thought about where you'd like to go on Wednesday?"

"*Prime Time*," I said, naming my favourite Canberra steakhouse. They did the most fantastic slow-cooked steaks there, with different toppings. Yum. I wasn't one of those eat-like-a-bird girls; I liked my food too much.

"Done. I'll be there at six. Tell your aunt."

"Okay."

I'd no sooner sat down and picked up my pen when my mobile buzzed its way across the table. Sarah tried to grab it, but I was faster.

Unknown number. My heart jumped into my throat again.

"Hello?"

"Hi Isla, it's Dominic."

"Hi," I said, hoping I didn't sound as strangled as I suspected I did. I gave Sarah a thumb's up. She grinned back.

"How are you feeling after last night?"

"I'm fine. My wrists are a bit achy, but no lasting damage."

"I'm still angry about that." There was a pause, and it dawned on me that Dominic might be nervous too. The thought made me feel a bit better.

"Well, if you see him, you can go all superhero on his butt," I said. Sarah groaned, but Dominic's laugh sounded genuine. I poked my tongue out at her and went to my room, shutting the door—although I had no doubt she'd tiptoe up and press her ear to it.

"So, I heard it was your birthday soon. Got anything big planned?"

"Just a family dinner on Wednesday. That's the big day." I lay on my bed.

"No party?"

"Nah. I might have a joint party with Sarah next month, but no big party just for me. You saw how spectacularly I went last night." The idea people might still be talking about me storming out of the séance made my face burn.

"That was my fault," Dominic protested.

"Not really. That sort of stuff always happens to me."

"Crazy ouija board stuff?" he teased.

"Well, okay, not *that* sort of stuff." I laughed. "But I'm happy with something smaller."

"Hmm." Another pause. "How about I take you out for coffee and birthday cake after dinner on Wednesday night?"

I closed my eyes for a second and successfully suppressed a squeal of delight. Go me. "That'd be … really nice. I'll probably have cake at the restaurant, but I could always have seconds with you."

"Second desserts are made of win."

We organised for him to pick me up at *Prime Time* at nine o'clock, and talked for a few more minutes before he had to go.

After I hung up the phone I lay there for several seconds, heart racing. He'd just asked me on a date. I couldn't believe it!

It was going to be even harder to concentrate on studying now.

# CHAPTER THREE

*O*n Wednesday, Dad arrived right at six. I was sitting backwards on one of the dining chairs, arms resting on its back; Sarah stood behind me with a hair straightener. She'd refused to let me just put my hair in a ponytail. At this point I was too jittery to care.

"Happy birthday, pumpkin," Dad said as he strode in the back door. Despite living almost two decades in Australia, he still had a noticeable Queen's English accent, more obvious than Aunt Elizabeth's.

His blue eyes sparkled, surrounded by deep laugh lines. He'd forgone his usual scruffy jeans and flannel for black slacks and a forest-green, collared shirt that made him look years younger. "You look great," he said at the same moment I did. We both laughed.

After much consultation with Sarah and our friends from school, Kim and Natalie, I'd settled on a black lace-knit top and boot-cut jeans, as well as the same black leather boots I'd worn to the Halloween party. They had a bit of a heel, making me taller than my flat-footed five foot two. As Sarah pointed out, that was a plus if there was going to be more kissing. Kim, who was no taller than me, had agreed emphatically.

"Thanks, Dad." I smiled, turning my face up so he could kiss my cheek. Sarah grumbled, adjusting the straightener. "Did you see my bracelet?" I knew he hadn't, but I wanted to show off my gift. I held out my arm with a grin.

Sarah had given me the silver charm bracelet for my birthday. Two sterling silver beads were strung on the snake-like chain when I opened Sarah's gift. Kim and Natalie had added two, leaving space for at least a dozen more. Cherishing the glittering treasure wasn't hard.

"Very nice." He turned to Sarah. "Where's your mother?"

"Her room, I think," Sarah said.

"He could have at least pretended to be interested," I grumbled once he'd disappeared down the corridor.

Sarah turned my head with one hand so she could keep steaming my hair. "They're discussing your present, probably. They have something planned, but they wouldn't tell me what."

"That's 'cause you're no good at keeping secrets."

"Am too," she protested. "I kept the secret about the bracelet, didn't I?"

"True. But I think your mum's still blaming you for blabbing about Ryan's new bike."

"I was seven!" She sounded wounded.

"I didn't mind," Ryan grinned, coming in the door. His hair stood in damp spikes from the shower, and he'd dressed in clean jeans and a black shirt. He looked much less scruffy than usual. "It gave me something to look forward to. Hey, cuz, looking good."

"Thanks." I winced as Sarah tugged my hair.

Soon we were ready to go. I brushed my now straightened and loose hair back from my eyes as we trooped outside. My stomach didn't know whether to be hungry or nervous. I hoped my nerves about meeting Dominic didn't ruin my appetite—I'd been looking forward to this meal all week—and then had to laugh at myself. If all I could do was fret about my date, better to put it from my mind until it was time to meet him.

Or try to, at least.

Sarah, Ryan and I started towards Aunt Elizabeth's sedan, but my father and aunt hung back. When we turned back, they were both smiling. "We thought we might take two cars to the restaurant," Dad said, holding out a set of keys.

Sarah twigged before I did. "Are you giving her a *car*?"

"Well … yes."

"Where is it?"

Dad pointed down the driveway to a small hatchback parked at the curb under the lone streetlight. I ran over to get a closer look, my cousins on my heels.

The car was a cute little four-door in medium blue, and I loved it instantly and completely. I jumped into the driver's seat as soon as Dad handed me the keys, running my hands over the steering wheel and dashboard, admiring the soft grey upholstery. I was unable to believe the generosity of the gift. It was an older model and smelled of air freshener, but I didn't care. I had a *car*.

"So what do you think?" Dad bent to look through the open door.

"I love it," I beamed, getting out and wrapping my

arms around his neck. "I love it. But..." I took a deep breath. "Dad, are you sure about this?"

"Of course I am," he replied, gently disengaging my arms so he could look me in the eyes. "I've saved for this since you were sixteen, and your aunt paid for the registration and insurance as her gifts to you."

"They're paid up for twelve months," Aunt Elizabeth added, standing a few feet back up the driveway. "After that, you're on your own." She smiled to soften her words.

"That's fine," I said, stepping closer to wrap my arms around her slender neck. "Thanks so much, both of you."

"Are we going?" Sarah called from the front passenger seat, peering out the driver's door at us. She and Ryan had sorted out the matter of shotgun; Ryan was wedged into the back seat, a disgruntled look on his face.

I glanced at my benefactors, and Dad waved me towards the car. "Go. We'll meet you at the restaurant."

"Thank you," I said, kissing him on the cheek before dancing back to the car. My car!

I cherished every moment of getting in: putting on the seatbelt, adjusting the seat and mirrors, turning the key and listening to the engine purr to life.

"It's got a tape deck," Sarah pointed out as the dashboard lit up.

"That's okay," I said, fiddling with the dial. Dad had programmed it to one of the local AM radio stations, so I flicked it to the FM band and found my favourite music station. "That's what Triple J's for."

"That's got to be the first time your father hasn't given you a sculpture or something else he's made," Sarah said, riffling through the glove box.

"Probably not the first time ever, but recently, yeah,"

I agreed. Dad's main hobby, other than obsessively following his football team, was ironwork. I had a daunting collection of coat hooks, towel racks, heavy jewellery, bells and particularly candleholders. I loved my father and that he enjoyed his hobby, but there was a limit to how many candleholders a girl needed. Most of mine were on a shelf in the back of Aunt Elizabeth's shed. It was a wonder there was room in there for Ryan's paint supplies.

The drive to the restaurant was hair-raising for someone who still lacked confidence in her driving, given we were on the tail end of peak hour and it was dusk. But I also felt a pang of regret when I parked the car. Burgeoning affection made me pat the blue hood as I walked around its front. My cousins didn't bother to stifle their laughter at that.

Dad and Aunt Elizabeth were already in the restaurant, sitting at a booth along the back wall. They waved and we headed over, inhaling the delicious smells of cooking meat and Cajun spices. I slid in beside Dad and Sarah sat beside me.

*Prime Time*'s decor was based on the pun of their name. Heavy timber furniture padded with dark cushions provided the foundation, gleaming softly under the subdued lighting you'd expect from a steakhouse. In contrast, the walls were lined with bright posters and memorabilia from popular television shows. Novelty clocks, autographed posters, props in glass cases and even a street sign filled the spaces between tables. Actual televisions were mounted at various points around the room, showing reruns, but the sound was muted. We wouldn't have been able to hear them anyway. While I loved the timber furniture, the scraping of chairs on hard floor contributed to the noise made by conversation and clinking cutlery on plates.

We chattered as I pretended to look at the menu. I'd decided what I wanted days ago—medium-rare steak smothered in béarnaise sauce. It didn't get any better than that—taste-wise, at least. I'm sure a health nut would disapprove. But it was my birthday, so screw it.

I did order a Coke Zero though.

Once we'd ordered, Ryan reached into his jacket pocket and produced an untidily wrapped gift. "I hope you like it," he said, sliding it across the table.

With clamped lips, I held back the squeal building behind my teeth when I saw a pretty purple MP3 player in a black case. He'd painted a tiny rose on the back of the case. I ran a wondering finger over its scarlet petals and sharp-looking green thorns, feeling the subtle contours of the paint.

"Once you get some portable speakers you have an alternative to the car's tape player." Ryan grinned.

"Wait a minute." Sarah's voice rose. "You knew she was getting a car *and you didn't tell me?*"

"Coincidence," Ryan replied, but the sparkle in his eyes indicated he was lying.

Sarah inhaled to say something explosive, and Aunt Elizabeth opened her mouth to scold, but Dad cut in over both of them. "I have another gift for you as well," he said.

"Dad, you've been too generous already."

"Well, I can't let a special occasion go by without inflicting some of my 'art' on you," he teased. It was so close to what I was thinking on the drive over that my ears burned. Ryan snorted, and Sarah kicked him hard under the table. He winced.

Dad handed me a gift bag, and its weight gave away its general contents even if I hadn't been forewarned. The present was a circle of dark metal as wide as the span of my hand, with a numeral 18 in the middle. The circle and the number were all one piece. He'd attached a separate loop to the top, so I could hang it from the wall if I wanted to. Unlikely, but I admired his optimism, as well as the talent it took to make the gift in the first place.

"Thank you, Dad," I said, giving him a kiss on the cheek.

"You're welcome, Isla Rose." He smiled. "I'm so proud of you, honey. You're all a father could want in a little girl."

"She's not a little girl anymore," Ryan pointed out, fidgeting with his napkin. "That's sort of the point of this dinner."

"Children are always little boys and girls to their parents," Aunt Elizabeth said, brushing Ryan's hair behind his ear.

"Muuuum!" Ryan did sound like a little boy then, and we all laughed.

Dinner was delicious, and Dad managed to refrain from telling too many embarrassing stories from when I was a kid. I almost managed to forget about my date, although I did regularly peek at my watch to make sure I wasn't going to miss meeting Dominic. When it came time to order dessert I held off; despite my earlier jokes about having two desserts, I didn't want to get to wherever we were going and discover I was too full to have something. Or, worse, eat something to be polite and then feel sick.

Everyone else ordered, though. I was a little jealous at the idea of the giant fudge sundae Dad requested with a grin. Fortunately I would have to go before it arrived, so at least I wouldn't have to watch him eat it.

When I got up at quarter to nine to freshen up my makeup, Sarah followed me into the bathroom.

"Oh my god, are you excited?" She hovered behind me as I leaned forward to check my eye shadow in the mirror before fishing my compact out of my bag.

I rolled my eyes at her, which she took as assent.

"I wish I could come with you," she said.

"Awkward."

"Not to sit at the table! I could watch from across the room."

"And you think that somehow makes it less awkward?" I raised an eyebrow at her reflection.

She thought about that for a moment. "Good point. Will you text me if anything interesting happens?"

"Probably not."

"Cow." She punched my shoulder and I laughed.

When we got back to the table, Dad was standing. "Do you want me to come and wait outside with you?"

"No," I gasped, taking a breath and trying not to look horrified. Poor Dominic would be frightened off by my bear of a father in a heartbeat.

"I don't like the idea of you waiting alone outside," Dad said.

"David, she's an adult now, remember?" Aunt Elizabeth pointed out. I tried to hide my sigh of relief. When Dad continued to look reluctant, Ryan spoke. "I'll go wait with her."

"Ooh, me too," Sarah volunteered quickly.

"Just Ryan will be fine, thanks," I replied just as quickly. Sarah's capacity for overwhelming enthusiasm was as great as my father's was for looming. As much as I loved them both, I didn't want them making me feel any more awkward than I already did. Not to mention the effect they'd have on Dominic. Ryan was so relaxed he wouldn't be intimidating, and he and Dominic knew each other.

"But—" Sarah looked rebellious.

"Sit!" Aunt Elizabeth said.

Sarah flounced into her chair, looking petulant as Ryan stood to follow me.

I knew she'd forgiven me when I got a text from her as we were walking out the door. *Cow.*

*Moooo,* I sent back.

Full night had settled but, when I craned my neck to look at the sky, I could only see a handful of stars. The rest were bleached out by city lights. I slid my hands through the sleeves of my trench coat, bristling at the satin lining's chill. The air was cooling rapidly. There might even be dew on the grass by dawn.

I felt silly asking Ryan to stand with me, but knew if I sent him back in I'd have to cope with Dad or Sarah. Or both. So instead I smiled. "Thanks for this."

"No worries. Good to get some fresh air." He slipped his hands into his jeans pockets and rocked back and forth on his heels. I went back to scanning the car park across the street for Dominic.

"So are you eighteen yet?" Ryan asked me after a few minutes of silence. I gave him a puzzled look. "I mean, has the actual time passed when you were born?"

"I don't know. Probably." I glanced at my watch again. It was one past nine.

"Feel any older? More mature or anything?" His eyes sparkled.

"Nope." Even though I'd known it was silly, I'd wondered if maybe I would. But I felt the same as I had the day before. It was a little disappointing. I guess part of me had hoped there'd be some flash of insight: a revelation of what I was meant to do for the rest of my life. Or next week's lottery numbers. Something.

"Isn't that Dominic?"

Ryan's question startled me from my reverie and I peered towards the car park again. He was right. My date—*eep*—was making his way across the lot. My stomach rolled over and tried to hide behind my spine.

"Relax. Dominic's a good guy." Ryan took my hand, squeezing it reassuringly. My fingers sparked, as though an electric shock had leapt from me to him.

"Ow," Ryan said. I felt dizzy, grabbing his arm for support. "Are you okay?"

Even as he spoke, the vertigo evaporated. I released his arm, embarrassed. "Uh. I'm fine." Did Aunt Elizabeth's coat have a nylon lining? I'd been sure it was satin. That'd be my luck. For my next trick, I will electrocute my date with the power of static electricity.

Dominic wore the same Chucks he'd had on at the Halloween party, this time paired with stonewashed jeans and a grey, collared shirt. A leather jacket was slung over one arm, and his hair was neat except for a spiky fringe. Would the fringe would be crunchy or soft to run my fingers through? Would I get to find out?

"Happy birthday." Dominic grinned and leaned forward to kiss me on the cheek. He smelled of aftershave and mints. A different kind of tingle fluttered in my belly.

"Thanks." Was I blushing again? Or still? Dammit!

Ryan and Dominic shook hands and exchanged greetings. My phone buzzed in my pocket. *He looks good.* The message was from Sarah. I glanced over my shoulder to see her peering out the restaurant window, her phone in her hand and a grin on her face.

*Stalker,* I sent back. The window was thick enough to block her squeal of outrage.

"So where are you going?" Ryan asked Dominic.

"I thought we could go to *Jean-Claude's*," Dominic replied, naming one of the better French patisseries in Canberra. He turned to me. "I figured we could walk there, have cake, and afterwards I could drop you home."

"I've got a car." I tried to sound cool about it, but my fresh excitement betrayed me. "It was a present from my dad."

"Wow, your dad's awesome."

"No kidding." I grinned.

"Where are you parked?" he asked. I pointed across the road, to the same car park he'd come from. "Okay, well I can walk you back to your car instead."

"Done."

"Have fun," Ryan said, giving me a hug. "Call if you need anything," he whispered in my ear. He was taking his impromptu role of protector seriously. It was reassuring, although I didn't get the sort of vibe off Dominic that made me think I needed it.

I nodded to Ryan and he went back inside, shooing Sarah away from the window as he entered the restaurant.

Within a few seconds, Dominic and I were alone on the street.

"Ready?" Dominic offered me his arm and, smiling, I looped mine through his. Goosebumps shivered along my arm.

"So how has your day been?" he asked.

"Good," I replied. "I'd have preferred not to go to school, but at least my friends were there."

"You should've taken the day off."

"Finals start next week." I shrugged. "It's my last year. Some of my teachers have started reviewing, so I can't afford to miss it."

"Fair enough," he said after a moment. "I remember how freaked out I was during my last semester."

"How'd you cope?"

"Caffeine. Lots of caffeine." His smile flashed bright under the streetlights.

When we arrived at *Jean-Claude's*, my heart sank. All the tables were full or had reserved signs. But Dominic had planned ahead. One of the reserved signs, in a small two-person booth in the back corner, was for us. Sliding in to sit beside him, I hid a grin behind my hand at the realisation he'd thought ahead. Maybe I wasn't the only one who'd been nervous.

The café wasn't as noisy as *Prime Time*, despite crowding a similar number of people into a smaller space. The decor was a combination of brown and cream that made me feel like I was inside a chocolate éclair, and the air smelled of sweet baked goods and cooking fruits.

A pretty waitress with blond hair tied back in a braid brought us a menu. She handed it to Dominic with a wide smile, ignoring me. Was she hitting on him?

Hips swaying rather more than was necessary, the waitress walked away to serve another table. *Yep, definitely hitting on him.* I smiled when Dominic didn't seem to notice. After a brief glance, he handed me the menu. "Ladies first."

"Why, thank you, sir."

The menu contained all of the usual, delicious, suspects—croissants, danishes, éclairs and tarts, as well as savoury items like quiches. "Should I have chocolate lava cake or mocha cake?" I wondered aloud.

"Why don't we get both and share?" Dominic offered.

I beamed at him. "My hero."

We ordered cakes—*moelleux au chocolat* and *gâteau moka*, the blond waitress corrected when I ordered them in English—and coffee. Conscious of the fact I'd already overshared about my family on our previous meeting and not wanting to seem self-centred, I quizzed him about where he'd gone during his backpacking adventures. It turned out he'd travelled around the United Kingdom, working in pubs to pay his way. His favourite place was Ireland, because of the friends he'd made.

"So what are you going to do now?" I asked him.

"Not sure," he shrugged. "I'm thinking I'll try and get a job in a pub or restaurant to start with. Maybe look at getting a hospitality diploma. I enjoyed working with people when I was overseas. You?"

"Me?"

"Yeah, you said your father was hoping you'd go to uni, but have you given it any thought?"

I looked down at my hands. "I haven't decided. I think I'll do okay, entry score-wise, but … it's such a huge decision. What I want to do for the rest of forever."

"I know." He took one of my hands in his. "That's why I went abroad for a year. I had no idea when I graduated."

Tension flowed from my shoulders at his touch. I curled my fingers around his, and deep questions about my future vanished like Hamish at bath time.

"Your desserts," the waitress said, arriving at the worst possible time and plonking the two plates down between us so we had to let go. She sounded a little annoyed—she was far less attractive when she scowled. Dominic frowned as the waitress swished off to get our coffees.

Still, both desserts looked fabulous and smelled even better, chocolate creations that almost made me forgive the waitress for flirting with my date. Almost.

"I don't think we're going to be able to cut the lava cake in half," I said, mouth watering as I curled my hand around my spoon. "How about you eat half and then we swap plates?"

"Okay," Dominic agreed. "But where are we going to put the candle?"

"Candle?"

He reached into his pocket and pulled out a small pink candle sitting in a plastic stand with a spike on the bottom, like a tiny golf tee. "Candle, see? Can't have birthday cake without a candle."

"Oh. Um. In the mocha cake, I guess. But please don't sing."

Dominic looked hurt. "Did someone warn you about my voice?"

"No!" I gasped. "It's the soul-crushing embarrassment of everyone staring at me. I hate it. I'm a wimp, I know."

"It's okay," he laughed, "I'm kidding. But I won't sing, I promise. It's better for everyone that way."

He wedged the candle into the gooey top of the mocha cake before producing a lighter and lighting the wick. "Quick, blow it out before Grumpy comes back and scolds me," he urged, eyes sparkling.

I closed my eyes to make a wish, and blew out the candle with a quick puff. A thin tendril of smoke unfurled.

"Happy birthday." Sliding the cake back, Dominic leaned across the corner of the table and kissed me. I shivered at the soft warmth of his lips, the brush of his tongue against mine.

"Are you okay?" he asked, in a low, teasing voice when we parted.

"Sure. Just didn't expect my wish to come true quite so soon." I laughed, flustered.

He grinned, and kissed me again. I could get used to this whole kissing thing.

"Your coffees," said Grumpy. I started to move away, but Dominic kissed me for another couple of seconds before looking up at the waitress.

"Thanks," he said brightly.

She huffed and walked away.

"She got out of the wrong side of the bed this morning," he said.

"She was trying to flirt with you," I pointed out.

"She was?" He sounded surprised.

I nodded, cutting a piece of cake off the slice with my spoon and popping it into my mouth so he wouldn't see the anxiety on my face.

"Hmm." He looked after her for a moment before shrugging. "Well, she's not my type anyway."

"What type is that?" I held my breath.

"It's an Isla-shaped type," he said, smiling.

It was a wonder I didn't melt onto the floor.

After we'd eaten, Dominic surprised me with a present. The familiar blue pouch nestling in his hands was a pretty big clue—it bore the same jewellery store logo as the ones Kim and Natalie had given me earlier. Sarah *was* meddlesome.

Sure enough, the gift was another silver bead for my charm bracelet, this one a tiny elf clutching a daisy-like flower. It was adorable.

"Thank you so much."

But when I went to put the bead onto my bracelet with the others, the bracelet was gone. It wasn't under the table, either, or in my purse. My stomach sunk through the floor—it was such a thoughtful gift from my friends; what if I couldn't find it? "It must have fallen off after we left the house," I moaned.

"It's okay, we'll find it," Dominic said, trying to be reassuring as he scanned the aisle between our table and the door. "Let me pay and we'll walk back to *Prime Time.*"

"I can pay for half," I offered, reaching for my purse.

He waved my offer away. "It's your birthday."

The walk back to the steakhouse was nowhere near as pleasant as the walk there; although Dominic held my hand, I was too busy scanning the path and verge for hints of silver to enjoy the moment. The closest thing I found was the silver foil from the inside of a cigarette packet, which I threw into a bin in disgust. What if someone had already found my bracelet and taken it?

The others had already left, but the waitress who'd served us helped check under the table and in the booth where we'd sat. No luck. Almost in tears, I gave them my details in case anyone found the bracelet. I considered texting Sarah to ask her to check around the house, but I didn't want to tell her I'd lost my present. Not until I'd searched everywhere.

The walk back to the car also produced nothing; Dominic had a small flashlight on his key ring and ran its beam along the ground between the cars. When we got to my little car, I hugged him, sad not just because I'd lost my gift but because I felt like I'd ruined the end of our date. "I'm sorry." I apologised, wiping away a tear.

He looked surprised. "What on earth for?"

"For getting all emo on you."

"Rubbish," he said, kissing the tip of my nose. "This isn't emo. You should meet my sister."

I nodded, scuffing the gravel with the toe of my boot.

"Hey, chin up. I'll walk back to *Jean-Claude's* one more time, to make sure we didn't miss anything in the dark. Text me when you get home so I know you got there okay?"

"Okay." I watched him walk away, cheered a little by how sweet he was being.

My hand brushed along the rough carpet under the driver's seat, checking for my treasure. Nothing. Even the pleasure of driving my own car couldn't lift my heart from my boots. Sarah would be upset that I'd lost my gift, especially since she'd gone to so much trouble making sure everyone chipped in. By the time I parked out the front of our house, I felt two inches tall. The bushes rustled; I scowled at them. I'd almost welcome another confrontation with my attacker from Halloween. It would suit my mood. But nothing emerged from the screen of plants, so I trudged up the driveway.

When I saw the telltale gleam of silver sitting in a small pile on the doormat, I gasped. Sure enough, my bracelet was there, glittering under the porch light. I scooped it up and checked to make sure it was intact. It had come unfastened right on our doorstep. How lucky! I resolved to buy a safety clasp the next day.

Sarah was waiting inside the door when I came in.

"How was it?" she demanded.

"Wonderful. Until I made an idiot of myself." I explained about the lost bracelet, still embarrassed, but relieved

I'd found it.

"I'm sure I would've seen it if it'd been there when we got home." Sarah frowned.

"I guess you were distracted. It's lucky no one stepped on it and broke the chain."

"True." She looked dubious, but then shrugged. "But how sweet of Dominic to go back and check again."

"Yes, it was. And look what he got me." I handed her the extra charm and she feigned surprise, turning it over in the palm of her hand and grinning.

I fished my phone out of my purse, noticing as I did several increasingly impatient messages from Sarah that I hadn't heard over the ambient noise at *Jean-Claude's*. "I better let him know I found it."

About thirty seconds after I'd sent him the message, as I was threading the new bead onto the charm bracelet, I got a reply.

*Great news! Had a good time tonight. Call you tomorrow?*

*Okay,* I replied, smiling.

# CHAPTER FOUR

*O*ver the next few weeks the weather gave us the first taste of summer. The entire exam period was marked by hot days and warm nights. Sarah and I often studied on the back porch in the evenings, enjoying the warm breeze and turning the back light on after sunset. The evening sounds were relaxing: the distant traffic; the *tick-tick-tick* of a moth throwing itself at the porch light; a magpie carolling its evening serenade; and even the thrashing metal of Ryan's music, audible despite the closed window of the shed down the back of the yard. The air smelled of pine and eucalypts, grilled steak and the lit citronella candle perched on the porch's railing in a ceramic dish.

The night before our final exams, Sarah and I studied on the porch. Sarah's battered copy of *A Midsummer Night's Dream* lay open in front of her on the glass tabletop, several pages folded to mark key passages—or maybe bits that tickled her fancy—and I was rereading Poe between casting sneaky glances at the beautiful orange and purple sunset. We'd finished dinner: lasagne and a garden salad. Ryan hadn't emerged from the shed to join us despite being called, and Sarah and I had read at the table while we ate, so it wasn't much of a family gathering.

That's probably what Aunt Elizabeth was thinking when she saw me fidgeting at the table. "Be a dear, Isla, and tell my oldest if he doesn't come and get his dinner soon, I'll be taking it to work tomorrow for lunch and he'll be having toast. I'll make us some tea." We hadn't seen paint-stained hide nor dyed hair of Ryan for days. Sarah and I were pretty busy, and he was a night owl at the best of times. Even his job usually had evening hours.

I slipped on my shoes, walking down the wooden stairs and along the path to the shed. The music was loud enough the metal walls vibrated. How could Ryan concentrate? The sound coming off the small building reminded me of a shoe stuck in a dryer. Thump, thump, *kerplunk*, thump, thump, *kerplunk*. Maybe loud music was part of his "artistic process" or something.

I banged on the door and waited, wondering if he could hear me over the growling singer.

My knuckles stung as I rapped them against the metal walls a second time. A third.

"Just go in," Sarah called from the porch.

I hesitated a moment longer. It went against the grain to go into anyone's private space uninvited. Besides, what if he was doing something I didn't want to see? *Ew*.

When I squared my shoulders and opened the door I was hit by the strong smells of paint and turpentine, by the volume of the music, and by the stored heat in the shed. Feeling suddenly nauseous, I took a deep breath to settle my stomach. It didn't help.

Ryan was sleeping, slumped in a foldout camp chair. He looked paler than normal, sweaty from the heat, and his limp fingers were stained with black paint.

"Ryan? Are you okay?" He didn't respond. I looked around for the stereo and thumbed it off. My ears rang a little in the sudden almost-silence: the only sound was an old pedestal fan that rattled in the corner, trying unsuccessfully to take the edge off the heat.

Ryan's easel had a large canvas resting on it, the surface still glistening. At first I thought the painting was of me, a wilder, darker me with thorns in my hair, wearing a too-revealing dress of glittering, fragmented glass. Some of the glass was silvered, like a mirror. The colours were almost all washed out: black, sooty grey, powder blue, white, a pale cream for the flesh. The only spots of vivid colour were on the woman's forehead, where blood beaded around the thorns that pricked her skin, and on her ruby lips. My jaw dropped. The painting unsettled me deeply.

What bothered me the most was it didn't look like the real me so much as it did the strange doppelganger I'd dreamt of at Halloween. Seeing her, the details of the dream came back to me, bobbing to the surface like twigs in a stream. The woman stared out of the canvas and straight at me in a way that made the hair on my bare arms stand on end.

"Holy crap," said Sarah from the doorway, her eyes wide, her demeanour radiating shock. "That's messed up." She looked ill, turning away from the painting and from me, taking Ryan's shoulders and shaking them aggressively. His head lolled to the side and a paintbrush clattered to the concrete floor. But he didn't wake.

"Ryan?" Panic threaded through her voice.

I reached past her and checked for a pulse in his throat. It was there, beating faster than it should, but strong. His skin was hot and slick with sweat. "He's alive," I tried to reassure Sarah.

She brushed me off. "I know that." She went to the door of the shed. "*Mum!*" When she turned back to me, her expression was dark. "Help me get him to the house."

We each took one of Ryan's arms and draped it across our shoulders, lifting him from the chair. His fingers and hands were still tacky, but now wasn't the time to worry about getting stains on my T-shirt.

Aunt Elizabeth rushed down from the house as we emerged from the shed, Ryan hanging between us. He was taller than either of us, and his feet dragged along the ground. "Ryan! What's wrong with him?"

"Unconscious," Sarah panted. "Hot in there. Maybe he passed out?"

Was it the combination of heat and fumes that had caused his collapse? My own queasiness began to fade once I emerged from the shed, taking a deep breath of fresh air.

Aunt Elizabeth helped us manhandle Ryan up the stairs, holding the door open so we could get him inside. We laid him on his bed. She ran a face washer under some cool water and placed it on his brow. I remembered what she'd said on my birthday, about how Ryan would always be her little boy, and could see it in the fear in her eyes.

"I'll get a bottle of water." I fled the room before I cried.

Sarah followed. She grabbed my arm as we entered

the kitchen, pulling me around to face her.

"What's going on?"

"With what?" The fury on her face made the urge to cry even stronger.

"With you and Ryan? Are you seeing each other behind our backs? Behind Dominic's back?"

"No. Gross!" Ryan was more like a brother to me than a cousin, and I would never cheat on Dominic. Or anyone.

"How do you explain that painting?"

"I don't. I ... can't."

Some of my own unease must have shown through, because the sharp edge of her rage blunted a little. She dropped my arm. "It's just weird. Shit."

"I know." I got a bottle of water from the fridge. "Should we call an ambulance?"

"I don't know. Maybe?" Sarah took the bottle from me and hurried back to Ryan's room. I grabbed the phone from the charger and followed.

But when we went in there, Ryan was stirring, blinking up at the overhead light. He looked confused, and protested when his mother and sister blanketed him in a hug. "Where...? What happened?"

"We found you unconscious in the shed," Sarah scolded him. "Dumbarse."

"Sarah," Aunt Elizabeth remonstrated gently, taking the bottle from her and handing it to Ryan. He guzzled it down.

"Thanks," he said when he'd finished, handing it back. He tried to sit up, swaying.

"When was the last time you ate?" Aunt Elizabeth asked with narrowed eyes.

"I ... don't remember?"

"Dumbarse," Sarah said again. "No wonder you fainted."

"I didn't faint."

"You did. Like a silly girl in an old movie."

"Sarah," Aunt Elizabeth warned again, this time more forcefully. "Please go and dish up dinner for your brother. Ryan, you need to wash up. You're covered in paint."

I stayed out of the way as best I could while my aunt herded Ryan to the bathroom and supervised as he scrubbed his arms. He mentioned wanting a shower, but she said she wasn't letting him out of her sight until she was sure he was recovered, so he opted for a quick wash at the sink instead. Sarah clattered around in the kitchen, frowning, but as well as serving Ryan dinner she also poured him some orange juice and added ice.

With Ryan eating under Aunt Elizabeth's watchful eye, I went back out to the porch, ignoring my textbooks. I couldn't shake the uneasy feeling the intense stare of the woman in Ryan's painting had given me. It had looked like she'd wanted to step out of the painting and ... I wasn't sure what, but it wasn't anything good. When Sarah joined me, I was leaning against the balcony, staring at the shed like it contained something dangerous that needed to be watched. A snake, maybe. The sun had set and the stars were sparking to life above us. In the poor light the shed loomed.

"That painting is even weirder than you know," I murmured without looking at her. Then I told her about my nightmare.

When I was done, she asked, "How could he be painting someone you dreamed of?"

"I don't know. But it's freaking me out." I squirmed at even entertaining the notion Ryan had somehow seen the woman from my dream. "Maybe it's a coincidence? I mean, the black hair, pale skin, red lips thing—it's Snow White, right? He painted Snow White, and I'm imagining it looked like a woman in a dream I'm probably recalling incorrectly anyway." The more I talked, the more my confidence in my explanation grew, steadying my nerves.

"Snow White wearing a dress made of a broken mirror, like from your dream?"

"In the dream she was wearing black. The mirror broke at the end, when I woke up."

Sarah rolled her eyes but persisted. "Snow White looking a lot like you?"

"I ... I guess so. Maybe she didn't look *that* much like me, and we imagined it." The other logical option was that, when Ryan was painting his sexy Snow White, he'd modelled her loosely around my appearance. The notion unsettled me, although not as much as the idea he'd somehow seen into my dream.

What other dreams might he have seen into? My eyes widened. That didn't even bear thinking about. I'd had some ... interesting dreams since I'd started dating Dominic.

"Well, there's one easy way to find out," Sarah said, determined. She pushed away from the railing. I blinked, wondering what she meant. She was already marching down the stairs to the footpath, and I hurried after her.

But I hesitated before entering the shed. Sarah barrelled in, flicking the light on. The fluorescent lights buzzed overhead. I took a deep breath, told myself not to be stupid, and followed her.

The shed was starting to cool, the metal roof ticking as it contracted, but it was still warm and reeked of turpentine. The nauseated feeling returned in full force.

# ISLA'S INHERITANCE

"It does look a lot like you," Sarah said. She stood in front of the canvas, seemingly unaffected by the oppressive atmosphere. "I suppose at least the reflective bits of glass are covering your privates." Talk about looking on the bright side.

"They aren't *my* privates," I insisted, but it was hard to argue that the woman did look like a more refined, attractive version of me.

"So he must have seen into your dream."

I disagreed, but bit my tongue rather than saying the words aloud. Sarah needed to believe her brother wasn't attracted to their cousin. I could understand that.

A sobering thought shook me. Was I so determined to believe it was modelled off me because I found the idea of someone seeing my dreams so unpalatable? No, that was silly; it was because it was impossible. Unpalatable had nothing to do with it.

Gritting my teeth and breathing slowly, I studied the painting. The glass fragments of the dress seemed to jump out, moving beneath the light as I inched closer to the image. The picture's background was indistinct, drawing my gaze back to the woman. Her dark eyes burned as they glared out of the canvas, substantial, almost three-dimensional.

The crown of thorns was made from vines woven together in an intricate braid. The thorns were identical to those on the rose Ryan had painted on my MP3 player case; the curved shape and the wicked point were the same. I wondered if that was significant. Presumably there were only so many ways to paint a thorn.

"Sarah," Aunt Elizabeth called, coming down from the house. Her shoes slapped on the path. "I'm going to take Ryan to the after-hours doc—"

She entered the shed. Her gaze settled on the painting and she stopped short, her skin blanching almost as pale as that of the woman on the canvas. Sarah and I stared at her as she turned and hurried—almost ran— back to the house without saying another word.

"What the...?" Sarah trailed off, following her mother. I hurried after, head spinning, but also relieved when the nausea again dropped away like an unwanted, bilious cloak falling to the floor.

When we entered the house, she was interrogating Ryan. He was still sitting at the kitchen table, empty plate in front of him. He looked confused. "The woman in the painting. Where did you see her?"

"Painting?" He struggled to remember. Maybe he'd hit his head when he passed out. The painting must have taken days. How could he have forgotten? He blinked slowly. "I, uh, it was a dream I had." He didn't even glance at me.

Sarah, on the other hand, shot me a triumphant, relieved look.

And Aunt Elizabeth looked horrified. She rushed out of the kitchen, again without saying anything, and disappeared into her bedroom. The door slammed.

There was a moment of silence. Sarah pointed at the phone, back in its cradle. The light had gone on to indicate that the line was in use. There was another handset in Aunt Elizabeth's room. Sarah picked up the phone, holding a finger to her lips as she held it to her ear. I stood beside her, and she tilted the receiver so both our ears were pressed against it.

I was the serious, studious and—yes, I admit it— square one among my friends. But I wanted to know what prompted this uncharacteristic reaction from my aunt. The woman in the painting looked like me. Didn't I have the right to know?

Sarah pressed the *talk* button on the phone and we both held our breath.

"You're sure?" It was my father.

"Yes." Aunt Elizabeth sounded angry. "He says he saw her in a dream, but that's impossible. He must have seen an old photo or something. She hasn't aged a day."

"It's not *that* impossible." Dad sounded scared.

"Of course it is," Aunt Elizabeth retorted. "It was eighteen years ago. He hasn't seen her on the street."

A cold feeling crystallised in my stomach. Eighteen years?

"I hope," Dad said. "Look, you're sure it's her?"

"I'm positive. The painting is of Isla's mother."

# CHAPTER FIVE

When Aunt Elizabeth came out of the bedroom five minutes later, Sarah was sitting beside Ryan at the kitchen table, feigning innocence. I stood at the sink, rinsing his plate. I had a worse poker face than Sarah did—and hers was pretty bad—so I thought it better to keep my hands busy until I got my emotions under control.

*My mother?*

"So ... what was all that about?" Sarah asked. Her casual voice was even worse than her innocent look. Her mother wasn't buying it.

"All what?"

"You know. You saw the painting and freaked."

"I did no such thing." Aunt Elizabeth put a hand on Ryan's forehead to check his temperature. He was watching the interplay with a frown. "How do you feel, Ryan?"

"Bit better," he mumbled.

"It looked like you freaked to me," Sarah said. I willed her to pursue the subject, widening my eyes, but she shot me a helpless look in return. She didn't want to reveal we'd been eavesdropping.

*Hell with it*, I decided, jamming the plate in the dishwasher before turning to confront my aunt.

"I listened in on the phone call," I said. There was no point in ratting us both out.

"Isla!" Aunt Elizabeth's mouth fell open.

"Well, that painting looks a lot like me. But I heard you say it's of my mother. Why?"

Aunt Elizabeth tugged a chair out from under the kitchen table and slumped into it. Her mouth pulled down at the corners and her shoulders rose and fell in a sigh. "Because it is."

"Why would I paint a picture of Isla's mother?" Ryan asked, bewildered.

"That's the sixty-four thousand-dollar question, isn't it?" She grimaced. "Are you sure you didn't find an old photo somewhere?"

"No, I had a weird dream of her. She wouldn't stop staring at me."

"When?" I asked. Sarah glanced at me.

"Um." He frowned. "It was the night of your birthday dinner."

"Not Halloween?"

He shook his head.

I'd had my dream days before Ryan had his. I guess he wasn't seeing into my head after all. Thank god.

"The painting looks a lot like me," I said slowly, turning to my aunt. "You're sure it's her?"

"It's the spitting image of her." Aunt Elizabeth rubbed her temples.

"You haven't seen her for eighteen years. Maybe you're

remembering wrong?"

"No. She's not the sort of woman you forget." There was an uncomfortable silence, before Aunt Elizabeth added, "Your father's driving in now."

Admitting I already knew that would amp the tension. The air was already thick, laced with uncertainty. I fought to keep the edge out of my voice. "Why?"

"He's worried about you."

"But it's just a painting. Right?"

She shrugged. She either didn't know or didn't want to tell me. There was another silence, and I decided to approach the subject from a different direction. I grabbed the last kitchen chair and sat so I could see her face. "Tell me about her. My mother."

"That's something you should talk to your father about, not me."

"He won't talk to me about her. Until today I didn't even know what she looked like." My frustration wasn't feigned. I'd tried for eighteen years to be patient with my father and his sensitivities about my mother, but this was too much.

Aunt Elizabeth's expression softened. "You're right." She nibbled her lip for a moment, then began to speak. "Your father met your mother when he was on a trip to Scotland. He brought her home, and it was clear from the first time we saw them together that he was besotted. She loved him too, but it was hard for the rest of us to get to know her. She was distant, I suppose. Cold. Our mother didn't like her, and I have to admit I wasn't a fan either." Sarah gasped, and Aunt Elizabeth's eyes widened. She reached over to pat my hand. "I'm sorry, sweetheart. Melanie just wasn't very friendly. She was private, I suppose, and we were a tight-knit family. But she was beautiful. Breathtaking." She said this like it was a consolation prize, but added a little sourly, "Almost every man who met her fell a little in love with her.

"They got married after returning from Scotland. There were rumours, of course; everyone speculated she was pregnant, and we discovered a couple of months later that we were right. Your father was over the moon. I've never seen him as happy as he was that year. He had everything he had ever wanted: a beautiful wife, a daughter on the way..."

"And she died giving birth to me." That was the one part of the story I did know. I'd never shaken the guilt, not since Dad told me when I was four the reason why I didn't have a mummy.

Aunt Elizabeth hesitated, and I gave her a sharp look. "What?"

"You have to understand, I was distracted too. I was pregnant with Sarah; my due date was about six weeks after Melanie's." She looked down at her hands and murmured, "And three days after you were born, Andrew died."

Andrew was Sarah and Ryan's father. We knew that part of the story too. He'd been jogging at dawn one morning and had tripped, hitting his head. A silly accident, but one that meant he'd never met his daughter. Sarah arrived a month later. After all these years my aunt had never remarried, although she had dated a few times, and once saw a man for almost six months before breaking it off.

My father had never even dated.

"Distracted from what?" Sarah asked, drawing me back to the conversation.

"It's just that something occurred to me when I was at your father's funeral." She turned to me. "David was cradling you, Isla. Such a tiny, solemn baby, you were. He looked as sad as I've ever seen him. And I realised..." She hesitated.

"What?"

"I realised there was never a funeral for Melanie."

There was never a funeral for my mother?

*She. Is. Not. Dead...*

The reply spelled out at the séance. An upturned scotch glass and a cruel practical joke ... or so I'd thought. But what if my father never had a funeral for my mother because she hadn't died at all? What if she'd run off after I was born, leaving me in the hospital nursery like unwanted baggage? What if the séance was real?

And if Emma had tapped into some supernatural thing, what else was possible? Had Ryan really dreamt of Melanie? Had I? Why?

*She. Is. Not. Dead...*

"Isla, are you okay?" Sarah's voice sounded concerned, and very far away.

"I think I need to sit down," I whispered.

"You are sitting down."

Oh. So I was. The others were staring at me from afar, as though they were sitting at a different kitchen table on the other side of a great hall. Sarah got me a glass of water; when she handed it to me I curled my fingers around it but didn't drink. The glass weighted my hand, too heavy to lift to my mouth.

"What do you think happened? To Melanie?" Ryan was saying.

"I don't know. I never saw her again, so I thought I

was being paranoid—making nothing into something. David applied for a visa to come to Australia shortly afterwards, and for citizenship for Isla and himself when he was able. I thought he was fleeing the place where he had such painful memories." She looked down at her hands and added softly, "Goodness knows I could understand that." My aunt had moved to Australia with her two small children five years after Dad and me.

"I'm sure you *were* being paranoid," Sarah declared. She always was a bad liar.

"I think I'm going to rest for a bit," I said, putting the glass down. Water slopped across the battered tabletop.

"Do you want me to come with you?" Sarah asked.

"No. Thanks. I'm just going to lie down."

Kicking off my shoes, I crawled onto my bed and curled on my side. I left the bedside lamp off. The hall light was on, providing more than enough illumination for my mood. I could hear murmured conversation in the kitchen, and the sliding door to the back porch being opened and closed.

I tried to still my swirling, incoherent thoughts and be rational. Séances weren't real. Dad probably didn't have a funeral for my mother because she'd said in her will she didn't want a big fuss. Or because he couldn't afford it. Or because it pained him too much. Who knew how anyone would react in that situation, grief-stricken and with a newborn baby?

My father never lied to me about anything.

*That I know of.* That treacherous thought wouldn't be silenced. If he'd lied to me about this, what else could he have lied to me about?

It wasn't possible.

Of course, it wasn't also possible Ryan and I had both

dreamt of the same woman. I racked my brain, trying to recall whether I'd ever seen a photo of my mother. But I was sure I hadn't.

Sarah appeared, silhouetted against the hall light. "I'm just bringing your books in from outside," she whispered, leaving my study things in a pile on the desk. She hesitated. "Do you need anything?"

"No, thank you."

"You know where I am if you need me."

"Okay."

I heard her pad barefooted down the corridor to the lounge room. The television came on. A moment later Hamish appeared, jumping onto my bed and snuffling my face before scrambling over me and settling against my stomach, his small head resting on my waist. He sighed. Sarah must have turfed him off the couch, knowing he'd come in here. She was looking after me even when I hadn't asked her to. What would I do without her?

"I'm not sure which is worse," I whispered to Hamish, stroking his fur, "believing I killed my mother, or believing she abandoned me … and that Dad lied about it." Hamish didn't answer. He was already asleep. "Well, you're no use."

Against all odds, the steady rhythm of Hamish's breathing lulled me into a doze. It seemed like no time had passed when I awoke to a change in the light: my father's large frame was in the doorway, blocking the glow from the hallway.

"Isla? Are you awake?" His voice was tentative.

"Yes." I sat up, rubbing my eyes. Hamish grumbled a protest.

"Can I turn the light on?"

"Sure."

I blinked and stared at my father as the light clicked on. He looked dishevelled and his eyes were wide, like he'd seen a ghost. He was holding the gift bag he'd given me on my birthday. "You left this at the restaurant the other week, when you went out for dessert with that boy," he said, his voice strained.

As confused and resentful as I was feeling right now, I still loved him, and his appearance worried me. "Dad, what's wrong?"

"Nothing," he said. He was an even worse liar than Sarah. He came into the room and sat on the edge of the bed. "Here." He tried to hand me the bag. Vomit burned the back of my throat, and I flinched back.

He saw the flinch, and his face grew even more drawn. "Isla, take it." There was an urgency in his tone that I neither understood nor liked.

"No. Dad, what's going on? You're freaking me out."

He looked around the room. "Do you have any of my work in here?"

The question confused me. I felt my cheeks warm. "Um, I'm not sure." The answer was no. Pretty much every piece of ironwork he'd given me was in the shed. The rest I'd given away to friends.

"Here." He upended the gift bag. The heavy iron circlet tumbled into my lap.

My stomach twisted with nausea so severe I clenched my teeth, afraid I'd throw up. Where the iron touched my thighs through the denim of my jeans it felt ice-cold, and yet it burned at the same time. I gasped, shoving it away from me and onto the floor. It singed my hand.

"*What the hell are you doing?*" I jumped to my feet.

Hamish leapt up too, yapping.

Dad said nothing but the look on his face was wild, despairing.

"You're crazy," I cried, fleeing the room.

"Isla, wait," Dad yelled after me. But I ran, snatching my bag from the hallway before rushing out the front door. I ignored the bite of tiny rocks on the soles of my feet. I had to get away from him, from everything.

"Isla," Sarah called as I jumped into my little car. I hesitated, but Dad was right behind her, clutching that stupid circlet like a talisman. Seeing him made me feel sick and confused all over again. I had to get away.

My hatchback's tyres squealed as I sped around the corner at the end of our street. My heart pounded and tears stung my eyes as I drove, the pedals cold against the soles of my feet. What had happened? Why had my father attacked me?

*How* had my father attacked me?

# CHAPTER SIX

After a few minutes of directionless driving—fleeing—through the suburbs, I took a deep breath and pulled over. My hands trembled, and pain radiated from my burnt palm where it gripped the steering wheel. I was going to get myself killed if I wasn't careful, and my bare feet were freezing. I flicked on my hazard lights and, hurrying across the rough surface of the road, scurried around the car to check the boot.

To my relief, my gym bag was there. I threw it onto the passenger seat and, sliding my seat back, put my socks and sneakers on. Then I stared out the windshield at the quiet street.

My mobile phone rang. Home. I tossed the phone onto the passenger seat, unanswered.

What I wanted was somewhere quiet, somewhere I could gather my thoughts... Mount Ainslie. Located north of Lake Burley Griffin, the mountain reserve boasted a lookout facing the city and a gorgeous view. And at this time of night there wouldn't be too many people.

I tried not to think on the drive in, concentrating on the road. When my mobile rang again I turned the radio up, listening to a too-enthusiastic pop song instead. There wasn't a lot of traffic at this time of the evening so the drive only took about twenty minutes.

When I turned off Limestone Avenue and onto the winding road that climbed to the top of the mountain, I flicked my headlights onto high beam and slowed down to well below the speed limit. The drop to the car's left loomed in the moving shadows cast by the headlights.

At the top of the mountain, I pulled into a car park and stopped the engine with a relieved sigh. There was one other car at the lookout: an older-model green sedan with steamed-up windows.

My phone beeped a text message alert. It was from Sarah. *Are you okay? Where are you?*

I thought about calling her, but I couldn't be sure Dad wasn't using her phone. He'd never done that before … but he'd never hurt me before either. So instead I replied, *I'm safe. Talk later.*

My palm throbbed in time with my heartbeat. I flicked the car's interior light on and stared at my right hand. A faint red mark curved from the base of my pinkie finger to the mound beneath my thumb. So long as I didn't move my hand too much it only ached, and not as much as it should have given the intensity of the pain I'd felt when I pushed the iron circlet to the floor.

I jumped when my phone rang again, and started to push it away—but then saw Dominic's name and grabbed it.

"Hello?"

"Hi, Isla, it's me."

"Hey, you."

There was a little pause. "I just got off the phone with Sarah. She said you had a fight with your dad and took off. Are you okay?"

Sarah *was* an interfering wench, but I couldn't find it in me to be upset at her. "I'm alright. I just needed to get out of there."

"What happened?"

"I ... I don't want to talk about it." *Because I don't know what happened.*

"Did you want some company?"

I thought about that for a moment. "Sure."

"Where are you?"

"At the Mount Ainslie lookout. I just got here."

"Okay, I'll be there in about a half hour," he said. "Did you want me to bring anything?"

"Um. A hot drink?"

"Can do. Cappuccino with one sugar, right?"

"Yes. Thanks." He remembered. The ache in my chest eased a little.

"See you soon. And be careful up there."

"I'll be fine. There's hardly anyone here." I decided not to mention the people making out in the other car.

"That's sort of what I was worried about," he replied.

After I hung up, I put my phone on silent and slid it into my jeans pocket before flicking off the overhead light and sliding out of the car. The last of the spring day's warmth was fading and the pleasant breeze I'd enjoyed while I studied on the porch a couple of hours ago—it seemed a lifetime ago—had cooled. At least I had jeans on, but I was still in my baby doll tee, complete with its black paint smudges. My gym bag was not so well stocked that it also contained a jumper. I hadn't needed long sleeves during the day for weeks now.

Hugging my arms to my sides, I walked down from the car park to the lookout area clinging to the edge of the mountain.

The bejewelled lake spread out below me, ringed with national monuments and strung with bridges: diamond bracelets sparkling on an outstretched arm. The bright, distant lights of vehicles moved like red and white fireflies, far enough away that I couldn't hear traffic noise. The airport was a series of orderly lights to my far left; an airplane took off like a cast spear, its wingtips aglow.

I took several deep breaths, the cool air filling my lungs and the tumult inside me fading to silence as I absorbed the serenity. Drifting to the right-hand side of the lookout, I could see the built-up glow of Civic through the trees. Touching the cold railing eased the pain in my hand. How had Dad burnt me? And *why*? It couldn't have been deliberate. Not once in my eighteen years had he ever shown me anything but love. Sure, we'd had arguments. I'd always thought he was overprotective compared to other kids' parents, and a lot more strict, but I knew it was his way of looking out for me. As I'd grown older I'd assumed it was because of what had happened to my mother: that losing her had made him more afraid than most people of the harm that can befall a loved one.

But was Aunt Elizabeth right? Was there some significance to the fact my mother hadn't had a funeral?

I turned my back on the view, leaning on the rail and looking up at the stairs to see whether there was any sign of Dominic's car. The area was deserted. Looming above the car park was a huge pole topped with a rotating beacon to warn off low-flying aircraft. Tiny insectile specks swarmed around the light in a chaotic, joyful dance.

"You should not be up here alone," a voice said.

Heart in my throat, I spun so quickly I nearly fell. Standing a few metres away from me was a figure in baggy jeans and a soft grey jumper. A hood was pulled up to cover his head, casting his face into deep shadow.

"I'm not alone," I lied, squaring my shoulders and putting one hand on my hip. The other I slipped into my jeans pocket, getting a good grip on my car keys. Natalie had told us after she did a self-defence course that the individual keys, protruding from a clenched fist, could serve as an improvised weapon.

My heart raced so hard I was sure the stranger could hear it.

"You are," he corrected me. At least, I thought it was a he, judging by the voice.

"My boyfriend's just gone to the bathroom." Absurd; there were no public bathrooms up here. Before he could call me on it, I added, "It's none of your business anyway." He wasn't any taller than me, which made me feel a little more confident.

"It is not safe for you, lady."

*What?* "Who are you?" He hesitated, and I took a step forward. It was foolish, but I'd had enough tonight. "Tell me!"

The stranger pushed his hood back.

His dark eyes, fixed on my face, were the first things I noticed. They were large, like those of a baby animal that hadn't grown into its skin. In the poor light I couldn't determine their colour. His nose was on the small side; his chin pointed; his skin pale and covered in delicate wrinkles, especially around the mouth and eyes; and his hair straight, either dark blond or light brown. And his ears...

They protruded from the fall of his hair, long and pointed, the tips a good hand span away from his skull.

I stared. He stood there, waiting.

"You're the one who sniffed me and pushed me over," I exclaimed at last. "The kid from Halloween."

"I did not mean for you to fall," he said.

"But you *sniffed* me!"

"I had to be sure you were the one I had sensed, lady. It could have been your male companion."

"I'm sorry, what?"

"Earlier that evening I had sensed the presence of an unknown *duinesidhe*, but your heritage confused me. I am not usually so rude."

I frowned. I knew what most of the words he had said meant—although what was a "din-ah-shee?"—but the way he'd put them together made no sense.

I gave up on that for the moment and raised another point. "Your mask. It's very good."

"It is not a mask, lady."

"Of course it is." My insistence felt hollow.

He stepped forward and I jumped. "I will show you. Give me your hand?" He held his own out, fine-boned and fair. "I swear I mean you no harm." The words, soft-spoken and intense with meaning, shivered across my skin.

Even though my burned right palm ached, I tightened my grip on my keys, which were still in my pocket. I laid my left hand in his. My skin, I noticed, was almost as pale as his. Children of the sunscreen generation.

His fingers were warm, despite the cool air. He curled them around mine and lifted my hand. He touched my fingertips to his face, running them across his features.

I felt the fine indentations of the wrinkles; the softness of his cheek and chin, both free of stubble; the seamless transition to the gentle curve of his lips. He lifted my hand and placed it in his hair, so I could feel that there was no edge of a mask hidden in his hairline. His hair was fine, like a baby's: silken to the touch. Finally, he ran my hand along the length of his ear so I could feel the flex of the cartilage and the flawless skin. There was no mistaking any of it for rubber or another synthetic material.

Touching his skin was overwhelming and strangely intimate, and when I took my hand back, my fingertips tingled. I cleared my throat before I spoke. "Who are you?" I asked him again.

He bowed and, because he was standing so close to me, we almost touched. I took a step back, feeling the cold metal of the railing against my back. "I am Jack the Unsworn," he said.

"*What* are you?" I whispered. The question felt ridiculous. *Was* ridiculous. But I had no doubt this was real, not an elaborate hoax.

"I am a *duinesidhe*." When I didn't say anything, he elaborated, "One of the fae." Another pause; then he grimaced. "A faerie."

"A ... faerie."

"Yes." His eyes grew wide. "You do not know, do you? About us?"

I shook my head. His shocked look prompted me to speak in my defence. "Well, I've read about fairies in kids' books. The tooth fairy and stuff like that."

He smiled, showing a flash of even white teeth. "Any resemblance those books bear to the real thing is coincidental at best, I am afraid."

"Oh."

"Your ignorance... Forgive me, but it makes it even more dangerous for you to be up here alone," Jack said. "You should leave at once, return to your home."

"I can't right now."

"Why?"

For reasons I couldn't have begun to explain, I told him about the scene with my father. And he nodded as though it made perfect sense. "He knows what you are, or at least suspects. Iron burns our kind."

"What do you mean, what I am?" Frustration bled into my tone. Our conversation verged on madness, but it seemed this Jack understood me better than I did.

His next statement confirmed it.

"You are an unheard of thing, the child of a human and a *duinesidhe*."

"... pardon?"

He repeated his outlandish claim.

"You think I'm some sort of faerie half-breed?" My mouth fell open with shock.

"I would say half-blood, but yes, I suppose you could say that, lady. Can you not feel the power in your blood?"

"The only thing I feel is a burned hand."

"Show me."

That meant letting go of the keys and, as ridiculous a weapon as they made, my grip on them gave me some comfort. After a moment I pulled them out of my pocket and transferred them to my left hand. I held my right hand out, palm upwards, for Jack to examine. My fingers trembled.

He gently took my wrist and turned it so the light fell across the curved red weal. "Does it hurt much?"

"It aches."

He looked up at me. "Do you want me to take it away?"

"What do you mean?" I leaned in closer, looking from my palm to his large, serious eyes.

"I can take the wound from you."

"Heal it?"

Jack hesitated before nodding.

"Okay. I guess."

I'd imagined he might pull out a pot of salve and a bandage. Or wave a magical faerie wand. What he did instead was to lower his face to my palm and lick the length of the wound. Startled, I tried to pull my hand away; his grip tightened on my wrist so I couldn't free myself. But before I could panic, he stood straight, releasing my hand and stepping back.

"It is done," he said.

I examined my palm; the skin was unbroken and smooth, showing no sign of the burn. It glistened with saliva. I really wanted to wipe it clean against my jeans, but that seemed rude. Of course, he'd just licked me, so maybe his idea of rude was different than mine.

"How did you do that?"

"It is a gift of my blood."

"Is that the sort of thing I might be able to do?" I had a sudden mental image of myself in a nurse's uniform, licking my way through a hospital ward. A hysterical laugh bubbled up and I took a breath, willing it away. If I started, I might not be able to stop.

"Maybe. It depends on the blood in your veins, and who your *duinesidhe* parent was."

"You don't know?"

"No, although I suspect he or she was *aosidhe*." Another strange word: "ay-oh-shee". He elaborated, *"Aosidhe* is one type of *duinesidhe.* Would you like me to see if I can find out, lady?"

"Sure. One more thing, though. Can you stop calling me 'lady'? I have a name."

"What would you prefer I call you?"

"My name's Isla." I held my hand out for him to shake and he looked at it, holding his right hand cradled against his chest like a wounded animal. My eyes widened. "Show me your hand."

The curved burn mark that had ached against my skin now stretched across his palm.

"You shouldn't have done that," I said, feeling guilty even though I hadn't known what would happen, what his offer entailed.

He shrugged. "I heal quickly." Then he reached out—with his left hand—and touched one of the charms hanging from the silver bracelet I wore around my wrist. "I am pleased you found this again," he said.

I knew a change of subject when I saw one. But... "Did you leave the bracelet on the doorstep?"

"Yes."

"Then thank you," I said. "It means a lot to me."

"You are welcome, Isla." I liked the lilting way he pronounced my name. It was musical.

A car rumbled into the turn at the top of the mountain road, tyres crunching. Its headlights swept through the air above us.

The car pulled in next to mine and one person got out. "That's Dominic," I told Jack. "My boyfriend." I wasn't afraid anymore, but I did feel uneasy at the idea of Dominic's reaction to Jack's strange appearance.

"The one who had gone to the bathroom." He smiled. "I will go."

He turned and walked away, towards a flight of stairs leading down to one of the walking tracks that girdled the mountain. "Wait a minute," I called after him. He looked over his shoulder. "Where will I find you again?"

"Go to the park across the road from your house. I will be there."

"When?"

"Whenever you like." He smiled again, and was gone.

# CHAPTER SEVEN

**D**ominic and I left Mount Ainslie shortly after Jack vanished into the night. I searched the shadows for the strange boy's presence. Was he still watching? The idea made the hairs on the back of my neck stand on end and, as soon as we'd finished our coffees, we headed back to Dominic's place. I felt bad for dragging him all the way up there only to leave straight away, but he said he didn't mind.

"My parents are away so it won't be a hassle if you want to crash there," he told me. "You can stay in the spare room." I was relieved when he added the last part; I wasn't ready for anything serious between us, even though Dominic was sweet. I certainly didn't think I was in the right headspace to be making relationship decisions.

If Dominic was disappointed when I agreed to the offer of the spare room, he didn't show it.

Before we left the mountain, I typed a text to Sarah. *Crashing at D's,* I sent, being cryptic in case my father or aunt took the phone from her. *Can you bring a change of clothes tomorrow?*

*And your books?* she replied. I'd forgotten about the exam! If I needed any more proof of what a crazy night I'd had, there it was.

*Yes please.*

*Okay. Will let Mum know you won't be home. Have fun! ;),* she replied. Typical Sarah. I knew I was going to get the third degree from her tomorrow. I didn't mind sharing about Dominic, but I wasn't sure what to tell her about why I'd run out of the house.

I followed him to his place, turning the evening's events over in my mind as I drove. I was a half-blood fae? I still wasn't sure I believed it, but I'd seen at least two things tonight I couldn't explain: my father burning me with plain, unheated iron and Jack healing the burn. Even if I could come up with some kind of rationalisation for Jack's strange appearance, neither of those could be explained by normal means.

By the time I pulled into Dominic's driveway, I'd decided it was time to take Jack at his word. Dad had taught me to be sceptical about anything that couldn't be explained with logic and science, but he must have known something about Jack's world if my mother was part of it. That meant his advice was hypocritical, even if he was trying to protect me.

It struck me that, as well as being hypocritical, his efforts were also misguided. Wasn't I better protected by the truth? Ignorance wasn't bliss if you got blindsided by something you had no idea was coming.

Dominic's parents lived in one of the nicer suburbs in the south of Canberra, a ten-minute drive from Aunt

Elizabeth's place. The house was two storeys; the ground floor was a beautiful reddish-brown brick, the upper level cream-painted timber. A eucalypt towered on the front lawn, taller than the house.

We were greeted in the hallway by a furry, white shape that turned out, when the light was switched on, to be a cat. "This is Casper," Dominic told me, scratching the cat behind the ears. "Casper, meet Isla."

"Pleased to meet you, Casper," I said. The cat stared back at me with pale blue eyes and then licked a paw with feline indifference.

"Did you want something to eat?" Dominic asked as I followed him up the hallway into a spacious kitchen with a grey granite bench. Casper trailed along behind us.

"I'm okay." I smiled, hiding a yawn behind my hand. "Would you be offended if I said I just wanted to go to sleep? It's been a stressful day."

"No problem," he said. "Did you want a clean shirt to wear to bed or anything?"

"Um, yes, that'd be great."

He showed me to the guest room, the first bedroom off the hallway at the top of the stairs. Dominic's room was on the same floor, on the other side of a shared bathroom. From the décor, which ran to hot pink and dark purple, I guessed the spare room was once his older sister's bedroom. I could hear him rustling around in his wardrobe as I fidgeted in the middle of her room, feeling like an interloper.

"Here, will this do?" Dominic handed me a neatly folded T-shirt. It was grey and had Animal from the Muppets on the front.

I held it up in front of me; it fell halfway down my

thighs. "It's perfect."

I caught my reflection in an oval mirror on the low chest of drawers. My skin, a paler-than-normal shade of alabaster, almost glowed in the dim light. My eyes shone with a feverish tint. I flinched, clutching the T-shirt to my chest, and wondered miserably what Dominic must be thinking. I looked a mess. "Ah, do you mind if I freshen up first?"

"Not at all." Dominic led me to the bathroom and rustled around under the sink, pulling out a multi-pack of toothbrushes. "Help yourself." Then he withdrew, closing the door behind him.

I dug the pink toothbrush out and put the packet back under the sink; the toothpaste was in a cup on the basin. There was also a hairbrush and a stick of men's pine-scented deodorant. I took advantage of all three items—I didn't think Dominic would mind—and splashed some water on my face, feeling a little better when I emerged from the bathroom.

Although the mirror told me the startled look hadn't diminished. Maybe I was putting too much faith in the power of clean teeth and tangle-free hair.

Dominic's bedroom door was open, and he was sitting on his bed when I poked my head in to say goodnight. His bedroom was painted in neutral colours; the walls were grey and the ceiling was the same stark white as in the rest of the house. A couple of rock posters hung on the closet doors, a fat, old TV sat on top of a chest of drawers that matched the one in the guest room, and a guitar sat on a stand under the window.

"I didn't know you played."

"I don't, not really." He grimaced. "I mean, I took lessons

at school, but I don't have any talent."

"Sarah's a guitarist," I said. "She's pretty good."

"I remember."

There was an awkward silence. I took a breath, crossed the room, and gave Dominic a hug. He stayed sitting, so I could rest my chin on his head. It was nice. "Thanks for looking after me tonight. And for not asking lots of questions."

He shrugged. "You said you didn't want to talk about it. I figure you'll tell me when you're ready. And if you don't... Well, that's okay too." He smiled.

I leaned down and kissed him.

His lips were soft, and his tongue, when it flicked over mine, tasted like sweetened coffee. For a moment I lost myself as his arms wrapped around me, pulling me close. One hand massaged the small of my back; the other drifted lower, brushing the top of my backside. I curled my fingers in his hair, loving its softness.

It reminded me of Jack, of him guiding my hand across his face and through his hair.

Drawing a shuddering breath, I released Dominic and stepped back. He let go of me reluctantly.

"I'm sorry, that wasn't fair." My face felt hot.

"Don't be," he said, his lips quirking in a smile that made me want to kiss him again. He shifted uncomfortably on the bed.

"It's just that I—"

"It's been a crazy night for you."

"Yes."

"It's okay, we don't have to rush into anything."

"Yes. Okay. Good." I could feel the blood heating my cheeks. And elsewhere.

"I understand. Although, if you change your mind, you know where I am." He laughed breathlessly.

I laughed too, and the tension was broken. "Goodnight, Dominic."

"Goodnight, Isla."

Still laughing to myself, I went into the guest room and closed the door. Casper had set himself up in the middle of the bed with the air of someone who always slept there. "Do you mind, cat?" I turned my back on him to get undressed, slipping the oversized T-shirt on. It smelled of apple-scented fabric softener.

I turned the bedside lamp on and the overhead light off, and climbed into bed; Casper claimed a spot in the curve at the back of my knees, purring. "Hamish would be upset that I'm cheating on him with a cat," I told Casper. He purred a little louder. I guess the notion of annoying a dog amused him. "Okay, well, I won't tell him if you don't."

Switching off the bedside lamp, I lay there for a long time, thinking about Dominic's lips and Jack's soft, fine hair, before I fell asleep.

I woke up from a confused dream about my mother. She was dressed as she was in Ryan's painting, but with pink and purple butterfly wings sprouting from her back, and she kept trying to steal my teeth. My phone was chiming on the bedside table; I wasn't usually happy to hear the alarm go off, but this time it was a relief. It was just past seven.

Casper jumped off the bed, hurrying down the corridor

as soon as I opened the bedroom door. A cat on a mission. There was no other sign of life in the house. Dominic was probably still asleep.

Although I was hungry, I decided against making myself breakfast in Dominic's house. Going through the kitchen cupboards felt way too invasive. Clearly stalking wasn't a potential future career for me. I scribbled a brief message on a notepad I found next to the phone, leaving it sitting in the middle of the bench where Dominic couldn't miss it.

On the way to school, I detoured to get a drive-through coffee. Unable to stomach bacon or eggs at this time of the morning, I bought a yogurt instead.

Sarah's car wasn't in the car park yet. I found an empty bench on the eastern wall, facing the oval, and sat in the sun to have my breakfast, eyes squinting against the glare even through my sunglasses. I kept an eye on the car park entrance, hoping to see Sarah when she arrived. The sun had banished the overnight chill from the air with a warm, dry hand that promised to be uncomfortable come midday. But for now it was pleasant; the breeze carried the rich scent of cut grass from the newly shorn oval, as well as the sound of a magpie being harassed by a couple of smaller magpie-larks. I felt sorry for it.

It was about ten minutes before Sarah arrived, parking her car next to mine. I walked over to meet her and she gave me a fierce hug. "I'm glad you're okay, cuz."

"I'm fine," I said.

"And how's Dominic?" She wiggled her eyebrows and grinned.

"He's fine too. The perfect gentleman," I added, embarrassed.

"Disappointing," she said. "I need to give that boy a stern talking-to."

I squirmed at the thought of her confronting Dominic, and she laughed.

We got the bags out of the boot: both of our backpacks, laden with textbooks, notebooks and stationery, and her gym bag, which she thrust at me. "Your clothes, madam."

"Thanks. Change rooms?"

"Yup."

We shouldered our packs and set off around the side of the building. The gymnasium and change rooms were accessible through a side door, which was already unlocked. The first classes started in fifteen minutes, and a few students—no one we knew—were sitting in groups, talking. A couple of jocks came out the door as we were going in and set off at a jog around the oval. I admired their enthusiasm; Sarah admired more than that. I elbowed her in the ribs and she laughed, unabashed.

The change rooms were empty. If you've got gym first period you tend to come in your gym clothes, so we had the room to ourselves. I looked through the bag. Sarah had packed a pair of black denim shorts and one of my favourite tank tops: it was white, with a stylised woman's face done in pink and gold across the front. She'd also packed clean socks, two different pairs of shoes, my toiletries bag and a towel.

"No wonder this was so heavy," I teased her, laying out the items on one of the benches.

"I wasn't sure if you'd need to have a shower here too," Sarah shrugged. "I'm a good Girl Scout."

"Thanks. I appreciate the thought. Although you never were a scout."

"Don't bother me with details." She sat on the bench, worrying at a fingernail while I got changed.

She managed to hold her tongue until I sat down to pull on my socks. "What happened last night?"

"With Dad, you mean?"

"Duh. What else?" She rolled her eyes.

"You could've been talking about Ryan."

"I was there for that part."

"Or Dominic."

"You already said he was a gentleman. *Bor*-ing."

I pulled on one sneaker and laced it up before answering. "Dad and I had a fight."

"We heard you scream. I thought he hit you or something."

"No!" The idea horrified me, even though I'd spent a large part of the previous evening wondering why Dad had injured me. "He startled me is all." Her gaze was steady, radiating scepticism. "Really," I added.

It felt weird, lying to Sarah, but I couldn't tell her he'd burned my hand without sounding crazy. Especially given my hand now showed no evidence whatsoever of a burn.

"Did you ask him about your mother?"

"We never got that far." That was true, at least. "I'm going to ask, though, next time I see him. I'm sick of not knowing." Also true. Go me. I put on the other shoe. "What happened after I left?"

"Your dad was pretty freaked out, but he wouldn't talk about what happened," she said. "He wanted to get in his car and look for you, but Mum convinced him to stay at our place. He slept on the couch." She hesitated. "He was holding that circle thingy he gave you at your birthday party. I think he even fell asleep holding it. It was weird."

I busied myself repacking the gym bag with my dirty clothes, so I wouldn't have to meet Sarah's gaze. "What about Ryan? Is he all right?"

"Well, by the time Mum had calmed Uncle David down, Ryan had recovered. She decided not to take him to the doctor, but you should've heard the lecture she gave him about working in the shed during the hottest part of the day and not eating." Sarah's grin was fierce.

"Did ... did Dad see the painting Ryan did?"

She looked thoughtful. "No. They forgot about it, what with everything. After I got the text from you and we knew you were safe, Mum remembered it, but by then Uncle David was asleep, so she left it alone." She added quietly, "I think she gave him something. To get him to sleep, I mean."

My heart was a rock in my chest, trying to pull me down. They must have been so worried. Even though I'd thought Dad had attacked me, running out of the house like that was irresponsible. I was grateful to Aunt Elizabeth for stopping Dad from chasing me into the streets like a madman.

"I want to put this in my boot," I said, hefting the gym bag. "We've got time before class."

"Sure."

We walked back around the building to the car park in silence.

Sarah spotted him first, as we came around the corner. "Isla?" she murmured, grabbing my arm to get my attention. "Your dad's here."

I looked over, startled, and saw him standing between my car and Sarah's. He hurried across the car park, calling my name.

He looked terrible. His hair was unbrushed, a wild, strawberry-blond thicket on top of his head, and his face was unshaven. Even his clothes were crumpled; it looked like he'd slept in them.

And he was still holding that blasted iron ring.

When I saw it I took a step backward, nauseous, feeling a ghost of the searing pain in my hand. He saw my reaction and stopped a few feet from us. Then he turned to Sarah. "Can you hold this?" he said, holding it out to her.

Frowning and biting her lip, she took it.

I braced myself for it to burn her the way it had me but, of course, nothing happened.

Dad held his arms wide open to me, not coming any closer, and I hurried forward into them. "I'm so sorry I ran away," I mumbled into his shirt, hugging him as fiercely as he hugged me.

"No, I'm sorry. I didn't mean to... I never wanted to hurt you," he said back, his voice trembling. I looked up; there were tears in his eyes. My father never cried. "I just wanted to protect you," he said, and a tear tracked its way down his cheek into the stubble on his jaw.

"If you want to protect me, you have to tell me the truth," I said. "About Mum. *Everything* about her."

He caught the emphasis and gave me a penetrating look. Conscious that Sarah and a half-dozen other students, including a couple of the meanest gossips in our year, were watching, I held my right hand up so he could see the place where he'd burned me the night before. My healed palm.

His eyes widened briefly, and then his shoulders slumped. "Yes, of course. You're right. Shall we go back to your aunt's?"

# ISLA'S INHERITANCE

I hesitated. I wanted to hear what my father had to say. Desperately. But my final exam was in less than an hour. "I can be there at lunch time," I told him after a moment. Sarah scowled; she'd have blown off the exam if it were her. But the idea of having to take it later made me want to curl up in a ball with a pillow over my head. I wanted it done.

Dad walked me to my car, Sarah trailing behind us, still holding the iron circlet. I heard the whisper of gossip start up behind us and wondered how long it would take for news of the strange little scene to spread around the entire school. Of course, after this exam I wouldn't care anymore.

I put the gym bag in my car, and turned to give my father a kiss on his grizzled cheek.

"I've been a fool," he told me. "But you know everything I did was because I love you and your mother."

"I know, Dad," I said. Sarah handed him the circlet in uncharacteristic silence. He got into his ute and drove away.

# CHAPTER EIGHT

*I*t was lunchtime when my friends and I emerged from the school building. The dark lenses of my sunglasses cut the midday sun's glare and the air was warm in my lungs. A smile tugged at my lips. No more assessments!

When I turned towards the car park rather than the trees where the four of us usually ate lunch, Kim looked surprised. "You're heading off?" Beside her, Natalie, a blond-haired, blue-eyed china doll with all the subtlety of a brick to the head, was busy checking something on her phone.

"Yeah, I'm meeting Dad for lunch," I said.

"Want me to come?" Sarah asked. Kim gave her a quizzical look, tipping her head to the side. Her glossy black hair gleamed.

"Nah, this is a daddy-daughter date." I tried to smile, but it felt strained. The butterflies in my stomach were undermining me. Stupid butterflies.

"Will you be back?"

"Not sure." Our computer science teacher, Mr Holbrook, had threatened our class with a failing grade if we didn't attend, even after exams, and we had his class during fourth period.

Now Natalie was looking at me strangely too. "Are you nuts? You can see your dad any time."

"I haven't missed any of Holbrook's classes this term. I've got a couple of absences up my sleeve, and Dad and I have some catching up to do. I'll get him to write me a note."

Kim patted me on the shoulder. "If there's anything you want to talk about, you know where we are," she said, shushing Natalie when she opened her mouth to object.

"Thanks," I said, although the idea of sharing the embarrassing details of last night with even these, my closest friends, made me cringe inwardly. Still, I was grateful they'd offered.

Sarah extracted a promise that I'd talk to her tonight before letting me walk to my car. I felt her eyes on me until I pulled out of the car park.

The drive home was short but gave me enough time to build up a knot of nerves before I pulled into my spot out in front of my aunt's house. The knot twisted tighter when I saw Dad's ute wasn't in the driveway. I grabbed my bags from the boot and let myself into the house, keys jingling.

"Dad?" I manoeuvred the gym bag and backpack into the house and left them in the hallway. Hamish ran up to sniff my legs, nose twitching as he tried to figure out where I'd been. Could he smell Casper on me?

"He's not here," Ryan called from the lounge room. I poked my head in and saw him sitting on the couch, watching daytime television in his pyjamas. He shrugged at my raised eyebrow. "Mum insisted I have a day off work to recover. I didn't think I needed it, but you know her."

"Did Dad come back here after nine or so this morning?"

"He popped in, yeah. He went out to the shed. Then he told me he was going back to his place to get something, but that he'd be back here by lunchtime. He'll be back soon, I guess."

Disappointed, I sent Dad a quick text to let him know I was home. Then I stuffed my phone in my pocket; Dad never answered right away, if he answered at all. The mobile phone reception at the farm was bad, so if he was still there he might not receive it.

He'd almost certainly gone out to the shed to see the painting. Was that why he'd decided to drive back to the farm? He'd have enough time to get there and back in a morning, but it'd be a rush.

To keep myself busy, I unpacked the gym bags and put my washing in the machine, dumped my school things on the desk in my room, then made myself a salami, cheese and tomato sandwich. Ryan started hovering when he heard me in the kitchen, so I rolled my eyes and made him one too. He poured us a couple of glasses of apple juice and sat at the dining table, waiting.

When he'd had a couple of mouthfuls I asked casually, "So, you know how you said that painting was based on a dream?" He grimaced, which I took as assent. "What was the dream about?"

He didn't answer at first, taking a couple of extra mouthfuls of sandwich. I scowled.

"I don't remember much of it." He sighed. "I woke up in a cold sweat, like I'd had a fever during the night, and all that stayed with me was that image. I painted it as best I could. I don't know if I did it justice."

"Don't be silly. That's the best painting you've ever done."

"I know," he said, ducking his head with embarrassment as he accepted the praise. The red roots were showing beneath the black dye of his hair. "But the way she shimmered and sort of glowed? I don't think I captured that at all. She was like a firefly."

His words sunk into the depths of my soul. Like a firefly. Was that how she'd looked in my dream?

"I've never seen a photo of her, you know," he told me, pushing a bit of crust around his plate with a finger. "I know that's what Mum thinks happened, but it didn't. I know it sounds freaky, but..."

"I believe you," I said. "Sarah does too."

"You do?" He was surprised. "I mean, I figured Sarah might. She's always loved mystical stuff: ghost stories and dreams that come true. Whatever. But you're Sensible Isla." He smiled. "I remember you telling Sarah Santa wasn't real."

"I made her cry."

"Yeah." He punched me on the shoulder, trying to look stern. His sparkling eyes gave him away. "Don't you know that's the big brother's job?"

"Sorry."

I was, too. I remembered the lecture I'd gotten from Dad afterwards: about how sometimes it was better to let someone believe in something we knew wasn't real, so long as their belief wasn't hurting them and made them happy. "Even if it's a lie?" I'd demanded of him with a five-year-old's righteous indignation.

"Yes, even then," Dad had told me.

Was that what he'd been telling himself all these years?

"So why do you?" Ryan asked me. I gave him a blank look. "Believe me, I mean?"

"It's been a weird couple of days," I sighed. "Right now I'd believe it if you told me the sky was pink."

"Would you believe me if I said you owe me twenty dollars?" He sat up straight, expression hopeful.

I laughed. "Not likely."

After we ate, I spent some time cleaning the house, burning off restless energy. My phone remained in my pocket, where I'd feel it vibrating even if I didn't hear it over the vacuum cleaner or while I was emptying the bins.

By midafternoon I still hadn't heard from Dad, and my anxiety about our promised conversation—and irritation that he'd stood me up after I skipped school to be here—turned to worry. What if he'd had a car accident? I rang his mobile phone and the phone at the farm, but there was no answer at either one. I left messages at both numbers, trying not to sound shrill.

I considered driving out to the farm to look for him, but what if he arrived here after I left and I missed him?

Ryan, who had finally showered and dressed, eyed me with a frown. "You're worried." It wasn't hard for him to tell; he had eyes. "Do you want me to drive out there for you?"

"You can't," I protested. "You're sick."

"I am not!"

"You passed out from heat exhaustion after not eating and having weird dreams. What if you have another dizzy spell and crash your car?"

"I'm neither hot nor hungry," he pointed out, his tone sharp.

"What if it's more, though?"

"Like what?" He stared at me. "Do you think I've got a brain tumour or something?"

Before I could answer, someone came in the front door. My heart skipped a beat, but it was Sarah, not my father, who came into the lounge where Ryan and I were glaring at each other. "Who's got a brain tumour?"

"Me, according to Isla," Ryan said.

"I never said that. I meant what if you have a virus or something? You should take it easy."

"Now you sound like Mum," Ryan said.

"You do," Sarah agreed. She looked around. "Where's Uncle David?"

"He never showed." I grumbled. Sarah gave me a hug.

"That's what we were arguing about," Ryan told his sister. "He was here not long after you left for school, but he left to go to the farm. He said he'd be back here a couple of hours ago, and Isla can't reach him on the phone. I was going to drive out there to make sure he's okay."

"I appreciate it, but—"

"Yeah, I know; I have a brain tumour and shouldn't be driving."

"Why don't you call Mrs Wilson and ask her to see if he's home?" Sarah asked.

Lily Wilson was a widow who lived on the farm across from Dad's place. Her husband had died of a heart attack fifteen years ago, but she still called herself "Mrs". She said she was too old to be a Miss. She kept alpacas and horses and bred Russian Blues. She'd babysat me occasionally when I was little, before I'd moved in with my aunt and cousins.

"You, Sarah, are a freaking genius." I kissed her cheek.

"I know." She buffed her nails against her shirt, a twinkle in her eye.

I didn't have Mrs Wilson's number. Fortunately she was listed in the White Pages online.

The phone rang a few times before she answered. It felt like at least an hour. "Hello?"

"Hi, Mrs Wilson, it's Isla Blackman. How are you?"

"Very well. One of my queens, Bluebelle, had her babies four weeks ago, so I'm up to my neck in kittens. You should come out and visit, dear. See if any of them take your fancy."

"You're very kind," I said quickly, before she started giving me a rundown on the names and personalities of each kitten. She'd done it before. "I was wondering for now if you could do me a favour?"

"What's that?"

"Dad isn't answering his phone, and he's running late for an appointment. I was wondering if you could—"

"Go over and check on him for you? Of course, dear. We single farm folk need to look out for each other." I'd often wondered if she was interested in my father, but nothing had ever come of it. He might not thank me for sending her over there, but screw it. He was either in some kind of trouble or ignoring me—which would still get him in trouble, only with me. "Let me get my boots on and I'll head right over," she continued. "What number shall I call you back on if he's not home?"

I gave her the numbers for the house phone and my mobile. We hung up after a round of polite goodbyes.

I hated waiting at the best of times. These weren't the best of times. I stared out the front window, biting my lip.

"This isn't how it's meant to work," Sarah told me,

perching on the arm of the couch.

"What do you mean?"

"You're the teenager. He's meant to worry about you, not the other way around."

"I'll make sure to tell him when I see him."

"He was worrying plenty last night," Ryan added.

"Shush, you," Sarah scolded, chasing him from the room. I heard her tell him off in a low voice before she came back alone. "Sorry. He's a doofus."

"It's okay. He's right. Maybe this is Dad paying me back."

"As if he'd do that." She was right, but I shrugged anyway. Sarah decided to change the subject. "Class this afternoon was a total waste of time. Holbrook didn't do anything except mark the roll. Then he sat at his desk and read the paper. So rude."

"Was he angry I wasn't there?"

"I told him you'd gone home sick, but he didn't say anything. Half the class was missing, so you weren't alone. The rest of us spent the time surfing the net or chatting." She grinned. "It was kind of fun. Best class he's run all semester. And no homework."

I smiled absently, twirling a lock of hair around my finger and clutching my mobile phone in my other hand. After a long moment, Sarah stood. "I'm going to make a coffee. Want one?"

"No, thanks. I've had way too much caffeine this afternoon." If I had anymore I'd start climbing the walls like Spider-Man.

Cabinets slammed, water ran and soon the house filled with the sound and rich aroma of percolating coffee. I stared out the window. Across the road, at the park, a couple of kids were going up and down endlessly on a seesaw while a woman in shorts and a white shirt sat on the nearby bench, watching them. Jack had said if I wanted to find him I should go to the park. Did that mean he was somewhere nearby, watching? How else would he know I was there? Some sort of fae trick?

Jack could do any number of strange things. Would he be able to tell me where my father was?

When, a couple of minutes later, the woman herded the kids home, I went into the kitchen. Sarah was on a stool at the counter, sipping her coffee and flicking through a trashy magazine. Hamish was curled up underneath the stool, asleep.

"I'm going to get some fresh air," I told her. "I'll be across the road. If Mrs Wilson calls on the landline, can you come get me?"

"Sure," she said. "You're taking your phone, just in case?"

I nodded, holding it up.

Across the road, the park was still deserted. I looked around, trying to spot Jack, but he was nowhere to be seen. After a moment I sat on one of the two swings, moving back and forth in a small arc, scuffing the tanbark under the swing with one toe. Soon my sneakers were powdered with fine brown dust.

This was silly. As if Jack was going to show up.

"Are you okay, Isla?"

I jumped, nearly dropping my phone. Jack came around the climbing frame beyond the seesaw, walking towards me. He wore the same soft grey jumper and loose-fitting jeans as he had the night before, although they didn't look any dirtier. The hood was up, covering his long ears, but a golden-blond lock of hair had escaped to fall down the side of his face. His skin seemed smoother than it had: the wrinkles were extremely fine, barely noticeable.

"Jack," I gasped. "Do you live around here?" The park was in the middle of an open, grassy space ringed with footpaths and tall shrubs. Beyond that were the back fences of several houses. I hadn't seen him coming. And I should have.

He shrugged, smiling, and sat sideways on a plastic bouncy frog near the swing set. I twisted on my seat to look at him. "In a manner of speaking," he said, eyes sparkling. They were a deep blue, like a pair of sapphires: almost black except where the direct light struck them. Then they lit up with brilliant flecks of light.

"How's your hand?"

He held it up, palm towards me. A faint pink line gleamed where the burn had been the night before. "Almost healed. By tomorrow that mark will be gone."

"Wow. You weren't kidding when you said you heal quickly."

"No," he said, smiling a little. "I was trying to find out more about your mother. So far all I have determined is that she is from the Old World, a mid-ranking *aosidhe*."

"What does that mean?"

"She is, among our kind, nobility. A ruler of the *dui-nesidhe* people more broadly." The latter term must describe all of the fae. And my French teacher had claimed I would never be able to learn a foreign language. Take that, Mr Fournier. "But we already knew she would be *aosidhe*," Jack continued.

"We did?"

"Well, yes." He blinked those strange, wonderful eyes. I tried not to stare. "I am sorry, I forgot. I should say *I* already knew she would be *aosidhe*." He gestured at me as though that would be explanation enough.

The fact my mother was some sort of fairy princess made me want to laugh out loud at the absurdity. It felt like I'd stepped into the pages of *Cinderella* or something. And if faeries were real, what about other supernatural creatures? Was it possible Dominic had seen a ghost all those years ago? Had the séance at the Halloween party genuinely contacted a spirit guide named Daniel? Would Dracula be annoyed Sarah had dressed up as him for a party? My mind whirled as Jack continued.

"So I asked around for rumours of an *aosidhe* woman who had birthed a child to a human. There was such a one, in the Old World. She sought her child for many years."

*She wants to find me?* I felt the tiniest stirrings of something inside my heart, something I'd never imagined was worth dwelling on—a hope, or a desire, for a real mother. Someone who'd look at me with the same loving pride as Aunt Elizabeth did her children.

Jack watched the emotions play across my face and stood, stepping over to brush my hand with his fingertips. His expression was sympathetic. "Isla. Do not dream too wildly, not yet. Let me find out more first."

"But you said—"

"We do not know *why* she is seeking you." His soft voice contained a warning. I shuddered, feeling as though a cloud had passed in front of the sun despite the empty azure sky.

"You think she might want to … hurt me?"

"It is too early to say. But yes, it is possible. My people are not always, or even often, known for their kindness. That is true twice over for the *aosidhe*. They are powerful and often cruel. Do not leap to conclusions either way yet."

"Oh." Well, that was sobering. If I were going to step into the pages of *Cinderella*, I would prefer it be the sanitised Disney story rather than the Brothers Grimm version, with its self-mutilation and angry doves pecking people's eyes out. The Brothers Grimm had based their stories on old folk tales rather than film rating systems; the hair standing up on the back of my neck told me which version my gut thought more credible.

I guess I'd stick to just having a father. At least until Jack could find out more.

Speaking of which. I couldn't believe I'd forgotten about him, even for a moment. I was the worst half-human daughter in the world. "I was wondering if you could help me with something," I asked.

"If it is in my power," he nodded, hooking his thumbs in his pockets.

"Dad was meant to meet me at lunchtime. He never arrived, and now I can't get in touch with him. Do you have some way to track him down or make sure he's okay?"

"I could, but it would take time."

"How much time?"

"That would depend where he is. At least several hours."

"You found me." I indicated the park with a nod of my head.

"I did. But you are *duinesidhe*, and I knew you might come here. Your father is not. And he surrounds himself with iron, which makes him even more difficult to sense."

I paused. "You know about that?"

"I have been watching you since the night you tried to summon your mother." He meant the séance. "That was unwise, by the way. It drew attention to you as clearly as if you had lit a signal fire atop a cliff."

I nibbled my lip, looking past Jack to Aunt Elizabeth's house. There was no sign of movement over there, except for a tree swaying in the breeze. "You know, saying you've been watching me makes you sound pretty stalkerish."

"I am not sure what you mean." He frowned.

"Like a crazy person. Or a Peeping Tom. You say your people aren't known for kindness. How do I know you don't plan to hurt me?"

His expressive mouth thinned. "Because I gave you my word I meant you no harm."

"No offence, Jack, but how do I know you're the sort of person that keeps your promises?"

"Because I am *duinesidhe*," he said solemnly. "And *duinesidhe* that break a sworn oath grow sick and die, *aosidhe* or otherwise."

I searched his face for a lie, fingers tightening on the swing's chains, but couldn't find one. "You're serious, aren't you." A statement, not a question.

"Yes. It can take hours or months, depending on the strength of the oath and the seriousness of the violation. The only way to prevent it is if the person the fae swore to releases them from the oath, or if they somehow make amends to that person."

I swallowed hard. "Would the same thing happen to me?"

"It might," Jack said, voice gentle.

"But I... Don't think I'm a bad person for this, but I've broken promises to people before, sometimes, and nothing like that has happened."

"Agreeing to something is not the same as swearing to something," Jack said. "To swear an oath requires a formal statement, like *I swear* or *I promise*."

"Even so…" I could think of a couple of awkward high school moments where I'd promised to do something and hadn't—not always through any fault of my own, but it had still happened.

"It may be…" He trailed off, eyes growing distant as he thought. "You also used to touch your father's ironwork before and not suffer ill effects, did you not?" I nodded. "You celebrated your coming of age this month, Isla. It was after that time the iron burned you. It is not a *duinesidhe* thing, for the power to manifest itself after a coming of age, but I think in your case that may be what has happened."

"So if I break a promise to someone now, I could die?" Goosebumps shivered along my arms.

"You may merely grow ill," he said. "Your reaction to the touch of iron was less than mine would have been."

It was macabre, but I couldn't help but ask. "What would've happened to you?"

"My skin would have blackened and burned and, if the contact was prolonged, the bone would have turned to ash and crumbled away." He said it like it was a straightforward thing. I stared up at him, horrified. He tried to smile reassuringly, but he looked uncomfortable, as if he'd seen someone burned away by the touch of iron. "Do not worry," he continued. "Real iron is rare now, and steel does not hurt as much. It scalds, that is all—similar to the way the iron affected you."

"Oh, is that all?" My tone was sarcastic.

His smile was real then, lighting up his eyes. "Indeed."

"It doesn't make sense, though. Isn't steel made of iron?"

"Yes. Something about the process dilutes the—"

The screen door across the road bang closed. Sarah was heading down the stairs, Ryan behind her. Jack bowed to me, a slight incline of the head and shoulders. "I will see you later, Isla." He strode away.

Sarah was holding the phone in her hand. Had Mrs Wilson called? I leapt up, the swing swaying wildly, and rushed across the street to meet her.

She looked upset. So did Ryan. "Did she call?" I asked, heart in my throat.

"Yes, just now." Her voice cracked. She swallowed and tried again. "She found him on his driveway, near the gate. She said it looked like he got out of his ute to close the gate on the way out. She called for an ambulance before she rang us."

"Is he...?" I couldn't bring myself to finish the sentence.

"He's alive. But she couldn't wake him. They're taking him to Canberra Hospital."

I was running for my car before the words finished leaving her lips.

# CHAPTER NINE

My fingers shook, jingling the car keys in my hand. The metal wouldn't fit in the car lock. I tried again. Ugh. Why wasn't it cooperating?

"I'm driving." Sarah snatched the keyring. I stared at her. The firm set of her jaw matched the steel in her gaze. "I am. You're too freaked, and I don't need a phone call telling me you're on the way to the hospital too."

Words eluded me. My mind had stopped functioning the moment my cousin relayed what Mrs Wilson had found at Dad's house. He was lying on the ground. Was he alive? Or dying? A lump formed in my throat.

Would I get to the hospital before he passed?

Sarah tossed Ryan the phone. "Call Mum. Tell her what's going on."

He nodded and hurried inside.

The drive to the hospital felt hours long. Sarah sat right on the speed limit. I wanted to object, but she was right: we wanted to get there in one piece. And being pulled over by police would hardly help. So I gritted my teeth and said nothing, instead staring out the window at passing houses, trees and light poles. My hands clenched into fists, between glances at the clock on my phone to confirm time wasn't moving as slowly as I thought.

It wasn't.

It only took us twenty minutes to reach the hospital, and another ten to find a spot in the multistorey car park, in a two-hour parking zone. We hurried out of the garage and through the main entrance into the hospital.

Sarah steered me through the current of visitors and slow-moving patients, following the signs to emergency. The bright fluorescent lights dazzled my eyes as I followed her, grateful she'd come. The nurse working the desk in the emergency department clicked a few times at her computer before telling me, not without sympathy, that my father was being brought in on the Careflight helicopter and they weren't expecting him for another ten minutes or so.

A helicopter. That made sense, given how far his farm was out of town. He'd be excited about going in a helicopter. If he was awake to notice it. I took a deep breath to stop myself from crying.

The nurse was still talking to me. Luckily, Sarah was paying attention, giving her my name and mobile number. My mind whirled like the blades of the helicopter carrying my father. Morbid visions of him, unconscious, lying still on a gurney, filled my brain. Would he be awake when he arrived?

"We'll page you when we know anything," the nurse told me.

"Come on." Sarah took me by the elbow. "Let's go get

a coffee or something."

"I want to stay here."

She didn't bat an eyelid. "Okay. Do you want me to get you anything?"

I shook my head, and she left in search of a vending machine.

All of the chairs in the emergency department were occupied. A man sat slumped over with his head in his hands, elbows resting on his knees; a woman beside him had her arm around his hunched shoulders. A worried-looking mother cuddled a limp toddler whose eyes were bright and feverish, flushed spots on his cheeks. A father sat with a teenage boy in a sports uniform who cradled his arm, trying to look brave, although he winced with pain every time his father shifted in the uncomfortable plastic chair. The atmosphere in the waiting area combined anxiety, frustrated impatience and sadness, laced with the scent of disinfectant. How did the nurse working behind the desk stand it?

I leaned against the pale green wall, closing my eyes so I wouldn't have to see the glacial pace of the second hand on the wall-mounted clock.

Sarah returned after a while, leaning beside me. "I got you some water. I know you said you didn't want anything..."

"Oh. Thanks." I took the bottle from her and had a sip.

And we waited.

And waited.

The mother and toddler were called in to be treated, replaced by a woman with curled white hair who continuously wrung her hands. Sarah slipped out to move the car into the long-stay part of the multistorey. Aunt Elizabeth and Ryan arrived, and we exchanged hugs. Ryan brought my bag from home; I slung it over my shoulder, feeling less naked. Aunt Elizabeth went to talk to the nurse at the desk again.

"What did she say?" I asked when she came back over to us. "It's been forever. He must be here by now."

"He is," she said. "They're running some tests and scans on him now. They'll page us when we can see him."

"When?"

Aunt Elizabeth put a sympathetic hand on my arm. "She didn't know."

"Is he still unconscious?" Sarah asked.

Her mother nodded. The lines around her eyes seemed more prominent than usual.

"Uh oh," Sarah murmured. I looked passed her to see Lily Wilson bearing down on us. She was dressed more neatly than I'd ever seen her, wearing slacks, a patterned blue shirt and sensible black shoes. A cardigan was slung over one arm and her steel grey hair was bound on the top of her head in a severe style that belied her good nature.

"I'm so sorry." She swept over to engulf me in a lavender-scented hug. "I wanted to come with him in the helicopter but they said no. I had to drive."

"It's okay," I mumbled, overwhelmed.

"Thank you for coming all this way." Aunt Elizabeth smiled graciously, drawing Mrs Wilson back from me. I gulped an appreciative breath. "David would be grateful. And thanks for checking on him."

"Not at all," Mrs Wilson said. "It was quite the shock to see him lying there beside his ute. The engine was still running, you know, and the door was open. I drove it back up to the house after the helicopter left. Have you heard anything?" She looked around, as though she expected him—or an informative doctor—to materialise before her eyes.

"Not yet. Soon."

Mrs Wilson clicked her tongue and looked past me to see Sarah and Ryan. "Goodness, Elizabeth, are these your children? Haven't they grown!"

"Yes." My aunt looked amused by the suppressed outrage of her adult—or almost adult in Sarah's case—offspring.

"I don't think I've seen them in … well, it's been years." She gave Ryan a disapproving look. "You look better with red hair." He smiled stiffly.

Aunt Elizabeth glanced at us and took Mrs Wilson's arm. "How about we go to the café and get you something to drink? You must be parched after such a long drive."

"Well, I don't mind admitting I am a little thirsty. Do you suppose they'd do a proper pot of tea?"

"Let's go find out. The children can wait here in case there's news."

Sarah looked like she was going to protest at being called a child, but Ryan pinched her arm. She jumped but said nothing as Aunt Elizabeth hurried the older lady away.

They were almost at the emergency department exit when Mrs Wilson stopped suddenly, escaping my aunt's grip and hurrying back to us. "Isla, dear, it slipped my mind, what with everything. I'd forget my head if it weren't screwed on some days." Out of the folds of her voluminous cardigan she pulled a large envelope the colour of worn ivory. She pressed it into my hands. "I found this on the passenger seat of your father's ute when I moved it back up to the house. I thought you'd best look after it for him."

"Thank you. I will," I said, the dutiful daughter.

She took my chin in her work-roughened hands, tilting my head so I looked up into her face. "Astonishing," she murmured. "You do look just like her."

"What?" I stepped back so she had to release me.

"Like your mother."

"How do you know what my mother looks like?" I asked, exasperated. It felt like everyone knew more than I did, although I knew it wasn't entirely true. At the very least, Sarah and Ryan were as in the dark as I was.

More, since I'd met Jack.

Mrs Wilson reached out and tapped the envelope that I held against my chest.

"You went through Uncle David's stuff?" Ryan stepped forward, Sarah flanking him.

Mrs Wilson had the grace to look abashed. "I had to check whether there was something important in there, something the paramedics might have needed to know. Or it could have been important papers."

"Right," he said, his eyes narrowing to icy slits.

"You should go get that tea," Sarah interrupted before he said anything else. His expression was thunderous. "Mum's waiting for you." Aunt Elizabeth stood near the sliding door that led past the ambulance station to the main reception. She was looking back at us with a frown.

"Right you are, Sarah," Mrs Wilson agreed, hurrying away.

"I never did like that old bat," Ryan muttered as soon as she was out of earshot.

"Her heart's in the right place," Sarah said. She'd been quite fond of Lily Wilson when we were younger and I

**106**

still lived with Dad. When she came to visit, we'd often go across to Mrs Wilson's farm and visit the latest batch of kittens or ride her fat old horses around the yard. "She did drive all the way in here."

Ryan grunted, turning to look at me. My fingers clutched the thick envelope, which felt lumpy in places. I didn't feel queasy, though, so it didn't have any iron in it.

"Are you going to open it?" Sarah asked.

"Yeah. I want to find somewhere quieter to sit down, though." The emergency department was still crowded and I'd been standing around for ages. Hours, maybe. My feet ached. And the nurse had said they'd page me.

"We can't go to the café," Ryan said. "She'll butt in again."

"Let's see if we can find some unoccupied chairs somewhere," Sarah said, leading the way.

After some searching, we found a set of four plastic-covered chairs set around a large potted plant. The nook was in direct view of the front desk but hidden from the door leading to the café, so we should be safe from interruption by Mrs Wilson.

I sat between my cousins. How much of their protectiveness was concern for me and how much was curiosity about what was in the envelope? It didn't bother me when it was them, though.

The envelope opened at one end. I reached inside to pull out a smaller, glossy envelope with an old photo lab logo on it. Inside, contained in a series of joined plastic sleeves, were half a dozen strips of photo negatives. A brief check against the fluorescent lights revealed the photos to be of people, the negative eerily reversing the colours and the images so small I couldn't make out much of them.

"Can I look?" Ryan asked when I slid them back into their envelope. I handed it to him and reached back into the larger envelope, pulling out a bundle of old colour photos of various sizes. I flicked through them slowly, my heart in my mouth. Sarah leaned her head on my shoulder to look. I barely noticed.

The photos were of my mother. I recognised her from Ryan's painting and my dream, but more so from looking at my own reflection all these years. The photos lacked the surreal, ethereal air Ryan had given her. These could easily be photos of a regular human woman.

Her hair was a few shades darker than my own, almost black, as were her eyes. But those were the only real differences between us, and I wasn't sure they'd be obvious to a stranger. Her skin was pale, and her face had the same fine-boned shape and smooth forehead. Her eyebrows arched above her eyes, and her lips were full, although hers had the red hue of lipstick in every photo, something I rarely wore.

There were a couple of photos of her in a wedding dress, holding a simple bouquet of off-white roses. The dress was antique-ivory satin, strapless, with a sweetheart neckline. The bodice sparkled with rhinestones and crystal beading. A chapel train curved behind her, and a veil hung back over her hair, which was also beaded with crystals in a way that reminded me of how my hair had been decorated in my dream.

In one photo my father stood alongside her, a huge grin on his face. He was slimmer, handsome in a black suit with a white shirt and an ivory tie. His hair was a brighter red, not yet faded to strawberry blond on its way to grey.

I wondered what he looked like now, unconscious in

a hospital bed. Tears stung my eyes. I flicked to the next photo.

My mother was sitting on a couch, wearing a loose-fitting top with black slacks; I realised after a moment that what I'd thought was an unflattering fall of fabric was actually the gentle curve of a belly early in pregnancy. Dad sat next to her, looking as over the moon as he had in the wedding photo, grinning fit to burst, eyes sparkling.

More photos of her as her pregnancy progressed, the belly growing more prominent. In the last one, her stomach was so round she looked as though she had a basketball up her shirt, but the rest of her body was still slender and elegant—although her expression showed some of the discomfort in a tightness in the jaw and around the eyes.

There were no photos of her in the hospital with me as a newborn. I looked at her face in the last photo. What was she was thinking? Had she abandoned me in the hospital, as Aunt Elizabeth had hinted? Was she really a fae, a *duinesidhe,* like Jack had told me? She looked graceful and lovely in the photos, even the last one, but she also looked human. There was no hint of the supernatural about her: no glowing skin or dresses made of fragments of broken glass.

"She didn't smile much, did she?" Sarah murmured. I startled. I was so engrossed in the photos and my own thoughts I'd forgotten where I was.

"She looks wistful," Ryan said, adding, "And your dad looks head-over-heels in love."

I nodded, lips pressed tightly together, before handing the photos to Sarah and reaching again into the envelope.

There was one thing left inside: a drawstring bag made

of navy-blue velvet. Inside it were dried rose petals, possibly from the wedding bouquet, and two plain gold rings. One was larger, sized for my father, and the other was small. It looked as though it would fit me, but I didn't try it on. Instead I gazed at it for a long moment, running a finger along the smooth, glossy metal. The ring gleamed from many years of care, with one small exception: on the inside, an engraving had been scratched out. I ran my finger across the frantic indentations, wondering what could have caused them. No accident I could imagine.

The sight of the scratches chilled me. I slipped the rings back into the drawstring bag, knotting it tight and dropping it in the envelope.

Sarah flipped back to the wedding photo in which my mother stood alone. "When you get married you should wear a dress that colour," she told me. "It would suit your skin tone."

I opened my mouth to answer, but the hospital paging system clicked and crackled to life.

"Isla Blackman, please come to the main reception. Isla Blackman."

Sarah and Ryan returned the photos and negatives to the envelope and we hurried over to the reception desk.

Dad was in the Intensive Care Unit.

We met Aunt Elizabeth in the foyer. Mrs Wilson was with her, but left when we were told only family would be permitted to see Dad. To her credit, she didn't make a fuss, just gave me a kiss on the cheek and my cousins a fond pat before leaving. Ryan glowered at her but, if she noticed, she didn't say anything.

We were given directions to the third floor of building twelve, on the other side of the emergency department from the main reception. I rode the lift without a word, clutching the envelope to my chest and trying to concentrate on breathing.

Unlike the one in the emergency department, the waiting area outside the ICU was empty. The door to the unit itself was locked; an intercom was mounted to the left of the door. I pressed the button.

"Yes?" asked a tinny female voice.

"Um. We're here to see David Blackman?"

"One moment please." There was a click as the magnetic door released to let us in.

"Wait here," Aunt Elizabeth told my cousins as I pulled the door open. Sarah began to object, but my aunt shook her head. "They have a two-visitor limit."

"Oh."

"Come on. Mum will let us know when it's our turn. We can have a coffee while we wait," Ryan said, faking enthusiasm.

Sarah gave me a brief, strong hug and I went into the ward, my aunt following behind.

We were met by a beautiful nurse with chocolate-coloured skin and neat dark hair pinned to the top of her head. "I'm Rachael," she said, smiling at us. "Have you been to the ICU before?"

We shook our heads.

"Well, the first thing we need you to do on entering and before leaving is wash your hands." She indicated a pump pack of hand sanitiser mounted on the wall. The pink liquid dried quickly on my hands, leaving a lingering scent of alcohol. "And please turn your mobile phones off while you're in the ward. They can interfere with our equipment."

She led us into the unit: it was a large, open room with a central nurse station near the doors and a ring of beds around the walls. Each of the beds was in its own alcove, an island in a sea of whirring, glowing machinery. Curtain tracks snaked across the entrance to each alcove, but none of the curtains were closed.

Rachael led us to one of the alcoves. In front was a smaller nurse's station, covered in charts.

Beyond the station lay Dad, his face relaxed and eyes closed as though he was sleeping ... if I ignored the intravenous line poking out of his left arm, the profusion of cables and rubber tubes snaking out from beneath the blankets, and the clear plastic oxygen mask covering his nose and mouth.

Although usually if Dad fell asleep on his back, he snored pretty loudly. Another sign things weren't right.

"Oh, Dad," I breathed, glancing at Rachael, who sat at the nurse's station. "Am I allowed to touch him?"

"Sure," the nurse nodded. "You can bring in music as well, if you like, so long as you provide headphones so you don't disturb other patients or visitors."

I took the single seat beside the bed. Aunt Elizabeth and Rachael spoke together in low voices.

It felt weird. I'd imagined Dad would be in a smaller room somewhere: maybe not a private room, but not a room with so many beds in it. He was separated from his neighbours only by a six-foot partition on either side, lined with shelves. There was also a surprising number of nurses—stationed at the entrance to each alcove, circulating throughout the room, checking the various machines, reading charts and talking to those patients who were awake.

I took Dad's hand and leaned in close, whispering. "Dad, I don't know if you can hear me..." I studied his face, but there was no reaction. "I have the envelope you had on the front seat of your car. The one with the photos of ... of Mum. I guess you must have gone home to get it for me. What happened? Did someone hurt you?"

He didn't answer. I looked down at his strong, callused hands, at my smaller ones wrapped around them. "You looked really handsome at the wedding," I said. "When you wake up you can tell me about it."

I sat there in silence until Aunt Elizabeth returned. She took my other hand and stood beside me. "The nurse said the doctors haven't made an official diagnosis yet," she said, "but he's in a coma. They've started running tests for toxins or some sort of brain injury. He'll be having an MRI soon."

Tears welled in my eyes as I stared at my father's face, trying to be strong. Across the room, a woman sat next to an elderly lady and began to sob quietly. Grief tightened the back of my throat and hot tears burned my eyes. One of the nurses began talking softly to the woman, laying a hand on her shoulder.

Looking away from them, I took a deep breath, and another, and felt myself regain a tenuous grip on my emotions.

"They wanted to know who his next of kin was," my aunt said. I gasped, my control slipping; she spoke quickly to reassure me. "It's not what you're thinking, sweetheart. It's so they have someone to talk to about his medical history."

"Oh." She was looking at me, waiting for something. The idea dawned slowly. "Am I meant to do it?"

"Only if you feel up to it. I can if you'd prefer."

The idea of being directly responsible for Dad's wellbeing was overwhelming. What if I forgot something? What if there were things—other things, medical things, not just personal ones—he hadn't told his daughter about? "Would you, please?" My voice was small with shame at my cowardice. "But you have to let me know if there's anything I can do to help. Phone calls and things?"

"Of course."

The talk of medical histories reminded me of something. "Sarah said she thought you gave Dad a tablet last night to help him sleep."

Aunt Elizabeth nodded, expression grave. "I did. It was an over-the-counter medication; I told the nurse about it. She's going to let the doctor know. She said it wasn't known for causing this sort of reaction. Especially not twelve hours later. But they can't rule out some sort of allergic shock either." She looked equal parts anxious and relieved. I squeezed her hand.

After a while, Aunt Elizabeth left and Sarah came in. She didn't say anything, just stood beside to me, hand on my shoulder. Then she went back out again and Ryan came in. He frowned at my father for a long moment, looking uneasy. Then he shook his head, snapping himself out of whatever dark place his thoughts had gone. "Hi, Uncle David." He took Dad's limp hand and shook it, then placed it back on the white sheet. I tried to smile.

"Mum's thinking we should head home soon. It's dinnertime," he told me. I blinked, surprised it was so late.

I didn't feel hungry. "She said we could come back tomorrow with some of his things."

"That makes sense." I reached down the side of the chair to collect my bag and Dad's envelope of photographs. I considered leaving one of the photos here for him but decided not to. Dad had never displayed the photos in his home; maybe he didn't want to see them. Besides, what if it got lost? Instead, I leaned over and kissed him on the cheek. "I'll see you tomorrow," I told him. "Don't go anywhere, okay?"

"A specialist came and talked to Mum while we were out there," Ryan told me as we walked across the ward to the exit. "He needed her to sign a form so they can contact Uncle David's doctor to get his records. But he said he doesn't have any of the typical physical signs of brain damage. Something about his posture and pupils being normal. I didn't understand any of it."

My heart lifted a little. I'd been trying to fend off dark thoughts about my vibrant and energetic father being a vegetable for the rest of his days. "That's good news, right?" I nodded a farewell to the nurse at the station as I applied more of the pink sanitiser.

"Probably," Ryan agreed, pushing the release button to open the door. Aunt Elizabeth and Sarah were standing on the other side, ready to leave. "But, well, the doctor was asking a lot of questions about whether Uncle David did drugs."

"What?" I stared at him. "No way."

"That's what we told the doctor," Sarah chimed in. "He barely even drinks."

"They're still waiting on the results of a few blood tests, so we'll know more then." Aunt Elizabeth sighed.

"How about we go home? Ryan, we'll pick something up for dinner on the way."

"Sure."

We split up at the hospital exit, Sarah and I heading to the multistorey car park. It was dark outside; the sun had set and a sliver of moon skimmed atop light clouds, visible between the tall hospital buildings. I took my car keys from her. She didn't protest.

My cousin was quiet for several minutes, finally speaking when we pulled up at a set of traffic lights. "I don't really know what to say," she murmured. "It's been such a crazy twenty-four hours."

"I know." And she didn't even know the half of it. The idea made me grimace, turning my face away so she couldn't see my strained expression. "I just want to go home and sleep."

"I'm not sure I can."

The light turned green and we set off. "I think I could. The bed at Dom's place was okay, but not as good as mine. I missed my pillow."

Sarah laughed. My smile was genuine then, glad my comment had achieved the desired effect. "That's right, I'd almost forgotten you were a dirty stopout last night."

"We've had other things on our minds," I pointed out. "And I slept in the spare bed."

"Ah, but where did *he* sleep?"

"In his room. Although," I added after a moment, "I didn't sleep alone."

"*What?*" Her voice rose with delighted shock.

"Their cat slept on the bed too."

She groaned.

"If it's any consolation, it was a boy cat."

"You're such a disappointment," she sighed.

"Sorry about that."

The conversation reminded me I hadn't called Dominic since that morning. Guilt gnawed at my stomach like Hamish with a bone, although it took me half the drive home to figure out why.

When I was worried about Dad that afternoon, I'd gone looking for Jack instead of calling my boyfriend.

*That's silly,* I scolded myself. I'd sought Jack because I'd hoped there was a way he'd be able to find my father, not because I'd rather confide in him.

Jack was also the only one I'd told the details of the confrontation I'd had with Dad last night ... but Jack understood that stuff, right? It would be unreasonable of me to expect anyone else—Sarah, Dominic, the others in my family or among my friends—to think that sort of talk was anything but crazy. Sarah and Natalie went through a crystals-and-chakras phase during early high school, but they'd both more or less moved past enthusiasm for the supernatural by now.

Dad would have understood and not thought I was crazy. Although he'd hardly needed to be told about it after it happened, either.

To shut my confused thoughts up, I resolved to give Dominic a call when I got home. At least that would ease my guilt, if not any of the other horrible feelings.

We pulled up in front of the house. Sarah walked up the drive while I locked the car, her own keys jingling in her hand. "Oh!" I heard her exclaim. "I wonder who these are from." She bent and picked something up off the doormat.

Someone had left a small posy outside our house: a

few pink and lavender flowers in full bloom, bound with a bit of string. There was no note, but I thought I knew who had left them. The flowers were in the same spot Jack had left my bracelet on the night of my birthday.

The guilty feeling returned.

# CHAPTER TEN

"We need to go out to David's farm and get a few things for his hospital stay." Even though it was first thing in the morning, Aunt Elizabeth looked tired. She'd gone back into the hospital after we'd had dinner to talk to the ICU staff and sit with Dad for a while; I'd wanted to go with her, but she told me I'd be more use to her functioning and rested.

I'd joked feebly that she wanted that single chair at his bedside all to herself.

Now she put a plate piled high with toast onto the dining table, next to the posy of flowers. Sarah had placed them in a glass of water the previous night, speculating about whether they were left by one of our friends who'd heard about my father, or whether one of us had a secret admirer.

What would she say if I told her I suspected my *duinesidhe* … mentor? friend? … had dropped them off?

"It'd be quicker to buy toiletries than to drive to the

farm." Sarah hooked her chair out from under the table with her foot, the legs squealing against the floor. She sat, cradling her coffee in both hands. Her eyes were shadowed with lack of sleep.

"True," my aunt agreed. "But the hospital wants any medications he may have been taking."

"Aren't they getting a record of his scripts from the doctor?" Ryan asked, eyebrows raised.

She nodded. "But he might have had other drugs. Over-the-counter ones. Also, I was thinking we should bring him some personal items like CDs, and pyjamas for when he wakes."

*When* he wakes. The optimism in her choice of words hung in the air. None of us disputed it, although Ryan did glance at me before grabbing a couple of slices of toast and the strawberry jam. His eyes were bloodshot, and the smudges of graphite on the sides of his right hand and his fingertips were only a shade darker than the bags under his eyes.

Was I the only one who'd slept last night? Exhaustion had taken over and I'd dropped off to sleep right after my promised conversation with Dominic. He had chattered, excited and nervous about his job interview today, but volunteered to take me out for coffee in the evening if I needed a break from the hospital.

"I still have my key to Dad's place," I said, sipping my coffee. I wasn't hungry, but Sarah put a piece of toast on my plate and scowled at me, so I nibbled at it until she looked away. "I can go."

"It's Friday. You're meant to be at school," Sarah reminded me. "We both are."

Aunt Elizabeth shook her head. "You've both finished

your assessments. I'll go in and have a word with the principal, explain the situation. I'm sure she'll understand."

"For me, too?" Sarah asked, trying to look dutiful rather than hopeful. She didn't do a very good job.

Her mother smiled a little. "Yes, I suppose so. Isla will need your support, and I may need you to run errands. You can come to school and show me where to find the principal's office."

"Sure."

"I'll go out to the farm with Isla then," Ryan volunteered.

Our plan settled, we each went to get ready for the day. After looking out through the curtains at the flat grey sky, I settled on jeans, with a hoodie, rather than shorts. A pair of sensible sneakers and I was ready to go.

Ryan wore jeans, with a black T-shirt that had a stylised drum kit on the front. If it weren't for the fact his dyed black hair was sporting red roots almost an inch long, he would've looked very rock and roll. "You need to go to the hairdresser," I said as we walked to the car.

He shrugged.

It was dry outside, but the high, pale clouds kept the heat down. I hoped there wouldn't be rain, because it would make the drive to the farm no fun. Some of the roads out that way weren't good at the best of times, and the reduced visibility made it harder to see livestock or kangaroos straying onto the road.

We decided to take my car, because I had an almost full tank of petrol. Ryan grumbled about the lack of a CD player as we pulled out into traffic but soon slumped back, thumbs hooked in his jeans pockets, and fell asleep. I grumbled under my breath, wishing I'd had time to buy the portable speakers for my MP3 player.

The drive was relaxing. I knew the roads well, although this was the first time I'd driven them myself. The only sounds were Ryan's steady breathing, the rumble of the engine and the hiss of the tyres on the road.

At least, it was relaxing so long as I kept my mind from thinking about the purpose of the drive. Or away from anything relating to Jack. Or my mother. I wanted to pretend I was on a normal drive out to Dad's house to see him, to think about normal things—not the bizarre series of events my life had become.

Pushing my worries to one side, my mind ran through a catalogue of options for Sarah's birthday present. I wore my bracelet every day, and wanted to give her something she'd cherish just as much. The problem with our birthdays being so close and mine being first was that she beat me to the best ideas.

I was tossing up between a wristwatch, a leather tote bag and a voucher for a facial when I turned onto the dirt road leading from the main road up to Dad's farm. Ryan awoke when my little car started juddering along the uneven surface. He groaned, stretching to relieve a crick in his neck. "Sorry."

"It's okay. Although you snored," I teased. We pulled up in front of the gate, and the mirth dropped away. This was where they'd found Dad, lying in the dirt beside his still-running ute.

"Do you want me to get the gate?" Ryan asked.

"Please." The gate had a steel frame with a galvanised mesh infill. It was secured by a crude twist of thick wire wrapped around the frame, binding it to a metal loop screwed into the wooden fencepost.

The wire was iron.

The telltale nausea churned in my stomach even at this distance. Although it was healed, my palm tingled with the memory of the burn my father had given me. I scratched it, watching Ryan walk over to the gate.

He hesitated before he touched the twist of iron, his hand inches from it. A frown creased his forehead. I held my breath, heart pounding, mind filled with wild speculation. Did he sense something about the iron too, some danger? Did Ryan somehow suffer the same affliction as me, even though we didn't share a mother? How could such a thing even be possible? I drew a breath to cry out, to stop him from touching it.

But I was too late. I waited for the yelp of pain, the sizzle of burned flesh...

Nothing. He unwound the wire and passed it through the gate, leaving the twist of metal hanging from the loop. The gate creaked on unoiled hinges when he swung it open; he stood to one side, waiting for me to drive through.

Heat crawled up my neck. He hadn't hesitated because the iron nauseated him. He'd probably been looking at which way to unwind the wire.

I sighed quietly, relieved, when he got back into the car after closing the gate. At least we'd passed the barrier.

My sense of reprieve lasted only for the drive through the paddocks, until we reached the farmhouse.

The ute was under the carport, and Sonya the goat looked at us over the back fence, probably wondering if we had anything good to eat or were going to come close enough for her bite us. She was better than a guard dog, that goat; when strangers arrived, she'd kick the side of a metal drum in her pen to raise the alarm. She regarded Ryan and me with grudging tolerance.

But there was iron everywhere.

Dad worked iron for a hobby; I hadn't realised why until I'd learned *duinesidhe* were vulnerable to the metal. And now I was growing sensitive to it too. Energy encircled the farmhouse and surrounding yard like a talisman, a physical barrier against someone with fae blood entering. There was an iron knocker on the door; an iron hook was mounted on the wall beside it, under the overhang of the veranda. His broad-brimmed leather hat hung from the hook. Fastened to the side of the chicken roost, an iron rack held a shovel, pitchfork and rake. A plastic rain gauge was mounted in an iron frame near the gate to Sonya's pen.

What was Dad so afraid of?

My stomach twisted up like the wire on the main gate. "I don't think I can do this," I gasped. If the outside was this bad, how bad would the inside be? Iron knickknacks were scattered throughout the house. If I went in there it would be as if I was walking through a minefield. A minefield that made me want to vomit.

Ryan misunderstood. How could he not? "Do you want me to get some things for him?"

"If you could." Shaking, I took my keys from the ignition and handed him the front door key. "I'll feed the animals."

At least outside I could see the iron to avoid it, and the fresh air and cool breeze helped quell the sick feeling in my stomach.

It took me a half-hour to feed the chickens and goat and to check on the sheep. By the time I walked back from the paddock, glad I'd worn sensible shoes rather than a pair of cute sandals, Ryan was waiting by the car with an overnight bag slung over one shoulder and a plastic shopping bag in the other hand. The latter was full of small bottles and boxes: the entire contents of Dad's medicine cabinet, if I wasn't mistaken.

"We should ask Mrs Wilson if she can feed the animals," he said as I approached him. "A two-hour round trip every day is a bit much." He didn't add we didn't know how long this would go on for. He didn't need to. "It's a bit weird going through another man's underwear drawer," he added, trying to lighten the mood as I opened the boot so he could sling the bags inside. "Choosing the CDs was cool, though. He's got some awesome old stuff. I grabbed some Eagles, Police and Beatles. And a photo he had on his bedside table."

"What's it of?"

"You, actually." He grinned, unzipping the bag and rummaging around inside it. "Here."

I was about six in the photo, standing at the top of a wooden fort at the local playground. I wore a Minnie Mouse tank top and shorts, grinning down at the camera.

The picture frame was iron. I hadn't felt its closeness over the farm's background nausea levels and nearly took it from Ryan before a warning tingle in my palm alerted me. I thrust my hands behind my back and stepped back. "Thanks." I tried not to sound flustered. It didn't work.

Ryan gave me an odd look, but returned the picture to the bag and closed the hatch without saying anything.

After squaring things away with Mrs Wilson, we headed home. Looking for something to focus on, I asked Ryan what he was getting Sarah for her birthday.

"I've got some sketches for a painting," he said. "It's her as a singer on stage. You know, guitar, lights, screaming fans. That sort of thing."

"Awesome." I was envious of him for being able to give her something so original.

"Remind me later and I'll show you the sketches. What are you thinking about getting her?"

"I haven't decided. I thought maybe a bag or a watch? Or a facial or something? Although a voucher feels lame." I touched the bracelet around my wrist. "I want it to be something that makes her feel special."

"The bag or the watch, I reckon," he said. "For an eighteenth present, you want it to be something you can look back on later and remember. Save the facial for Christmas."

I thought about it for a bit. "The watch then."

"Good call."

Rain began to sprinkle down when we were about fifteen minutes out, leaving specks of water on the windshield but doing little to wash away the dust from Dad's driveway. It was barely worth turning the wiper blades on and, when I did, they covered the windshield with streaks of damp mud.

Sarah was waiting for us on the front porch. She waved when we hopped out, and we all hurried inside, out of the rain.

"Did you sort out everything at school?" I asked her.

"Yup. There wasn't even any argument. Disappointing much? But guess what? You got more flowers." The sinking feeling in my stomach evaporated when she continued, "There's a bunch from Natalie, Kim and some of the other girls, and one from Dominic." She dragged me into the kitchen. The flowers were on the dining table, already in vases. There was a bunch of beautiful violet orchids, and another—the one from Dominic—of peach-coloured tulips. Both had cards attached, unlike the original bunch.

"Starting to get a little crowded there," Ryan remarked, leaning on the doorframe. "Soon we won't have space to eat."

"I should take them in to Dad. They're for him, really." I sniffed the tulips; they were beautiful but didn't have any fragrance. The original bunch, which I thought of as Jack's even though I hadn't confirmed it, gave off a delicate, sweet aroma. Had he picked them from somebody's garden?

We had a quick lunch before Sarah and I headed in to see Dad. Ryan wanted to come with us, but he had a shift at the supermarket in a couple of hours, and Aunt Elizabeth had gone to the bank to sort out getting some leave approved.

At the hospital, I shouldered my bag and hefted a portable CD player, Dad's medicines and one vase of flowers. To my relief, Sarah grabbed the other vase and Dad's bag of clothes. I didn't want to get close to that iron picture frame.

The nurse who buzzed us into the ICU wasn't the same one we'd met the night before; she was an older woman with a neat steel-grey braid trailing down her back and serious eyes. She frowned when she saw the vases. "No flowers," she said. "ICU rule. Cards are okay."

Flustered, we left the vases in the waiting area. My new least-favourite nurse pointed at the hand sanitiser before returning to her paperwork.

Dad was still in the same bed; I could see his red-and-silver hair from across the room. The sight was a fresh punch in the gut, leaving me breathless. Even though it was stupid, part of me had hoped he was awake, and that the hospital just hadn't called yet. Squaring my shoulders, I started across the ward.

We were halfway to him when Dad gasped and arched his back. His head flung backward into his pillows. His limbs thrashed in the throes of a convulsion so violent the intravenous line in his arm tore free. The needle dropped to the linoleum. An alarm squawked urgently.

Nurses swarmed. Sarah grabbed my arm when I took a step forward. The nurse from the desk appeared before us. "Out. Now." She took my other arm and, between them, they herded me back out the magnetic door.

"I'll come back out in a few minutes," the nurse said, and closed the door in my face. The lock engaged with a click, echoing in the quiet waiting room.

Sarah dropped the overnight bag on the couch. I stood there in shock, my heart pounding. I knew I should put everything down too, but my feet wouldn't move. Sarah took pity on me, relieving me of my burdens, putting them on the overstuffed table. With empty arms, she engulfed me in a hug. I don't know how long we stood there in the middle of the room, clinging to one another like children, but it felt like more than "a few minutes". I stared at the door, numb.

It was Rachael, the nice nurse from the night before, who came out to talk to us. She sat us down on the couches. I curled my legs up so I could hug my knees. "First of all, your father has stabilised," she told me. "The seizure didn't last long at all; he stopped as soon as you both left the room."

I gasped with relief.

"What took so long then?" Sarah frowned.

"We had to make sure he was fine first. Now we're running some additional scans to identify the cause of the attack. I'm afraid you're not going to be able to see him until this evening at the earliest." She reached across and patted my hand.

"We brought him music and things." My voice sounded hoarse. "And that one has his medicines from home in it."

"I'll take that," she said, retrieving the plastic bag. "But as for the rest, we'll have to ask you to bring it back next time, I'm afraid. Except for those flowers." She stood. "Would you like me to call you later, when he's able to receive visitors?"

I nodded.

"Thank you," Sarah said.

"Go home, get some rest," Rachael told us both. "You're no good to him if you're exhausted." I wanted to tell her I wasn't tired, but the words wouldn't come.

Rachael went back into the ICU, plastic bag rustling with her long strides.

We gathered our burdens and trudged back to the car. Sarah spent a large part of the drive on the phone to Aunt Elizabeth, letting her know what had happened, so I didn't have to speak much. I was thankful.

At least the weather had improved. The rain had dried up and the sun was even peeking through the clouds. When we arrived home, Sarah decided to take Hamish for his walk, asking if I'd like to go with her. I said no.

This was the first time I'd been alone in the house since they'd found Dad. Without the pressure to maintain a strong façade for my family, I went into my bedroom and cried into my pillow for half an hour, hugging Mister Monkey tightly.

Every time I closed my eyes I saw Dad thrashing in his bed, the drip falling to the floor, a small line of blood trickling down his arm and spotting the blue hospital tiles. Was Dad aware of his surroundings, scared and trapped in his own body? The staff had told us he was in a coma and may not be conscious of anything, but the niggling doubt wound around my heart, which was already heavy with regret. I shouldn't have let Sarah and the nurse pull me away. I should have gone to his bedside.

I knew I'd have just been in the way. But that didn't stop me feeling like the most neglectful daughter alive.

When my tears subsided I felt strangely numb, like the ocean on a still day: calm on the surface but with currents of emotion still lurking deep, unseen but potentially debilitating. I took a trembling breath. My eyes felt raw and my nose was red and sniffily—I was never one of those girls who looked pretty when they cried, like a character on television. I climbed off the bed and got a tissue.

A large sketchpad sat on top of my laptop. Ryan's. A yellow sticky note was attached to the cover. It read:

*Isla—*
*The sketch for S's painting is towards the back. Be careful to touch the edges of the pages, not the pencil, or it will smudge.*
*Ryan.*

He must have left it for me before going to work.

After repairing some of the damage from my crying

jag, including splashing some water onto my face, I took the sketchpad and sat on my bed. Feeling whimsical, I put Mister Monkey beside me so he could see the pictures too. He looked damp and bedraggled.

Dad had given me the bear to celebrate my first day of school. The toy was long-limbed and brown with a big sewn-on smile and, although he lacked a tail, his appearance had reminded me of a monkey and the name stuck. I wasn't one for toys these days; while Mister Monkey did live in the top corner of my bed, against the wall, I hadn't cuddled him for years. But he reminded me of Dad, so I was more than willing to ignore the minimal embarrassment of hugging a toy in the privacy of my own room.

Also, I figured Mister Monkey wouldn't tell anyone.

I'd seen some of Ryan's sketches before. He'd had this current sketchbook since the start of the year. The books that preceded it were lovingly stacked on a bookshelf in his room.

Some of the pictures were simple sketches, line art he'd later transferred to canvas once he was happy with the composition. Others were detailed drawings in their own right, with complex details: patterns, light and shadow. These drawings were rarely done in colour, but I was still astonished at the detail he could evoke with just a lead pencil. I didn't have an artistic bone in my body.

There were pictures of people, including sketches of some of his friends from school and of an old girlfriend; of objects, from a motorbike to Sarah's acoustic guitar, Amy; of plants; of cartoon characters; and of improbable-looking robots towering over small buildings.

When I got to the concept sketches for the rose he'd painted onto the cover of my MP3 player I paused, fascinated.

He'd drawn several versions of the rose across one page; the one in the bottom corner was the closest to what he'd painted in the shape of the petals, although the thorns resembled the second-last sketch.

The next picture was the composition sketch for the painting he'd done of my mother. The hair stood up on the back of my neck when I saw it. I should have expected to see her but still felt a jolt of surprise when I turned the page. After I'd seen Dad's photos, she seemed much more real to me. Even though the sketch wasn't fleshed out in the same way the painting was, the resemblance was eerie.

I shivered, turning the page.

The following sketch was the one he'd wanted me to look at, the picture of Sarah. The viewer looked up at her on an angle, as though standing in the mosh pit at a concert. She was on stage, depicted mid-motion: her shoulder-length hair few around her head and her mouth was open, singing into a wireless microphone attached to a headset. Short shorts, knee-high boots and a tank top flattered her figure, while a leather bracelet encircled her wrist. And she was playing an electric guitar.

I smiled. She would love the painting. Even the sketch was wonderful. I couldn't wait to see it once it was brought to life in colour on canvas.

I turned to the next sketch, the last one in the book before the blank pages began. This picture was half complete. An outline covered the entire page, detailing a reclining figure, lying on his back, eyes closed and hands on his chest. Funereal. The face and torso of the man were detailed, and my hands began to tremble as I recognised the subject.

It was my father.

The image wavered as my eyes filled with fresh tears. I blinked them away furiously. Dad's eyes were closed and his mouth was open in an echo of the gasping expression that had haunted me since his seizure. My fingers hovered above his forehead as if to smooth away the pained furrows. His hands clutched something over his heart. Whatever it was wasn't yet completed, but a black shadow rose behind it, spreading inky tendrils across his chest.

Horror curled in my gut. What was Ryan thinking, drawing something so awful? I remembered the smudged fingers, the tired eyes; he must have done this last night. Straight after seeing his inspiration at the hospital.

I stared at the half-finished drawing for a long time, my eyes fixed on that black shadow and the way it spread across Dad's chest, like the exposed root system of an old oak. An idea formed in my mind. It was a crazy idea, but it made a certain amount of sense too.

I rang Ryan's mobile. He didn't answer so I left a message, pacing my room. He phoned back a few minutes later. "Is everything okay with Uncle David?" he said as soon as I answered the phone.

"He had a seizure this afternoon."

"Do they know what caused it?" I heard muffled noises in the background.

"No. Listen, that's not why I called. I was looking through your sketches and saw the picture of Dad."

"Oh." He sounded abashed. "Listen, I'm sorry about that. I should have taken it out before I left the pad there."

"Where'd you get the idea from? The shadow and whatever it is he's holding, I mean?"

"I … don't really know. It came to me at two in the morning when I couldn't sleep."

"Right. Okay." I thought quickly.

"I'm really sorry, Isla."

"Don't worry about it. Look, can I keep it?"

"It's not finished," he said. Captain Obvious.

"I know. Can I keep it?" I repeated, biting my nail.

"Uh, sure. I guess." I heard a voice calling his name in the background. "Gotta go. See you in a few hours." He hung up before I could say goodbye.

I carefully tore the picture out before leaving the sketchbook on Ryan's bed.

Then I went out to find Jack.

# CHAPTER ELEVEN

*I* paced around the edge of the park, along the concrete border corralling the tanbark. My bag swung from my shoulder and Ryan's half-finished drawing was in my hand, rolled up in a manner that would have horrified my cousin.

Was this sense of pent up frustration what kept a tiger pacing its cage?

Jack arrived after fifteen minutes. He seemed different: younger, somehow. But he was dressed in identical clothes to last time, a hood covering his ears as always.

"Are you okay, Isla?"

The same question he'd asked me the day before. Only this time I answered it immediately, refusing to get sidetracked. "No. They found Dad unconscious outside his farm. He's in the hospital."

He blinked. "I am sorry."

"My cousin drew this." I unrolled the paper; the image was smudged from being furled, but the details were still clear. "That's Dad, but what does this mean?" I jabbed at the black stain Ryan had drawn across his chest.

Jack studied the image for several long moments. My gaze remained glued to his face, looking for signs of recognition.

"Did you ask your cousin what it is?"

"He said it just came to him," I replied, impatient.

"Has he drawn anything else that 'just came to him' recently?"

I nodded. "A painting of my mother. He said he dreamt of her, but he never even knew what she looked like before that." Jack stared at me with those strange sapphire eyes. It made me angry. "Look, so far I've tried to believe you with all the weird stuff you've told me. I've trusted you, and I haven't freaked out." *Much.* "So tell me. What the hell is going on?"

"Walk with me," he replied. I took another angry breath, but he nodded towards the street. Sarah had rounded the far corner, Hamish trotting in front of her, ranging like a fish on a line. Neither of them had noticed us. Yet.

Grumbling under my breath, I set off, heading away from the park and up one of the connecting footpaths that crisscrossed our suburb, choosing one that led towards the small local shops. Jack walked beside me.

The path cut through a small reserve lined with tall shrubs and a few trees. Long grass flanked the path. We walked until we were out of sight of the park.

I turned and put a hand my hip, scowling. "Okay, talk."

He left the path, swishing through the damp grass to one of the trees, a tall pine close to the back fence of a quiet suburban house. He sat beneath it, curling his legs under him with feline grace. I reluctantly joined him, cringing as I waited for water to soak through the seat of my pants. But the ground under the tree was dry. I put my bag down beside me.

"Your cousin is your *aislinge*," he said without further preamble. Another strange word, this one pronounced "ashling". When he saw my complete lack of understanding, he shrugged. "He is a ... a seer, a visionary. Some *aosidhe* can imbue the power of extraordinary perception onto one of their court. This cousin of yours is, well, yours."

"Ryan," I said, voice barely a whisper. The *this is crazy* feeling I'd had over the past couple of days returned in full force.

"I beg your pardon?"

"His name is Ryan."

He nodded, accepting that.

"You're saying I somehow made it so he can see the future?"

"Maybe not the future. Only time will tell, as far as that goes. But the present, yes, and with more clarity than a normal human, or even many of our kind."

"So I gave him the power to see things I can't even see?" That didn't make a lot of sense.

He nodded, a lock of hair falling from the confines of his hood. It hung across his cheek, a strand of gold.

"Right. Well, let's say that's true—"

"It is."

"—what is he seeing in this picture?" I laid Ryan's sketch flat in front of him so he could study it, the paper crackling as my hands trembled.

Jack looked at the drawing for several minutes. My impatience built like a scream inside me; when I thought

I might explode with it, he spoke again. "It looks as though your father has been elf shot." This time he didn't wait for me to ask. "Elf shot is a weapon available to some *aosidhe*. It causes paralysis in its target."

Someone had shot my father? Who made me terrible costumes for school plays and taught me to swim? Who laughed too loudly in the movie theatre, so that I ducked my head with embarrassment?

I didn't know of a single reason anyone, let alone an *aosidhe*, would want to hurt him. But I didn't know my father's history with the fae either, and cursed the rotten timing of the attack. It seemed unlikely to be a coincidence. The thought made the hair on the back of my arms prickle with anxiety. Jack had said the séance could have drawn unwanted attention. Was this what he meant?

*Is this my fault?*

"I'm pretty sure—" I swallowed the quaver in my voice and tried again. "If the doctors had seen an arrowhead on the x-ray they would have said something to us."

"They would not have seen it."

We both fell silent as an older woman and her fluffy black poodle walked up the pathway. She glowered, eyes narrowed with suspicion. I scowled back at her. I had nothing to be ashamed of here.

The poodle sniffed and moved on, taking its owner with it.

"If he's paralysed, does that mean he's awake?" I asked once the woman was out of earshot. The idea of being trapped in your own body, aware but unable to move or communicate... I shuddered. The summery air didn't feel so warm now.

"I do not think so."

"But you don't know?"

"I have never been elf shot. Or spoke to one who has. But the stories of those who are shot and recover speak of it as a deep sleep."

"Like Sleeping Beauty or that other guy … Rip Van Winkle." He stared at me blankly, and I grimaced, rolling up Ryan's drawing. "Can you remove it?"

"No."

"Why not?" The sudden ache of disappointment turned my voice into a wail. "You healed the burn on my hand."

"I can only heal injuries within a day of them being inflicted, and elf shot is not a normal wound in any case. The paralysis can only be healed by removing the arrowhead, and I do not have that kind of power."

"But it can be done?"

"Yes."

Hope flared in my chest. "Who has the power?"

"You do." His reply was simple, direct.

And ridiculous.

"I … what?"

"If you have the power to make an *aislinge* then you have the power to remove elf shot," he said.

"But I don't remember making an *aislinge*!"

"It probably happened around the time of your coming of age. Your birthday," Jack told me. "Do you remember having any physical contact with this Ryan around that time? Anything unusual?"

Suppressing a juvenile giggle edged with hysteria at the phrase "physical contact", I leaned back against the tree. We'd gone out to dinner that night, and Ryan had waited with me in front of *Prime Time* until Dominic arrived for our date. My cousin had squeezed my hand,

I recalled, sending an electric shock along my skin.

I explained all of this to Jack.

"That may have been it." He shrugged. "I must confess, I have never seen the process myself, only heard of it. But it is possible you were emitting energy as part of coming into your own, and you inadvertently channelled it into him."

The idea Jack wasn't all-knowing was alarming ... but reassuring, too. My sense of ignorance lessened. Even if I had accidentally turned Ryan into some sort of painting visionary by spilling invisible magic all over him.

"Have you seen elf shot removed before?" I asked him.

"Yes, once."

"Can you show me how, exactly?"

"I can explain what I saw. You will have to do the rest. But ... it is somewhat conspicuous. We will need privacy."

A vision of me conducting an arcane ritual naked by moonlight, like something from a Hollywood movie, flashed before my eyes. "Conspicuous *how*, exactly?"

"It will be flashy, in a manner that is not of human origin." His words did little to ease my mind. He patted my arm. "All that is required of you is concentration and your power. But it will be visible to anyone, not just the *duinesidhe*."

I thought about the busy ICU, crowded with patients, nurses and visitors. "That might be a problem. Dad's not in a private room."

"Can you get them to move him?"

"I doubt they'd listen. But they might move him out of the ICU on their own if he remains stable. Those beds are for high-risk patients." I tipped my head to the side. "Today when Sarah and I went to visit, he had a seizure.

Could that have been caused by the elf shot?"

"Possibly." He brushed that errant lock away from his face.

"We had iron with us."

He paled, eyes widening. "Then yes. The elf shot is a thing with a purely fae nature. It will react to iron as one of us would."

I pursed my lips. "I don't suppose we could use iron to destroy the elf shot, could we?"

"That would not be a good idea."

"Why?"

"It would almost certainly kill your father as well."

"Oh. Forget that then."

He smiled. "Indeed."

We sat in silence for a while. The sun and shadows played across the footpath as the clouds somewhere above our tree shelter raced across the sky, blown by a high-altitude wind we couldn't feel. How strange a turn my life had taken. Especially in the last forty-eight hours.

Although it was becoming apparent my life was always strange; I was just the last to know.

"There's one thing I don't understand," I said finally. "You tell me I have all this power I've inherited from my mother, that I've given Ryan magical visions and can somehow cure Dad's coma. But I don't feel powerful. Sure, iron makes me queasy and burns me if I touch it, but where's the upside to all of this? Shouldn't I be developing some sort of superpower or something? Walking through walls, invisibility—something like that?"

Jack laughed, loud and unexpected, throwing his head back. I smiled despite myself. "You seek further proof?"

"Superpowers would be better, but yeah. Proof would

be nice." I laughed.

As he had done the first time we met, he took my hand and touched my fingers to his cheek. "What do you feel?"

The first thing I felt was my ears burning with sudden embarrassment. "Um. Your skin is warm," I stammered. "And smooth."

"And smooth," he repeated patiently.

The penny dropped. "Wait a minute. When I met you, you had wrinkled skin. Now it's not." Awkwardness forgotten, I ran my hand across his cheek and forehead. No lines marred them. "Are you saying I had something to do with this?"

"Yes. That same power you are so sceptical about has allowed me to regenerate my skin."

"What caused the wrinkles?"

"My particular race of *duinesidhe* are like flowers. We thrive in the sunlight, and wither in the darkness." I opened my mouth to ask the obvious question, but he continued. "The *aosidhe* are the sunlight. You contain a source of power within you that enables us to thrive."

I frowned, trying to follow what he was saying. "So the reason your skin is smooth is that you've somehow recharged your batteries by being around me?"

"I do not understand the reference to 'batteries'," he said, "but the rest sounds correct."

"And I carry a, um—" my mind scrambled to find the right words "—power source around in me?" I had a mental image of radioactive-green light glowing out from between my ribs.

At least I'd be able to find my way to the toilet in the dark.

"Yes. After a fashion. You can probably also draw more 'power'—" he made air quotes with his fingers and I had to suppress another giggle. Seriously, who knows air quotes but not batteries? "—from an aspect of the human world. Each of the *aosidhe* is different. You may take after your mother in that regard, but it is difficult to say."

"You haven't heard anything more about her?"

"I am trying, but it is hard to get information without revealing too much about who is asking, and why."

I grabbed my bag, fishing around in it for the envelope of photos I'd received the day before. I pulled one of the photos out, more or less at random: it was a portrait of my mother in later pregnancy and showed her from the waist up. She wore a grey cardigan over a white top lined with horizontal black stripes, accentuating the roundness of her belly. Her hair was loose, falling over her ears and framing her face.

I handed it to Jack. "This is her."

He took the photo, looking at it for a long while. Then he nodded. "Can I borrow this?"

"Sure, so long as I get it back. Will it help find out who she is?"

"Definitely. There is someone I can take it to."

We both jumped a little when my phone beeped a text message alert. It was from Sarah. *Where are you? Everything okay?*

*Getting some air. Home soon.*

"I'd better go," I told Jack. "Thanks for talking to me."

"My pleasure." He stood and offered his hand, pulling me to my feet. He was stronger than he looked.

We walked back towards the park. "I'll let you know once they move Dad to a more private room," I told him. "Will you contact me if you hear anything about my mother?"

"Of course."

When we arrived at the end of the laneway he stopped. "I truly am sorry about your father, Isla," he said.

"Thank you."

I walked across the park, feeling his eyes on my back, but when I glanced back he was gone.

If Sarah was annoyed at me for going for a walk without her after she'd invited me for one, she didn't say anything. In fact, she was solicitous and kind, all of which made me ashamed I was keeping such a large—albeit insane— secret from her. It wasn't that I didn't want to tell her about everything I'd learned in the past few days, or even that I didn't think she'd believe me, because I was pretty sure she would. I just wasn't sure where to begin. And the idea of trying made me feel weary all the way down to my toes.

Feeling guilty, as soon as I had half an hour alone I ordered her birthday present off the internet: a custom watch from a website that would decorate its face to order. After some consideration, and thinking about Ryan's sketch of Sarah as a rock goddess, I chose an acoustic guitar theme.

Fingers crossed it arrived in time. Her birthday was in less than two weeks.

The next few days dragged.

I visited Dad at least once a day. Now that I'd removed the iron picture frame from the gym bag, wearing a pair of my aunt's gardening gloves to shield my hands from the metal and taking slow breaths so I didn't hurl, he didn't have any more seizures. But he also didn't show any signs of recovery. The doctors were baffled: the tests came back saying there were no drugs in his system and no signs of brain injury. He hadn't even scraped his head when he collapsed in the driveway. As far as they could tell, he was healthy.

Except no one could wake him.

The rest of my family were anxious, although they were trying to hide it from me. Aunt Elizabeth had called her mother, our nana, to tell her about Dad's condition. She was going to fly over from England and stay for Sarah's birthday. So Aunt Elizabeth was also anxious about getting the house pristine and keeping it that way; given we were no longer attending school, Sarah and I were drafted into helping scour the bathrooms and tidy the garden. She and I would have to share a bedroom while Nana stayed with us. After a brief inspection of each of our rooms, Aunt Elizabeth decided I could bunk in with Sarah, because my room required less work to get cleaned up.

I was anxious too, but the cause wasn't ignorance about Dad's condition. It was concern about what I'd have to do to cure him and whether I'd be up to the task.

Jack was positive I could do it, but I didn't share his confidence. I still hadn't detected any signs of "superpowers" in myself, although how they would manifest I had no idea. Jack had told me he'd contact me if he learned anything, but it hadn't occurred to me until after he left that I should have asked how. He didn't have a phone as far as I was aware—and, even if he did, he'd never asked for my number. I kept peering between the blinds to check the park but, although I grew to be quite familiar with the neighbourhood kids, I never saw him there.

Sarah cajoled me to go out for coffee and muffins with Natalie and Kim. Our friends regaled us with tales from school that, for the most part, made me glad we were excused from the rest of the year. Some of the end-of-school pranks sounded like fun, but I didn't have the heart for it right then.

Late the next afternoon, as Sarah and I were leaving the hospital, she took me on a detour via the short-term parking near the emergency ward. Head hanging with the weight of seeing my father so helpless, I barely even registered the change of direction.

"Afternoon, ladies," a voice said. I looked up in surprise to see Dominic, leaning against his car. He wore a black collared shirt and jeans, and his hair gleamed golden brown in a ray of afternoon sunlight that found its way through the towering buildings.

The sight of him made my heart jump in my chest. "Uh. Hi?" I stepped forward and he wrapped warm arms around me, kissing the top of my head. My gloom evaporated with the touch of his lips. "Not that I'm not pleased to see you, but what are you doing here?"

"I know, right?" Sarah said in a voice dripping with mirth. "What a bizarre coincidence."

"Totally," Dominic agreed.

I looked between them, a slow smile pulling at the corners of my lips. "So that's why you volunteered to drive, Sarah. You set this up!"

"Me? Never!" she said, the lie twinkling in her eyes. "But if I did, Mum's already fine with you being home late. You know, hypothetically."

"Hypothetically," I agreed, laughing.

Dominic opened the passenger door for me with a bow

and a wink. "Fair lady? Your chariot awaits."

I blinked at him, reminded overwhelmingly of Jack, and then shook myself and slid into the seat. "Thanks. What's that? Shakespeare?"

He walked around to the driver's seat. "Tarantino," he said as he opened the door.

I had a vague memory of Ryan forcing Sarah and me to sit through a gory action movie. "Oh. Wait, wasn't the guy who said it a serial killer?"

He thought about it, starting the car. "Good point. I take it back."

I mimed wiping the sweat from my brow. "So, where are we off to?"

"How does dinner and a movie sound? No serial killers, I promise."

"Awesome." I laughed.

"I hope you don't mind me springing this on you." We pulled out into traffic and turned right.

"No." The grin felt goofy but I didn't stop. "Since what happened with Dad I haven't had a lot of time off. I mean, I don't mind visiting him and everything, but…"

"Sometimes you just need to blow off some steam?"

"Yeah." I grimaced.

"He'd tell you the same thing, you know," Dominic said, reaching across to squeeze my hand as we pulled up at a set of traffic lights.

I thought about that as we drove into Civic. I couldn't shake the conviction my dad was aware of his surroundings—my chest feel heavy with guilt if I didn't stay with him as much as I could. But I knew Dominic was right. Dad would be horrified at the idea of me spending all of my time at the hospital.

Dominic took me to a tiny Burmese restaurant for curry. He kept the conversation light, funny stories from his backpacking adventure making me giggle until we earned a dour look from a couple at the adjacent table. Afterwards, we went to see a movie. As promised, there were no serial killers. His woodsy cologne filled my senses when I snuggled into the curve of his arm. I stole popcorn from him whenever he looked away, basking in the blissful feeling of being in a new relationship: a feeling I hadn't been able to enjoy since the dark cloud of Dad's illness descended on our lives.

The kissing was good too.

Dominic dropped me off after the movie. I was humming as I walked up the driveway, my voice stumbling to a halt when I saw Jack's signal. It was another small bunch of flowers, left on the doormat. This time two butter-yellow daffodils nestled in among green, leafy stems with tiny white flowers on them. They were tied into a posy with string.

Dominic was still waiting in his car, watching to make sure I got safely inside. Hiding the posy behind my foot, I turned and waved. He returned the gesture before driving away.

Once his taillights disappeared I scooped up the flowers. As I'd expected, there was no note. The lack of one confirmed my suspicions about the sender. I tucked the posy into my bag.

I looked from the front door to the park across the street. The house was quiet; Ryan was at work, Aunt Elizabeth would be in bed, and if Sarah was waiting up for me to see how the date went, she wasn't in the front room of the house. She probably hadn't heard me arrive.

The black pavement made no sound under my sneakers as I crept across the street.

I found him sitting halfway along the bench, as far as possible from the metal bolting the timber to the concrete frame. He wore the same clothes, which I hardly raised an eyebrow at by now, but had the hood back so his ears weren't confined. There was no moon and the illumination from the streetlight in front of our house was thin here. Given the park was deserted, there was little chance anyone would see his ears.

He stood when he saw me, a smile lighting up his eyes. The improvement in his appearance struck me; now that the wrinkles were gone he was, well, cute. I was even getting used to the long ears.

"I found out who she is," he told me without preamble, handing me the photo I'd loaned him. I sat on the bench, feeling like a deflated balloon. He sat beside me.

"Her name is Melpomene," he began. He pronounced it "Mel-*pom*-uh-nee".

I looked at the photo, at my mother's serious, unsmiling expression, barely visible in the poor light. "Not Melanie." It wasn't a question.

"No."

Another lie of my father's exposed. Resentment and sadness reared their heads, guilt in their shadow. I was being uncharitable. How could I resent him given his current condition?

However, I did promise myself that once he was awake I would yell at him. I might even gesticulate wildly.

"What else?" I braced myself.

"I confirmed she is *aosidhe*, out of Scotland."

"She's Scottish?" That would explain my father's choice

of name for me.

"No." Okay, maybe not. "But the shortest paths to her *sidhe* realm are in Scotland. The *duinesidhe* do not have nationalities."

"What makes the *aosidhe* the rulers? Is it inherited, like with human nobility?"

His smile vanished like a pebble tossed in a lake. "Power by virtue of their race. They are the most powerful, both in the *sidhe* and the human world. They can draw power from around them and use it to their own ends, or bend the *sidhe* to their will."

"And that's what makes them the sunlight to your metaphorical flowers?"

"Yes."

"But I haven't drawn power from the world."

"That you know of," Jack said.

"So how did … does my mother draw power?"

"She can siphon emotions to sate herself. And she can manipulate the emotions of others, human and fae alike."

I stared at Jack, horrified. "She's some sort of psychic leech?"

He nodded.

Nausea unfurled in my stomach, and not because someone had approached me with iron. My mother was able to manipulate emotions? The idea of invading someone's mind and making them feel a certain way, a way that went against their true self, left me cold. The idea of draining their emotions was worse. What was left inside a person if you drained their emotions? Would those feelings ever come back?

"Is—" My voice cracked. I cleared my throat and tried again. "Is my mother evil? Is she a bad person?"

Jack shrugged. "Those sorts of judgments do not apply to the *aosidhe*."

"What do you mean?"

"They are all the same." For the first time, resentment crept into his voice. His expression was grim. "Vain, powerful, selfish. Imagine a small child, and then give them power over their fellows. That is what they are like. Some of them have moments of kindness; others are always cruel. But they are all selfish."

"You sound like you hate them," I murmured.

"Hate is a strong word. But I do not *like* them."

*Vain, powerful, selfish.* I looked at the photo again, wondering what had enticed such a creature to spend almost a year with a human man, masquerading as his wife. What had enticed her to get pregnant?

Somehow I doubted it was love. If it were love, she wouldn't have left the day I was born.

I sighed, shoulders drooping as I stared at my mother's cool, indifferent gaze. It was easy to imagine she was looking through time at her unwanted daughter, rather than at the unknown photographer.

Jack reached across, turning the photo over so I couldn't see Melpomene's face. "You are not her. You may share some of her gifts, but you are not her."

"How do you know?"

"I just do." I looked away, and he caught my chin with his finger, turning my head back to face him. "There is a reason I live in this country. It is almost as far away from the *aosidhe* as one can get. But when I felt your power stir, your chrysalis beginning, I sought you out. I watched you, and what I saw made me want to help you. And not because of your *aosidhe* power. I was quite comfortable with my wrinkles." His eyes twinkled.

Our gazes remained locked for a long moment and then I laughed self-consciously and looked away. "You're sounding stalkerish again."

"Forgive me." He grinned. "I promise I have not looked in any bedroom windows. Or any other windows."

"Good."

We sat in silence for a few moments. A breeze stirred the tops of the trees, rustling the leaves, and a car drove along the road behind us, its headlights sweeping past. It was peaceful in the park, a marked contrast to the tumult of my thoughts.

But if I stayed much longer I'd be missed. I sighed and stood. Jack stood, too. "Thanks for finding out what you could. I'm grateful."

"Of course," he said with a smile, nodding his head.

"Once Dad is moved out of the ICU I'll come tell you, so we can organise … doing whatever it is we're going to do."

"I will be waiting."

His willingness to help was flattering, but also made me more than a little uncomfortable. I didn't know how to handle someone being so selfless. I said a hasty farewell and left.

Walking across the road to our house, I saw the curtains in the window twitch. My pulse skittered. Had Sarah or Aunt Elizabeth seen me in the park, talking to someone? I braced myself for questions as I unlocked the door, but when I peered into the lounge room it was dark. Hamish trotted up to me and snuffled the leg of my jeans, his tail wagging.

"Hi, boy. I'm glad to see you too." I ruffled the fur on his head and he followed me towards the bedrooms.

Sarah poked her head out of her room when I turned my light on. "So, how was it?"

"The movie? Good." I threw my bag on the end of my bed. Hamish jumped up and snuffled it with interest. I wondered if he smelt the posy of flowers and hastily picked him up, rubbing his tummy. I didn't want to have to answer awkward questions; Sarah would recognise the posy as being similar to the mysterious one I'd received previously.

"What about the rest of the date?" she asked, waggling her eyebrows. "The movie finished ages ago."

"That was good too." I grinned. Hamish wiggled so ecstatically I had to put him down for fear I'd drop him.

"Tell me everything!"

"Not likely."

But Sarah and I spent a happy half-hour gossiping about the details of my date with Dominic, before I brushed my teeth and changed into my pyjamas. It was nice to pretend I was a regular girl with regular things going on in my life.

I clung to the happy feeling as I drifted off to sleep, wrapping myself in it like a blanket.

# CHAPTER TWELVE

*O*ur nana arrived the next day.

Her flight was scheduled to touch down from Sydney—the final, mercifully short, domestic leg of a long international journey—late in the afternoon, and Aunt Elizabeth drove the three of us into a frenzy of last-minute cleaning. I moved my bedding and some clothes into Sarah's room. None of us had seen Nana since we were small. I couldn't remember her very well, and my aunt's panicked cleaning had us alarmed that Nana would be a neat freak. Why else would we be cleaning the grout in the shower and dusting the tops of bookshelves that were impossible to see without a stepladder?

Half an hour before we left for the airport, Aunt Elizabeth stalked around the house, conducting a final inspection a drill sergeant would be proud of. Her agitation was palpable. Sarah, Ryan and I stood in the lounge room, exchanging confused looks.

"Passable," she said when she came back into the

room. She relaxed visibly and smiled as though she hadn't dared to believe it.

"*Are you kidding?*" Sarah said. "This place has never been so spotless."

"Well, no, but she doesn't need to know that," Aunt Elizabeth replied, winking. "Now go and get changed. There's room in the car for two of you to come to the airport. Mum will be delighted to have a welcoming committee."

"I've got work soon," Ryan said, glancing at his watch. "I'd better go get ready."

"Don't mess anything up," Aunt Elizabeth called after him.

"I won't." His exasperated reply came from deeper in the house.

Sarah wrinkled her nose. "Guess that means it's you and me, Isla."

Wanting to make a good impression, I changed into one of my few pairs of black slacks and a black tank top under a loose lilac shirt. A pair of strappy shoes and a quick run of the brush through the tangled hair at the end of my ponytail and I was ready to go.

Sarah came out of her room dressed in her neatest pair of dark blue jeans and a green scoop-neck shirt with a matching malachite necklace and earrings. The colour brought out the emerald flecks in her eyes, like a cat's.

"Good." Aunt Elizabeth nodded approvingly.

Sarah called shotgun so I sat in the back, trying not to fidget. Sarah, Ryan and I received birthday cards from our grandmother every year, without fail, and we all signed the family Christmas card, but other than that we didn't correspond with Nana. She didn't have an email or social media account, and—although she sent Aunt Elizabeth long, handwritten letters several times a year, which I presumed my aunt replied to in the same fashion—my cousins and I didn't know her well. Or at all, really.

I twisted my hands together in my lap, staring out the window at the passing scenery. Dad didn't correspond with his mother either. How would he feel to wake up and find her standing over his bed? Had they had a falling out at some point? Or was my father just an unreliable pen pal?

A more exciting idea made me sit up straighter in my seat. What did Nana know about my mother? Would she be willing to talk about it?

We arrived at the airport only to discover Nana's flight was running late. Sarah and I wandered up and down the length of the terminal, flicking through a magazine at the newsagent and stopping to get overpriced soft drinks. Aunt Elizabeth waited by the arrival gate, near the luggage carousel.

We headed back to the gate when the arrivals monitor said the plane had landed, hanging back as a flood of businesspeople poured from the entryway. One weary-looking man in rumpled jeans and a T-shirt was greeted by a pair of exuberant girls. A beaming woman watched on as the man scooped the two children up and smothered them with kisses. Sarah and I smiled, exchanging a glance.

When she appeared, one of the last out of the gate, our nana looked similarly weary but less rumpled. I wondered how she'd managed it, given the flight from London to Sydney was about twenty-two hours. She was a small woman, about my height. Her hair was silvery white, pulled back from her face, and her eyes were blue, framed by neat glasses. She spotted us through the milling crowd around the carousel and came over, smiling.

Aunt Elizabeth enveloped her in a hug. "Mum! Welcome to Australia."

"It's good to be here," Nana replied with a Queen's English accent that reminded me of Dad's. My heart ached, but I forced a smile as she turned to regard Sarah and I. "And this must be Sarah," she said after a moment, kissing my cousin on the cheek. "How tall you've grown. You remind me of your grandfather. His height *and* his fiery hair."

"Hi," Sarah said, awkwardly hugging the smaller woman back.

"And this is Isla," Aunt Elizabeth said, indicating me.

"Yes," Nana studied me with less enthusiasm. She didn't say anything, but I was sure she was comparing me to my long-gone mother.

My heart sank, but I stood up straighter. If she was going to judge me because of something I couldn't control, then … I wasn't sure what. I tried not to scowl.

I suddenly hated the idea of her staying in my bedroom.

Nana broke the awkward tableau first, giving me a brief embrace. She smelled like breath mints and lavender. "I'm sorry about your father, Isla," she said. "Perhaps you will take me to see him tomorrow?"

"Okay, sure," I mumbled.

A siren sounded a warning exactly like the evacuation alarm at school, and the luggage carousel rumbled to life. Aunt Elizabeth went with Nana to look for her bags. Sarah ignored her mother's significant look and stepped closer to me to murmur, "Was it just me or was that a bit awkward?"

"It wasn't just you."

When we arrived home, Nana announced her intention to have an early tea and go to bed. I didn't feel up to a long evening of being sociable with her when she seemed so reserved with me. It was especially noticeable given she questioned Sarah about her plans for her birthday, and about her recent grades, with bright curiosity. Part of me wanted to wail like a petulant child that it was my final year of school too, and that she'd just missed my birthday. But I stayed silent, helping my aunt in the kitchen.

I was surprised when Nana turned to look directly at me when she finished her meal. "I'll give you your birthday present tomorrow, if you don't mind. I'm exhausted."

"That's fine." I forced a smile.

She turned to Aunt Elizabeth, effectively dismissing me. "Thank you for tea, dear. If you'd be so kind as to show me to the washroom so I can freshen up, that would be wonderful."

"Sure." The two of them left the room, chatting quietly.

"Well, that was rude," Sarah muttered to me as we tidied up, pitching her voice low so it wouldn't carry over the clinking plates and cutlery.

I shrugged, although I agreed with her.

"I wonder what crawled up her butt and died."

"I don't know. She seems to like you though." I tried to look on the bright side. Maybe Nana would avoid me and I'd be able to concentrate on Jack's and my secret mission to help Dad.

"I'm sorry," Sarah said. "If she keeps ignoring you so much I'm going to say something to Mum."

"Don't. Please. I don't want to start something. Maybe she's just crabby after such a long flight." I didn't believe it, though.

Sarah wrinkled her nose. "Her present for you better be good. Like a car or something."

"I already have a car," I said with a laugh.

"So? One for weekdays and one for Sunday best."

But, to Sarah's disappointment, there was no sign of any present the next morning when Nana emerged from her—my—room, dressed and groomed.

We ate a quick breakfast as a family; Nana gave Ryan the same polite but thorough questioning she'd subjected Sarah to the previous day, asking him what he did for a living, and whether he was considering further education or had a girlfriend. The answer to the last two questions was no. She disapproved of his passion for painting, which reassured me a little: it was nice to not be the only grandchild in the doghouse.

When she wasn't looking, Ryan rolled his eyes and grinned across the table at Sarah and me. Aunt Elizabeth glared. He ducked back, as if he were a vampire and she'd brandished a crucifix at him.

"Shall we visit David this morning?" Nana asked when the meal was complete, sipping the last of her tea.

Aunt Elizabeth nodded, looking across at her children. "Will either of you be coming with us?" No need to ask me, of course.

My cousins both looked reluctant, but after a moment Sarah nodded back. "I will." She squeezed my hand under the table, an unspoken declaration of support.

The drive into the hospital was familiar by now, but I still stared out the window of my aunt's car as though it were the most interesting thing in the world, listening with half an ear to the conversation going on in the front—talk of members of the extended family from England, whom I knew by name only. Sarah rode in the back with me, trying to look interested whenever Nana glanced back.

Once we arrived, Aunt Elizabeth and Nana went in to see Dad, while Sarah and I stayed in the waiting room. I didn't like the delay, but it would have been rude to make Nana wait to see her son after she'd travelled so far. And, to be honest, I didn't want to be the one with her when she saw him for the first time. Before she'd arrived yesterday I wouldn't have thought I'd mind, but after her cold attitude to me I wasn't sure how I'd cope if she started crying. Or whether she'd welcome any comfort I provided.

After about fifteen minutes Aunt Elizabeth came out and nodded to me, sitting down with Sarah to watch daytime television. Sarah mouthed "good luck" as I pressed the buzzer.

I'd visited the ICU so often in the past week that I knew most of the nurses, by face if not by name. The nurse who let me in that day was a hirsute man named Carter. He greeted me as I used the hand sanitiser, beckoning me over to the desk.

"Good news," he grinned, teeth flashing whitely behind his beard. "The doc said he's going to move your father out of intensive care and onto a ward." My stomach did a flip. I must have looked stunned, because he hastily added, "That means they think he's stable."

"Has he shown any signs of waking up?" I knew what the answer would be, but I asked the question every time I arrived.

"No. It could happen any time, though. Don't lose hope."

"I won't." I smiled. The expression felt strained, but not for the reasons Carter was probably assuming. The idea of having to perform fae—was "magic" the right word?—on my father made me tremble every time I considered it. What if I made things worse? Dad might be unconscious but at least he was stable, and the hospital was taking care of his physical needs. But I knew he wouldn't wake up on his own and, although we'd never discussed it, I was sure Dad would never choose to continue as a vegetable. He'd want me to take the risk. He'd believe in me.

Taking a deep breath, I shoved those worries under a mental rug and crossed the ward to where Dad lay, with Nana sitting at his bedside. The nurse station was unoccupied.

Holding his hand, Nana ignored my arrival—or maybe she hadn't heard my tread over the constant machine noises. Her head was turned in his direction with unwavering focus. Standing next to her, I shuffled my feet and wished the ICU had chairs for more than one visitor per patient. Biting my lip, I glanced at her out of the corner of my eye. She looked exhausted. Pity melted my irritation at her. It must be hard to see your child like this.

I cleared my throat and spoke as though my father could hear me. "Hi, Dad. Did you have a good evening?"

I went through this ritual every day. The nurses had told me to talk to him normally—or at least as normally as I could manage. Nana blinked and looked up at me with a frown, but I ignored her. "I brought you a new CD," I told him, showing him the case as though he had his eyes open. "It's a compilation of Queen songs. Do you want me to put it on?"

The only answers were the beeping and sighing of the machinery. "I'll take that as a yes. You really should wake up and choose for yourself, you know. Otherwise I might start choosing dance music. Or opera." I placed the headphones over his head, covering one ear but leaving the other uncovered so if we talked to him he would be able to hear us. Hypothetically. Once the music was playing softly, I arranged the cards on the shelf, feeling awkward.

I normally filled Dad in on things going on at home or on the news, such as how Australia was doing in the cricket—although I hadn't told him about Jack yet. I wanted to, and when he woke up I would, but I wasn't comfortable discussing the stranger aspects of my life in such a busy room. The hospital also had a psychiatric ward, and I wasn't angling for an admission.

But the main thing that had happened since I'd last seen him was the arrival of his mother and her disapproval of me. Given she was sitting in the hard plastic chair beside me, that didn't seem like the wisest topic. So I stood there, silent and self-conscious.

"How were you getting on with your father, Isla?" Nana asked then. "Before his illness, I mean?"

I looked at her, confused. She matched me stare for stare, blue eyes intense. "Fine."

"You moved in with Elizabeth and her family six years ago. I thought you might have had a falling out."

"I moved because of school."

"And you still see him regularly? Get on well?"

I took a deep breath to try and keep the rising irritation out of my reply. "Of course."

"Oh?" She raised an eyebrow.

"He gave me a car for my birthday," I said, and then wanted to kick myself. I didn't need to prove to her that my father loved me, or that I loved my father. And mentioning the car made me sound selfish.

"Elizabeth said you had a fight with him the day before he fell ill."

"So?" I couldn't keep the frown off my face any longer.

"What was it about?"

*He thought I might be turning into a supernatural being like my mother. It turns out he was right.* "It's private."

"Do you think this is the time to be keeping secrets?" She indicated Dad with a gesture and I realised what she was hinting at: that I might have something to do with his condition, or know something that may allow him to be healed.

The fact the latter was true did little to dampen my ire. "What exactly are you suggesting?"

"Just that I'm sure David raised you to be an honest child," she replied, folding her hands in her lap.

"He did."

"Well, then." She said it as though it concluded the argument.

"Yes." I looked across the room; Carter was watching us with narrowed eyes. I lowered my voice. "Trust me when I tell you that the argument we had isn't relevant." It was even sort of true. "I'm going to go tell Sarah it's her turn to come and see him."

I kissed Dad's grizzled cheek. "I'll see you later. I love you."

Carter looked up as I stalked past his desk. "Everything okay?"

"Not really," I said, cleansing my hands. "My father's in a coma, you know."

My black humour earned me a flicker of a smile. "I know."

"Do you know when he's going to be moved out of ICU?"

"Probably tomorrow morning, I'd imagine."

"Did you tell my aunt yet?"

He shook his head. "Do you want me to?"

"I'll do it. Thanks for looking after Dad while he's been here."

"You're welcome."

Aunt Elizabeth looked surprised to see me come out so quickly; Sarah, on the other hand, was standing by the door as though she was expecting it. "My turn?"

"Yup."

While we waited for Nana and Sarah to come out of the ward, I filled Aunt Elizabeth in on what Carter had said.

"That's great news!"

"It is," I smiled, trying to match her enthusiasm. I was pretty sure her emotion was as forced as my own: she was doing it for my sake, and I for hers.

Families were weird sometimes.

It was only a few minutes later that Sarah came out and nodded to her mother, holding the ICU door open to let Aunt Elizabeth slip through. Some of the nurses would frown on her for that but Carter wasn't one of them.

After the door clicked shut she slumped in the chair beside me, putting her feet up on the table.

Even Carter frowned about that. Lucky for her he was on the other side of the door.

"Weird," she grumbled. "I couldn't get out of there fast enough."

"Let me guess. She grilled you about me?"

Sarah's eyes widened. "She did. How'd you guess?"

"What did she say?" I asked, clicking the beads on my charm bracelet like a rosary.

"She asked about the fight you had with Uncle David the night before he got sick. She wanted to know what it was about, whether you and he got on and stuff."

"She asked me about it too."

"Well, I told her you and Uncle David adore each other," she growled. "Silly old bat, coming over here and causing trouble. Haven't you gone through enough?"

"That's your grandmother you're talking about," I reminded her with a grimace. I agreed with the sentiment, though.

"She's your grandmother too."

"Yeah." My tone was unenthusiastic. "I think she's looking for someone to blame for Dad being sick."

Sarah sat up straight, taking her boots off the table, and stared. Her blue-green eyes blazed with righteous outrage. "And she chose *you*?"

"She doesn't know me, remember?"

"But still—"

"I know. I think I remind her of my mother. And she doesn't … she didn't like her."

"Oh." Sarah thought about this. "That's dumb."

I shrugged. "Not much I can do about it."

She pursed her lips. "You could dye your hair pink. Or shave it off. That'd reduce the resemblance."

We were still laughing when Aunt Elizabeth and Nana came out of the ICU, packed up to go home. Nana gave me a suspicious look but I ignored it. She believed I had cursed Dad into a coma, but if Jack and I managed to wake him that should relieve her of the notion.

I hoped.

After dropping Sarah and I at home, Aunt Elizabeth took Nana to the mall, giving me a welcome break from her disapproving stare. I wanted to talk to Jack, but Sarah hovered around the house, leaving me no opportunity to slip away to the park to wait for him. I'd have to sneak out later.

It's hard trying to secretly meet a pointy-eared boy when you're bunking in with your nosy cousin.

Sarah and I sat on the back porch, feet up on the balcony railings, relaxing and doing nothing for the first time in what felt like weeks. Hamish was splayed along Sarah's legs, his front paws hanging off into the air on either side of her calves.

Saying it was too hot in the shed, Ryan had taken his easel out and put it on the lawn, under the shade of a bottlebrush that grew near the northern fence; the tall tree was dotted with red spikes of flowers that looked a lot like the fat bristles on a bottle brush. Funnily enough. He'd positioned his easel so we couldn't see what he was working on and warned Sarah not to look. She'd pouted but complied with a knowing smile.

Sarah often received little pieces of art from Ryan, gifts at birthdays and Christmases—her favourite was a sketch he'd done of her cuddling one of Mrs Wilson's kittens—so the fact he was working on a painting for her birthday wasn't a surprise.

Ryan's eyes were narrowed with concentration; he carelessly held a paint palette in one hand, which he tapped at with a brush before patting the bristles on the canvas. I'd seen the sketch of the painting, but it was black and white. I tried to guess which bit he was working on. Where did the bright green paint fit into the image?

He wouldn't mind if I had a look, but that would be cruel to Sarah. So I stayed where I was.

The screen door rattled open behind us, and Aunt Elizabeth and her mother came out onto the balcony. Hamish leapt off Sarah's lap, his claws scraping my cousin's skin; Sarah managed not to swear, biting her lip. I gave her a thumb's up.

"I've got your birthday present, Isla." My grandmother sat, putting a small box on the table. It wasn't wrapped, and the logo of the shop was on the side: a place called *Neve's*, one of the local alternative shops that sold everything from tie-dyed clothing and handmade, imported trinkets to incense and jewellery.

My surge of disappointment—and, I have to admit, lack of surprise—about her not having bothered to bring me something from England was matched by my curiosity about what my straight-laced Nana could have found in such a shop. What was she doing in one in the first place? I didn't even like those shops that much: some of the rings were pretty, but the incense made me sneeze and the clothing wasn't my style.

Sarah, on the other hand, was a loyalty card-toting member of *Neve's*.

Eyes narrowed, Nana slid the box across the table.

As soon as I took it, I knew she was up to something. I could feel a subtle twisting in my stomach, a faint warmth in my fingertips when I stroked the glossy cream-colored cardboard of the box. But the feeling was nowhere near as strong as the wrenching nausea I felt when I came close to touching iron.

This was a test, albeit one more subtle than the one my father used when he'd dumped an iron sculpture into my lap.

"Go ahead, open it," Sarah urged me.

"Yes, Isla, open it," my grandmother said, her eyes bright and cold as chips of ice. I hated her a little bit right then.

I lifted off the lid, revealing a pretty but rather strange necklace made of small, silvery-grey beads, each one no bigger than my little fingertip. The surface of each bead was glossy, dark rather than reflective. "Oh. Thank you." I smiled. The twinge of nausea grew a little stronger, but was still bearable. Whatever the necklace was made of, it wasn't iron.

"Oooh, pretty." Sarah leaned in to look over my shoulder. "Haematite."

"What's that?"

My grandmother answered. "It's iron oxide. In mineral form."

If I'd had any doubts, her words shattered them. *She knew what my mother was.* My heart ached. What if, instead of assuming I was tainted, my mother's daughter, she'd understood and opened herself up to questions? The things she could tell me, things I wanted—no, *needed*—to know...

The thought made me miss my father with a pain that tightened my throat and burned the back of my eyes. He had concealed the truth about my mother, but he'd agreed that day, in the parking lot, to tell me everything about her. I still believed he would, if he could.

And he loved me. I wasn't sure this woman did. In fact, I was pretty sure she didn't.

"Do you need help to try it on?" Nana continued, oblivious to my train of thought.

"I'm good." Bracing myself for a reaction, I reached into the box...

And almost laughed with relief. All I felt was an increased warmth in my fingers, like I was holding them near a candle flame, and another incremental increase of nausea in my stomach—but, again, still bearable. Worse nerves had rattled beneath my skin before my first date with Dominic.

Nana's face fell, a curious mixture of disappointment and confusion, when I fastened the necklace around my throat and smiled, genuinely this time. It rested against my skin, warm but not painful. Except for the nausea, it was sort of pleasant. It would be better than a scarf come wintertime. I turned to Sarah. "What do you think?"

"It will look great with that black shirt you've got. The one with the silvery lines through it?"

I nodded. "I think so too." I stood and walked around the table to Nana, bending to give her a kiss on the cheek. "Thank you for such a thoughtful gift," I said, possibly laying it on a little thick. "I'm going to put that shirt on."

Inside, I ducked into the bathroom and snuck a quick look in the mirror, lifting the necklace to make sure my skin wasn't reddening or doing anything else alarming. It all looked fine, and I heaved a sigh of relief. Nana would need no explanation if I had an "allergic" reaction, but I wasn't sure what she'd do next. Drag me by the hair to the hospital and demand I undo whatever I'd done, probably.

Awkward.

I went into my bedroom, dodging around the suitcase to get into my wardrobe, and retrieved the shirt Sarah had mentioned. I slipped it on and went back out onto the porch with a sigh.

# CHAPTER THIRTEEN

*I* spent the next twenty-four hours wondering how to escape my family in order to visit my father with Jack. Alone.

As Carter had predicted, Dad was moved onto a regular ward the next morning. Because of the more relaxed set of rules about the number of visitors, we all went in to see him. At least it denied my grandmother the opportunity to ask awkward questions when no one else was around, but, as I sat by his bedside and listened to my aunt make subdued conversation with Nana, I worried I'd struggle to find an opportunity to come in to the hospital without them.

It was Dominic who gave me the excuse I needed. We'd already returned home from the hospital when he called, asking if I wanted to go out for dinner that evening. He'd won the job he was after, working behind the bar at the Irish pub *Paddy's*, and wanted to celebrate.

Feeling like the worst girlfriend in the world, I begged off, telling him I had a headache. It was a lame excuse, but the first one that came to mind. "I'm sorry. How about we have dinner tomorrow night instead?"

"Great. I hope your head feels better soon."

"Me, too."

After I got off the phone I told Sarah and my aunt I was meeting Dominic in the city for dinner. They both agreed it was a good idea for me to have a bit of "me time". Nana, who was less overtly disapproving since I'd worn the haematite necklace, said nothing. I wondered what she thought now that I'd disproved her suspicion I was manifesting *aosidhe* traits. Or did she realise my reaction to the haematite was diluted because I wasn't a pureblood?

To avoid raising Sarah's suspicions, I went through my regular pre-date ritual, taking a shower and fussing over what I was going to wear. Conscious that I didn't know what the evening would involve, I chose denim shorts and a loose-fitting T-shirt with a scooped neck, as well as my canvas sneakers. They were less dressy than what I'd normally choose, but I hoped no one noticed. A little foundation, mascara and eye shadow, and I was ready to go.

"Don't be late," Aunt Elizabeth called after me.

"I won't." *I hope.*

Feeling excited and guilty, I drove around the block, leaving my car on the street at the other side of the park, out of sight of the house.

I had a brief dilemma when I neared the swings; it was almost six o'clock, and sunset wasn't for a couple of hours. If I sat where I'd normally wait for Jack, I'd be visible from the lounge room window if anyone looked. But visiting hours at the hospital ended at eight, so I couldn't hold off until the sun vanished below the distant

Brindabella mountain range.

I settled for sitting on the grass, putting one of the taller shrubs between me and the house. I closed my eyes and turned my thoughts to Jack, willing him to appear. I had no idea if it would help, but it couldn't hurt.

"Isla," he said from right beside me, making me jump. For the first time since I'd met him, he was wearing different clothes: knee-length baggy cargo shorts, sneakers and a plain black T-shirt. Instead of a hood, he wore a red Canteen bandana beanie-style, holding his golden hair back from his face and covering the points of his ears. His features were still striking and unusual, with large blue eyes and a slightly pointed chin, but he was not obviously inhuman.

"Wow!" I grinned. He looked good.

"Do you like it?" He held his hands out from his sides, self-conscious.

"It's nice to see you in something different. The jumper and jeans were nice, but a bit samey after a while."

"And long sleeves and pant legs are quite conspicuous in summer."

"True."

"What can I do for you?" He moved towards the bench, but I waved him off, standing.

"Dad's been moved off the ICU. He doesn't share his room with anyone, but I don't know how long that'll last."

"We should act immediately then," Jack said.

My stomach rolled with anxiety. "Is there, um, anything I need to bring?"

He shook his head. "The power to remove the elf shot comes from within you."

"Oh. Right." I swallowed. "Let's go, then."

We walked the short distance to my car. It wasn't till I was putting the key in the lock that I noticed Jack hanging back a little, his lips pressed together grimly. I opened my mouth to ask what was wrong and then it hit me. "The steel!"

"Indeed." His face was pale, but he squared his shoulders and walked forward. "I will be fine."

I searched his face for a lie. Steel didn't bother me—one of the perks of being a half-breed—but I'd seen him avoid touching it many times before. "Really?"

"Yes. I will be careful."

I opened the door for him; even though the door handle was mostly plastic, I decided not to risk it. He eased into the seat cautiously, sitting with his knees together, his hands resting primly on his thighs.

When I got behind the driver's seat he still hadn't put his seatbelt on. "Why aren't you buckled in?"

He gestured to the silvery tongue of the belt mechanism that hung from the sash.

"Pull it across by the belt and I'll clip it in." I wasn't going to let anyone ride in my car without a seatbelt. Even if I ignored the chance I might get pulled over—and I didn't imagine any police officer accepting the explanation that my passenger wasn't wearing a seatbelt because he was terminally allergic to steel—I was paranoid about the idea of getting in a car accident and Jack ending up through the windshield.

Being *duinesidhe* didn't make him immune to glass or to impacting with the ground at speed. I didn't care how fast he healed.

Jack took the belt gingerly, holding it high above his lap so the stainless steel tongue didn't drag across his pants. I took it as soon as it was within reach, sliding it into the buckle and clicking it in. Jack exhaled with relief.

"Are you sure you'll be okay? You look sort of like you're going to puke."

"I will be fine. Just ... please do not take overly long to get there."

"I'll do my best." I put the car into gear and pulled out onto the street.

Fortunately for Jack, we were heading north and most of the traffic was driving out into the suburbs, so we didn't encounter any delays beyond uncooperative traffic lights. He was quiet. I considered turning the radio on but it seemed rude, so I drove in silence, trying not to think about what might be expected of me when we reached our destination.

Jack visibly uncoiled when he got out of the car, as though he'd been trying to make himself smaller. "You okay?" I asked, shouldering my bag.

He nodded. "Are you?"

We started through the multistorey car park towards the main entrance. "A little nervous." I lowered my voice. "What if I can't do it?"

"You will be fine. It is your birthright."

"Technically it's only half my birthright," I pointed out.

He waved his hand dismissively.

We stopped at the little shop in the reception area. It sold newspapers, magazines, cards, toiletries and gifts. Rows of beady-eyed monkeys and rabbits, most of them pastel blue or pink, stared at me as I hesitated over what to buy. I eventually got Dad the most fragrant bunch of flowers on the stand. If what Jack and I were about to attempt didn't work, Dad wouldn't see the other gifts, but he might be able to smell the flowers. Small consolation.

We rode the lift to Dad's floor. It was the dinner hour; the sounds of clinking plates and cutlery emerged from open doors leading to wards. An orderly pushed a trolley further up the corridor. Dad's room, however, was quiet.

I went into the room first and Jack followed, nudging the door closed with the toe of his shoe. He must have had a fair amount of practice at navigating the human world, with its love of steel.

"Hi, Dad," I said, kissing my father on the forehead. He looked like he was sleeping. But, unlike Sleeping Beauty, a kiss wasn't enough to wake him up.

At least not mine. I couldn't speak for other kisses.

I put the flowers into a vase, throwing out the bunch I'd bought previously, and switched my mobile phone off so we wouldn't be interrupted. Then I turned to Jack. He was standing in the middle of the room, gazing around.

"I have never been in a hospital before. It is very..." He trailed off, wrinkling his nose.

"It is very," I agreed. "Once Dad's home I'll be glad to never set foot in one again. The nurses and doctors have been nice, but..." It was my turn to trail off.

"Shall we get started?"

"Right. Hang on a sec." I drew the curtains so they hung around the bed, allowing us a few extra seconds of privacy if anyone came through the door at a bad time.

We faced each other across my father's supine form, which was covered with a crisp white sheet and a blue woven blanket. Jack's back was to the window and the sun silhouetted his head. His hair was a golden halo where it had escaped the bandana.

"What do I do?"

"Remember Ryan's sketch of your father?"

I nodded. It was hard to forget: my father, gasping with pain, gripping the shaft of an invisible something piercing his heart. A black shadow spreading tentacled fingers across his chest.

"Hold your hand where he had his," Jack instructed softly.

Trembling, I held my hand over Dad's left breast, fingers splayed. I took a deep breath and willed myself to stillness. "Do I touch him?"

"No. Hold it higher than that. A bit higher. Good." He nodded, satisfied, when my hand was a good two feet above Dad's gently moving chest, at shoulder height. "Right." His voice continued. "The time I saw this done, the *aosidhe* drew the elf shot out by projecting a sliver of his own power. The elf shot responded to the lure and left its host."

"I'm going to be bait?" I squeaked and almost withdrew my hand, but Jack took my wrist in his fingers, steadying me.

"I suppose you could describe it that way. But it is more like calling the elf shot to its master."

"What happens when it comes out?"

"I will secure it for you. And then we will destroy it."

"What if—"

"You can trust me, Isla." He leaned forward to meet my gaze, his sapphire eyes earnest.

I wanted to trust him, but everything he'd told me about the fae made me wonder if that was the wisest course. It felt uncharitable given how much he'd helped me, but I was way out of my depth, and I didn't want to cling to something only for it to drag me under.

Then I remembered something.

"Swear."

He blinked, and I wondered if I'd offended him. Then he smiled—pleased I'd been listening, I guess. "Of course. I, Jack, swear to you that I will secure this elf shot and protect you and your father from further harm by it."

Shivering as though someone had walked over my grave, I considered his words for a moment, trying to see if there was a loophole. "Good enough. What next?"

"Close your eyes." I frowned and he added, "It will help you concentrate."

So I did. My world narrowed to the steady rhythm of our breathing and the warmth of Jack's fingers around my wrist.

"Imagine a glowing heat emanating from the palm of your hand," Jack said. "It is the colour of golden sunlight on a summer afternoon, warm as a laugh or a hug from a friend."

As he spoke, he placed his hand beneath my palm. His fingers were points of heat against my skin. Having them there helped me visualise a bigger, more encompassing heat spreading outwards. I pictured it originating from my palm and growing, like a flower opening its petals, to surround my fingers and Jack's outstretched hand in a bright sphere.

I don't know how long we stood there, holding hands, but I knew when something began to happen: I felt a wrench inside me, like someone yanking at an invisible rope tied around my chest. I staggered a little.

Jack's hand let go. Surprised, I opened my eyes. And stared.

The ball looked rather like I had imagined, yellowy

gold and centred on my palm, but it was shot through with glints of brilliant white, as though fragments of the sun were floating like motes of dust at my fingertips.

"Holy shit," I whispered. Jack beamed at me.

I felt another wrench and braced myself against the bed with my other arm. "I don't know how long I can keep this up."

"Just a little longer."

My father began to stir. His fingertips twitched on the bedcovers, barely noticeable, but more movement than he had managed independently since the seizure. My heart leapt, thundering inside my ribcage like a galloping brumby. It was working!

The elf shot, when it emerged from his chest, was shaped like an arrow but without the fitting for a shaft. It glowed white hot, leaving an afterimage on my retina when I blinked. It passed through Dad's flesh and the hospital gown he wore without leaving a mark and oriented itself on the luminescent sphere. On me.

The elf shot tensed like a snake ready to strike. But Jack was faster. He scooped the arrow up in a clear plastic container and screwed on a yellow lid.

"You can stop now."

I let the image of the ball that filled my mind go, and the glow dimmed. I'd imagined it flickering out like a candle being extinguished, but it faded, seeping into my palm the way water sinks into dry soil. My hand tingled.

Jack held out the container, which looked oddly familiar. It fit neatly into his hand. The elf shot lay in the bottom, no longer glowing, seemingly harmless. It had markings along its two sharpened edges that looked like writing. If they were, I couldn't read them.

Staring at the container, hysterical giggles bubbled up in my throat.

Jack looked puzzled. "I did something funny?"

"Uh huh," I told him. "Where'd you swipe that from?"

"Out there," he said, nodding towards the corridor.

"It's a sample container."

"What is that?"

Before I could explain, another wrenching feeling and a wave of dizziness overcame me. I sat on the edge of Dad's bed. "I don't feel so good."

Jack was at my side in an instant, slipping the container into a pocket of his cargo shorts as he moved. He put a finger under my chin and tilted my head up to look into his eyes.

"You are drained," he said after a moment.

"My battery needs recharging?" My voice slurred when I spoke and I blinked rapidly at him, trying to make him less blurry. Was this what being drunk felt like? And if so, why did people drink?

"Again with the batteries," he muttered, his expression a mixture of concern and exasperation. "But yes, you need to rejuvenate yourself."

"How?"

Jack didn't answer.

On the bed, Dad moaned.

"We should go." Jack slid one arm around my waist, pulling me to my feet.

"But..." I looked at Dad. He wasn't awake yet, but he was stirring. I wanted to be here when he woke. The idea of walking away now, when he was so close to coming back to me, brought tears to my eyes.

"How would we explain your current condition to the

healing staff? Your father will awaken, and they will think it was spontaneous. They do not need to know we were here."

His words made sense. Also, I was meant to be on a date with Dominic. The nurses mentioning to my family that I was here when Dad woke up would reveal my lie.

"Okay." My voice was hoarse. I swallowed and tried again. "One thing, though." I pushed the nurse call button. The idea my father wouldn't be alone when he finally roused loosened the knot of emotion in my chest. "Hopefully they'll think Dad did it. Let's go."

Jack pushed the curtain back on its rail and helped me to the door. I leaned awkwardly against him. The effort involved in pulling the heavy door open—Jack couldn't help because the handle was stainless steel—left me panting, and I was grateful for his support.

In the corridor near the lift, a nurse smiled at us, probably assuming we were a couple walking arm in arm. Concentrating on putting one foot in front of the other allowed me to ignore the flush of embarrassment. The corridor swam before my eyes, which were gritty with fatigue. Others' perceptions didn't seem that important right then.

Once we were back in reception, Jack led me to a chair. I sat, putting my head in my hands. The chair shifted as Jack sat beside me.

"You didn't answer my question," I said after a minute or two.

"Which one?"

"How do we ... rejuvenate me?"

He was silent for so long I sat up straighter in the uncomfortable chair, looking him in the eye. "Jack?"

"A couple of days' rest and you should be fine," he said. But there was uncertainty in his voice.

"I can't drive home like this," I pointed out, glaring—although the glare was undermined by the squint that brought him into focus. Even then, he looked a little blurry and was surrounded by a strange pattern of lights: flickering pink and yellow, a hint of red. Was I getting a migraine? I'd never had one before, but Aunt Elizabeth got them sometimes and she'd talked about seeing auras.

I closed my eyes, leaning back against the cool glass of the window behind me. "Sorry I snapped," I muttered. "But seriously, I'm seeing things. I can't drive home."

"What are you seeing?"

"A sort of rainbow around your head."

"Hmm." He was silent for a moment. "Do you remember how you said you wanted *duinesidhe* superpowers?"

"Yes."

"The colours you're seeing might be an expression of their development."

"I take it back."

Jack laughed softly. "It does not work that way, Isla."

"Figures." I opened my eyes to look at him again. "So what do I do about it?"

The flickering yellow was stronger in his aura. "I am not sure. If you have inherited your mother's talent for manipulating emotions, it might be that the colours you see are a manifestation of what people are feeling, your way of rationalising something your senses cannot otherwise perceive."

"What are you feeling right now?" I asked.

Jack blushed, his aura flashing a salmon pink. I realised the question was rude. But before I could apologise, he answered. "Uncertainty. Concern for you."

"How do I turn the colours off?"

"I am not sure," he said again. "I will have to investigate. But our priority right now is to give you the energy to get yourself home." I nodded, which set my head spinning. I took a deep breath to steady myself.

"I want you to draw one of the colours from my aura," Jack told me.

"That seems like a bad idea," I said. "A really, really bad idea."

"Do not worry. It will refresh you, not drain you further."

"That's not what I mean. What if I break something?" Was taking someone's emotions like pruning a shrub? Or more like uprooting it entirely and throwing it on the compost? "What if I take an emotion and it doesn't come back?"

"I do not believe that will happen."

"But you don't know for sure, do you?"

"Well, no."

"Is it possible to … take too much?"

He nodded. "I have heard of such things. But only when the *duinesidhe* goes too far and takes everything, all the emotions, leaving only a shell."

"But how—"

Jack placed a finger on my lips, cutting off further protest. "I insist. Here." He stood, helping me to my feet. We went out the automatic doors and onto the lighted walkway. "We should head back towards your car. There will be more privacy there."

We passed a few people on the way to the car park. Visiting hours would end shortly and people were starting to return to their vehicles. We were able to find a spot behind a concrete pillar that was well lit but out of direct line-of-sight of the elevators. A fire extinguisher and service door were to our right. I leaned against the side of a grey four-wheel drive, and Jack stood with his back to the pillar, avoiding contact with anything metallic.

His aura changed to a sickly yellow with patches of pulsating blue. The pink and red were interwoven with the other colours. A combination that would have made a circus clown proud.

"Do it," Jack told me.

"I don't know how."

The sickly yellow flickered with the brighter yellow from before. The colours were strange: I could see them but at the same time they didn't in any way obstruct my perception of Jack's features. The two images were perfectly overlaid. "Neither do I," he admitted.

"Great," I muttered. Then I squared my shoulders and reached through the pattern of light, which proved intangible, cupping his face with both hands.

The first time I'd touched his skin I'd noticed the fine net of wrinkles—now gone—and the silky, unnatural heat of him. He'd been so sure of himself.

His eyes were uncertain now, but filled with trust.

And my hands trembled with anxiety. Jack had become a friend. A strange friend, but a friend nonetheless.

"Do it," Jack whispered.

Swallowing hard, I chose the sickly yellow colour, because it seemed the most unpleasant. And there was a lot of it, so I figured he had plenty to spare. I wasn't sure what it represented ... but surely it was better to reduce the amount of the unpleasantly coloured emotion and leave him with the attractive blue and the intermingled pink and red—a sweet colour that reminded me of Aunt Elizabeth's roses.

Visualisation had worked to create the glowing ball before. Why not again? I imagined myself drawing the sickly yellow from Jack, siphoning it through my palms and into the core of my body, like water running down a drainpipe into a water tank.

The emotion that filled me as I drew the light from him was fear: the kind of persistent feeling that knots your stomach and leaves you trembling, so you have to clench your fists to hide your nervousness from others. At first I thought Jack was afraid of what I was doing—he wasn't alone—but as the emotion seeped into me I realised it was the constant fear of touching something with iron in its makeup. An ever-present fear of injury or death.

I finally appreciated the risk he took to see me, the danger every time he came out of … wherever it was he went.

I released him with a gasp, stepping backward and then twisting to avoid touching the car behind me. Right then, with Jack's fear bubbling inside me, the reaction was instinctive.

Jack beamed at me. His pose was more relaxed; he held himself apart from the metal, but was less concerned about it.

And my dizziness, that exhausted feeling, was gone. But the colours were still there. Disappointment sat heavy on my chest. The yellow was almost completely drained—I saw with relief I hadn't taken all of it—the other colours growing brighter. Again I thought of gardening as it reminded me of Aunt Elizabeth pruning a large shrub back so the sun could reach the smaller plants underneath.

"It worked," he said, his voice warm. "I knew you could do it."

"Yes, well. I wish I shared your confidence."

"You could if you wanted to." Jack grinned, and I laughed.

"Pass. I want to get home and sleep for, like, a thousand years."

"You are still tired?"

I thought about that as we walked back to my car. "Not physically. But it's been a long day. Drawing out arrows, sucking emotions: you know how it is." That reminded me. "What happened to the arrow?"

He reached into the pocket of his cargo shorts and handed the sample container to me. "Here. We will need to destroy it, but that can be done another day."

"Let me guess. Iron?"

He nodded. "That would be the most effective, if you can arrange it. Steel would work too, but it takes longer."

"I'll have to think about it." I turned the container over; the arrow clicked against the plastic as it fell on its side. "What does the writing on the edges say?"

He peered into the container. "It reads 'David Andrew Blackman'."

"A bullet with his name on it," I whispered, a shiver running down my spine as though an ice-cold finger had run along my skin. That was the single most disturbing thing about everything that had happened: someone had targeted my father. To what end? Elf shot caused paralysis, not death. Were they thinking he'd starve to death? If so, they didn't understand modern medicine.

"Who sent it?" I asked.

"There is no way to tell."

"It was probably her." *My mother.* "Who else has a grudge against Dad?"

He shrugged. "I would suggest, when you speak to him, you ask that very thing."

"I will." I put the container in my bag, swapping it for my keys. Despite everything, the reminder that I'd be able to talk to Dad again brought a little smile to my lips.

When I unlocked the car door and held it open for Jack, he took a cautious step back. The sickly yellow flared a little in his aura, although it wasn't as strong. Despite what it represented, I was relieved to see it react; it meant I hadn't drained the emotion to the point where it couldn't return at all.

"I will make my own way home, thank you," he said.

"You sure?"

"Yes. There are *duinesidhe* I would speak to about your new superpower." He smiled as he said the word, and I grinned back.

Jack stood by the car until I got in and closed the door, starting the engine. He turned and sauntered away through the car park, hands in his pockets, looking like any other guy my age.

I glanced at my watch. It was only eight. I wanted to go back and see Dad, more than anything, but visiting hours had ended—and the lie I'd told the rest of my family would be torn like tissue paper in a hurricane if I went back. Besides, he'd be swarmed by staff, and I might not even get to see him while they were running tests.

Likewise, if I went home now, Sarah in particular would want to know why I was so early.

I decided to give Dominic a call; maybe we could have that dinner after all, if he hadn't eaten yet. I had something to celebrate now, too.

I found my phone—it had made its way to the deepest corner of my bag, as usual—turning it on and drumming my fingers on the steering wheel while I waited for it to power up. I watched a couple walk past my car on the other side of the row. They were holding hands. Both of them had silvery grey auras: a sad colour.

My phone beeped a message alert, and then, as I picked it up, two more. I frowned, opening up the message app.

The first message was from Dominic: a missed call alert from about half an hour ago.

The second and third messages were from Sarah, both in the last twenty minutes. The first was a missed call, the second a text message: *Where the hell are you?!?!*

I bit my lip and debated whether to reply to Sarah's text or give her a call.

Whether to lie or tell her the truth.

I wasn't a deceitful person. And I trusted Sarah more than anyone else in the world. A weight lifted from my chest as I resolved to tell her everything I'd learned. I knew she'd believe it. She had a much greater faith in the supernatural than me. Than I used to have, anyway.

Hell, if she didn't believe me maybe I'd make my hand glow again, like I had in Dad's room. That ought to banish all doubt.

Smiling as I imagined the look on her face, I pressed the button to dial Sarah's mobile.

"Hello?"

"Hey, it's me."

"I know. I have caller ID," she snapped. "Dominic called not long ago."

My heart skipped a beat. "And?"

"He rang to let you know he'd reserved a table at that pancake place in town for tomorrow night. And he said to give you a get well soon kiss."

"What did you tell him?" I asked after a moment, my voice tight.

"I told him you were in bed," she replied.

My surge of gratitude confirmed my decision to be honest with her. "Thank you!"

"So where are you? And why am I lying to your boyfriend about it?"

"I'm just leaving the hospital."

"You lied about a date with Dominic to go see your dad?" Her voice was incredulous. I imagined her standing with one hand on her hip, jaw clenching and unclenching with frustration. "Don't get me wrong, I love Uncle David, but you saw him earlier today. You're taking daughterly devotion a bit far."

"It's complicated," I replied, staring out the windscreen of my car. There were more people entering the car park now, their auras in all the colours of the rainbow.

It *was* complicated.

"Try me."

"I will," I promised. "When I get home, I'll tell you everything."

"Are you coming straight here?"

"Yep."

"I'll be waiting," she said ominously.

We hung up, and I tossed my mobile onto the passenger seat of my car. Then I found my way through the twisting grey labyrinth of the car park.

I'd grown more comfortable with driving in the weeks since Dad had given me the car. But the trip home that night was as unnerving as my first drive around the block as a learner.

The sun had disappeared behind the line of mountains to the west, painting the sky vibrant pink and orange. The streetlights flickered to life, people turned their car headlights on, and, overhead, the moon was rising. All of this gave me enough light to see into the cabins of other cars on the road.

The colours in people's auras didn't glow with their own light, but when I saw them, their strangeness drew my eye. Some were a single, flat colour; others were a dizzying kaleidoscope. Once, as I was waiting behind a bus at an intersection, I saw a man whose aura was as black as tar being squeezed from a lung in a quit-smoking commercial. He was sitting on the bench seat at the back of the bus, staring out the side window with a stony expression. I was glad he didn't look back at me.

By the time I reached our suburb, whose roads were mercifully quiet, my hands were shaking with nerves.

Sarah was waiting out the front of our house when I pulled up. She leaned against the light pole with a hand on her hip, just like I'd imagined. The colours around her were an agitated swirl; I saw a bit of yellow and blue, similar to the colours I'd seen in Jack's aura, but not identical. The yellow was less sickly, the blue darker.

When I got out of the car she gave me a fierce hug. Then she punched my arm.

"Ow."

"That's for worrying me."

"What? Why?"

"Why was I worried? Because you're my sensible cousin, Isla. You don't lie. And if you do, you tell me about it." She rolled her eyes. But I saw the flash of that sad silver colour in her aura, and didn't have to guess what it meant.

"I'm sorry. It's been a weird week." I locked the car door and turned back to face her, wondering where to start.

"So why were you at the hospital?"

"Yes," said a voice from the shadows. "Why *were* you at the hospital?"

Nana stepped out from between Aunt Elizabeth's car and the neighbour's fence, bearing down on us.

"You were spying on us!"

"Not you, Sarah. Her." She pointed at me. The colours rippling around her ran to a furious red shot through with black, like the patterns you get on the inside of your eyelids after you look at a bright light. Blood and shadows.

I didn't have to guess what they meant either.

"That's outrageous." Sarah leapt to my defence. "You've been suspicious of Isla since the day you arrived, and for no reason. Just because she looks like her mother or whatever—"

"You don't know her, what she is capable of," Nana said. Did she mean me, or my mother?

Sarah frowned, sharing my confusion. "Of course I know her. Isla wouldn't hurt a fly."

"Then ask her what she was doing at the hospital," my grandmother demanded. She was standing close to us now, her voice low and intense, her accent growing more pronounced with the strength of her emotion. Somewhere in the house, the phone rang.

"She was visiting—"

Nana cut Sarah off with a sharp wave of her hand. "*Ask* her."

Sarah turned to me, the question in her eyes.

Before I could answer, the screen door banged open and Aunt Elizabeth came out onto the porch. "Isla! Mum! Great news." She almost sang the words. "The hospital rang. David's awake!"

Squealing, Sarah hugged me. I embraced her back, looking over her shoulder into my grandmother's eyes.

"Now you know," I said softly.

# CHAPTER FOURTEEN

We weren't allowed to see Dad that night. After we had impromptu, celebratory cake, Aunt Elizabeth stood and stretched until I heard her vertebrae pop. "This will be the first time I'll be able to sleep since—well, since David fell ill."

"I might stay up a while longer, dear," Nana said. When my aunt looked surprised, she added, "Jetlag."

"You poor thing. Would you like me to make you some chamomile tea?"

"No, thank you." Nana's contemplative stare turned to me. The angry red and black were gone from her aura, replaced with a complicated pattern of slate grey and the same blue as in Sarah's aura. Curiosity, maybe? Suspicion? "I'll sit up with the children for a while. Get some rest."

Ryan scowled at being called a child and stood, shoving his chair back. "I've got some stuff to do anyway. Night." He stomped up the hallway to his room.

He'd started painting in there rather than in the shed;

since his collapse he disliked being out there. I didn't blame him. Aunt Elizabeth normally objected to him painting in the house, but she either didn't notice or didn't care. I suspected the latter; the smell of turpentine carried despite the closed door.

Or maybe after his collapse she didn't like the idea of him painting out there anymore, either.

As soon as my aunt's bedroom door closed, Sarah and Nana turned on me, with identical, demanding stares. Their eyes were almost the same shade of blue, too, although Sarah's had a hint of green whereas Nana's tended more towards grey.

"Spill it," Sarah said.

So I did.

I directed my explanation at Sarah, who was a more sympathetic audience than my grandmother. I told her how Dad came to me with the iron ornament. How he'd tipped it into my lap. How it had scalded me as though it were hot, even though it wasn't. How I'd fled to Mount Ainslie.

How I'd met Jack.

How Jack wasn't human.

Sarah's expression went from amused suspicion to shock when she realised I was serious. She glanced across at Nana, who nodded at my description of Jack's appearance: the wrinkly skin; the long, pointed ears; the doe-like eyes.

"He's a hob," she said. We stared at her. "A type of fae that serves other, more powerful fae. That's their purpose."

I filed that information away for future consideration. "How do you know that?" Sarah asked.

Nana gazed at a painting on the wall with unseeing eyes. "When I was a girl I knew a member of the fae," she murmured. Her aura shifted from navy blue to deep pink. The silence hung for a moment before she shook her head and scowled. "They are dangerous. Not to be trusted."

"Jack told me," I said.

She raised her eyebrows. "He admitted it?"

I nodded.

"Just remember it applies to him too."

"He swore not to harm me."

Her mouth fell open with surprise, revealing a pair of pearly white dentures. I tried to suppress a smile; after what she'd put me through, I felt a certain amount of enjoyment at confounding her.

"Exactly what did he swear to?" she said.

"Does it matter?" Sarah folded her arms and glowered, her apparent dislike for being out of the faerie loop adding a light shade of red to her cheeks.

Having experienced that feeling myself, I was sympathetic.

"It does," Nana said. "Fae are bound by the oaths they swear, but as a result they are particular about the wording."

That night on the mountain seemed like forever ago. "I think it was, 'I swear I mean you no harm'."

Her expression of satisfaction and the smug pinkness in her aura annoyed me. "By wording it that way he was only swearing to his intent at the time he said it. He could change his mind and wouldn't be bound by the oath."

I shrugged, although I filed that away to think about later, too.

"So what happened next?" Sarah said, getting me

back onto the story.

I told her how Jack had healed my hand, and how I discovered my mother was a fae. It was hard to tell which of those revelations surprised my cousin more. She insisted on examining my palm for some sign of the injury or residual magic.

After pulling my hand from her eager grasp, I recounted in an abbreviated fashion how Jack figured out Dad's coma was caused by an elf shot. I left out Ryan's involuntary role in the discovery, as well as my inadvertently turning Ryan into an *aislinge*. I was certain my grandmother would be horrified and angry, even though I hadn't meant to do it.

What did Nana know about *aislinges*? I'd ask her another time, once I decided how to phrase the question without making her suspicious.

Sarah questioned me, rapt, about how we'd removed the elf shot. I tried to describe it, but my words seemed hollow. How to capture the warmth of the light Jack had helped me summon? The single-mindedness with which the elf shot had oriented itself towards my hand, as though ready to pounce?

"Can I see it?" Sarah asked.

I pulled the container out of my bag and handed it to Sarah. "Don't open it," I cautioned her. "I don't know what would happen if it got out."

She turned the container around, looking at the arrow from all sides. "What are the squiggles?"

"It's Dad's name. Jack told me," I said.

Nana stood, startling us. "We must destroy it."

I hesitated, and then nodded. The longer we waited, the more nervous I'd be that something would go wrong.

What if it escaped and went after Dad again?

Or maybe it would come after me?

"Jack said iron would do it," I told her.

She looked around as though expecting to see some iron in the lounge room. Actually, given my father's hobby, that wasn't an unreasonable assumption—although it was wrong.

"Out in the shed." Sarah led us out the back door.

The wind rustled the treetops with icy fingers that smelled like impending rain. I shivered. You wouldn't know it was almost summer from the feel of the air.

I waited on the back path, the porch light throwing my shadow before me, while Sarah and Nana went into the shed. They were taking a long time. There was quite a lot of ironwork in there; how long did they need? I tapped a foot but still couldn't bring myself to go inside to see what was causing the delay. I hadn't gone in there since the night of Ryan's collapse, when we'd discovered the painting.

Of my mother.

*Oh.*

Was it still in there? Had Nana seen it before now?

When they came out, Sarah was holding a long black candlestick. Nana looked pale, licking her lips repeatedly.

So that was a no then.

"Unnerving, isn't it?" I murmured. She nodded. There was no trace of suspicion in the look she gave me; if she'd heard of *aislinges*, it hadn't occurred to her Ryan might be one.

"I think this will fit inside the plastic container, like a mortar and pestle," Sarah said, showing me the candlestick.

I stepped back reflexively and she dropped her hand to her side. "Sorry."

"It's okay."

After a moment she continued, "Um. I figured we could crush it inside the container so none of it gets out."

"You'll have to be quick getting the candlestick in there once the lid's taken off, in case it animates," I pointed out.

"Me?" she squeaked.

"Well, I can't."

"True." She took a breath. "Okay, let's do it."

We went up onto the porch, where the light was better. I stood next to the railing, feeling useless, while Sarah placed the container upright on the glass tabletop. Nana stood beside her, holding the container steady. White creases formed around her lips.

"Good luck," I said as Sarah unscrewed the lid.

She didn't lift it immediately; instead, she held the candlestick beside it and closed her eyes, taking another, deeper breath.

In one quick movement, she lifted the lid aside and rammed the end of the candlestick into the plastic container.

Sarah had chosen her weapon well; it fit neatly inside the container, leaving no room for the arrow to escape up the side.

When the candlestick thumped down onto the elf shot, there was an instant where nothing happened. I had enough time to wish I'd asked Jack for more information, and then a high-pitched shriek broke the silence. The sound was both mechanical and human, like a steam whistle combined with a woman's scream. It went on for several seconds. There was a flash of light from beneath the candlestick, and then everything went quiet.

The first sound to return was the ringing in my ears. Slowly the sound of barking dogs—including Hamish, who leapt at the back door, trying to get out—returned, and I gasped with relief. For a moment I thought I'd gone deaf. Doors slammed inside the house.

Sarah whisked the container and candlestick behind her back before Ryan and Aunt Elizabeth appeared beside Hamish, sliding the door open.

"What the *hell* was that?" Ryan said.

I shrugged. Sarah tried to look innocent. "It came from over there," our grandmother said, pointing in the direction of the neighbour's barking dogs. "Perhaps a television?"

"It didn't sound like a TV," Aunt Elizabeth said, head turning as she took in every corner of the yard.

Hamish sniffed a path around us; Nana scooped him up and gave him a pat to calm him. He stiffened, surprised at the attention from an unexpected quarter, but her pats won him over. He was a whore for cuddles.

Ryan peered in the direction Nana had pointed, shivering. "You're all crazy, being out here without jumpers," he said. "I'm going back inside."

Aunt Elizabeth stayed outside a little longer, walking down to the fence line and poking around to see if she could identify the cause of the shriek. As soon as her back was turned, Sarah hid the container under the table, on the seat of one of the pushed-in chairs.

"Very strange," my aunt muttered, heading back inside. "Don't stay outside too long, girls."

After thirty seconds of silence from inside the house,

Sarah put the container on the table. The candlestick was wedged into the plastic sample holder. "Is it ... dead?" she asked. It was as good a word as any.

"I don't know," I said. "Turn it over so we can see underneath."

The bottom of the container was intact, but charred as though someone had held a lit match to the plastic, blackening it.

The elf shot appeared to be gone, but it was hard to tell.

"Should I take this out?" Sarah touched the candlestick with a tentative finger.

I nodded. "Just be ready to jam it back in if anything happens."

Sarah flinched as she pulled the candlestick out. When nothing happed, she peered into the container. "It's just some powder."

"Show me?"

She tipped the container so I could see the bottom. The arrowhead had been crushed into dust, although she hadn't hit it that hard. Not hard enough to destroy something made of metal.

Was that what a full-blooded *duinesidhe* would be reduced to if they came into contact with iron? Would the same thing happen to me if I held the candlestick for long enough? I shuddered. "Put the lid back on. I'll get Jack to look at it to confirm it's properly destroyed."

She obliged, ignoring Nana's frown at Jack's name, and slid the container across the glass tabletop to me. She picked up the candlestick and trotted down the stairs to the shed.

"So you mean to see the hob again?" Nana asked me.

"I don't see why not. He's been very helpful." *Unlike*

*some members of my family I could name.*

She frowned again. The expression came easily to her; was she always grim or was it a result of recent events? Having to travel halfway around the world because my son was in a coma would make me grumpy too, I supposed. "He will be sworn to an *aosidhe*, a high fae," she warned. "You don't know what his true motivations are, or those of his master."

"He's not, actually," I said. "He told me when we first met that he was unsworn." Not that I'd known what he meant at the time. And he'd since sworn a couple of oaths to me ... although neither of them were long-term service-type arrangements. Did that mean he was still unsworn?

There was still so much I didn't understand.

Again Nana looked surprised and opened her mouth to ask another, almost certainly awkward, question. But Sarah returned, saving me. "I think it's time for bed," she said, taking my arm. "Ryan's right. It's freezing out here."

"Good idea," I replied.

We brushed our teeth and slipped into pyjamas. Once we were in the privacy of Sarah's bedroom, I sat on the mattress on the floor and dragged a brush through my hair. After all my running around this evening, it was a snarled mess.

Sarah climbed under her blanket, lying on her side. Hamish jumped onto the end of her bed, snuggling down next to her feet. He heaved a huge sigh and fell asleep. Sarah propped her head up on her arm to look down at me. "You guys were talking about Jack?" she asked.

I nodded, still brushing.

"What's he like?"

I thought about that for a moment. "Odd," I murmured.

"He's polite, but I get the impression there's more going on beneath the surface."

"Do you think he's dangerous, like she said?" She gestured towards my bedroom with her free hand to indicate whom she was referring to.

"I don't know. I've never seen that side of him. But … I think he could be, if he was pushed."

"That statement could apply to anyone," Sarah pointed out.

"True." I put the hairbrush to one side and began braiding my hair.

"Is he cute?"

I raised my eyebrows at her. "Why? Are you looking for a date?"

"No," she laughed. "But you've spent a lot of time with him. And you did ditch a dinner with Dominic tonight to see him."

"I ditched dinner to help Dad." I threw the hairbrush at her. My hair unravelled.

She ducked, holding her hands up in surrender. "Kidding, kidding! But seriously, what does he look like?"

"He looks pretty much like any guy our age," I answered, starting over on my braid. "He's my height and has long ears and quite large eyes, but other than that..."

"I thought you said he was wrinkly?"

"I did." I hadn't told them Jack's revelations about my own powers. I shifted on the mattress, uncomfortable at the idea of discussing the part about me draining emotions. The thought of it made me feel dirty. "They've gone since I first met him. He said it was something about being around me. I didn't understand it, to be honest."

Sarah pursed her lips but didn't say anything more.

I twisted a hair elastic around the end of my braid and then took the hairbrush from the edge of Sarah's bed and put it on her desk.

Once I was curled under the blanket and reaching for the bedside lamp, she spoke again.

"Nana said Jack was a servant-type fae, right?"

"Yep."

"Maybe he got less wrinkly because he's doing servant-type things? For you? I know Nana was suspicious about his motivations, but if he draws strength from helping you, maybe that's his motivation? To serve?"

Her words made a great deal of sense, and matched up with some of what Jack said. He didn't like serving the full-blooded *aosidhe* because of their nature, but what if he needed to serve for his own sake, and I was the next-best thing?

I was impressed at my cousin's intuition. I should have made that leap myself, especially given I knew more, although not much more, than she did.

"You're taking all this very well," I said. "Magic and fairies and stuff."

She shrugged. "I always wanted to believe in magic. Maybe wanting to believe makes it easier to accept it when it turns out it's true." Her expression was wistful as she stared at the ceiling.

"Maybe."

"Can I meet him?" she said, startling me. From the beginning, I'd wanted to tell my cousin the truth about Jack and my heritage, but it hadn't occurred to me she might want to see more of it.

It should have.

"I don't know..."

"Why not? You said he looks more or less like a regular person. You could invite him to the party this weekend." Sarah, the massive extrovert and social butterfly, was having a big eighteenth birthday party. It was nominally a belated party for my birthday the month before as well, but most of the people going were more her friends than mine. I didn't mind, though; I'd been happy with our family dinner and a trip to the movies with my closest friends.

"I'm not sure he'd want to go," I said.

"Well, ask him. The worst he can do is say no," she pointed out.

"I guess." But the possibility of refusal wasn't the true source of my reluctance. I grimaced and explained. "I didn't tell him I was going to talk to you and Nana about the fae. What if he's angry at me?" The thought made anxiety flutter like moths in my belly.

"Tell him I promise not to tell anyone else. And it's not like you told Nana much of anything she didn't already know." Sarah sounded almost as annoyed about that as I was.

"I wonder what else she knows," I murmured, snuggling further under my blanket. My limbs were starting to defrost after the cold air outside. It was nice to lie in bed and talk with Sarah. I could almost imagine we were talking about boys and school gossip rather than family secrets and supernatural beings.

Sarah shrugged, looking up at the roof. "Dunno. But obviously her past with the fae didn't end well. She doesn't like them."

Okay, that made it a little harder to imagine this was a normal conversation.

"That may not be from her first experience with them, though," I said. "She also knew my mother. Maybe it was the fact she abandoned Dad and me that made Nana angry."

"So you think she's alive then? Your mum, I mean."

I nodded. "Jack says she is."

"Oh." She was silent for a long time. "I'm sorry," she said finally, compassion in her voice, her aura a soft pink. I knew what she meant: she wasn't sorry my mother was alive, but because the reality that my mother hadn't wanted me was in some ways much worse.

For me, at least. Presumably not for my mother.

Smiling grimly at that, I turned off the light.

# CHAPTER FIFTEEN

After speaking on the phone to Dad's neurologist the next morning, Aunt Elizabeth told me he was allowed to have visitors that afternoon. The doctor didn't want to overwhelm him with too many people at once, so he insisted only family visit for now.

By the time we were ready to leave for the hospital, I was a knot of anxiety, pacing the lounge with my hands balled into fists to stop them shaking. I wanted to talk to Dad in private, but the rest of my family were as keen to see him as I was. Worse, Sarah and especially Nana knew what I wanted to talk to Dad about, and were eager to hear his story as well.

At least, Sarah was eager. I found it hard to read Nana's emotions—they were a confusing swirl and not one I was able to interpret. But she was clearly intent on being in the room when I talked with Dad, which made my throat tighten with apprehension. Whatever he had to tell me about my mother was personal, and when I heard it for the first time I didn't want to feel like part of a drama production or a spectator sport. And I was sure Dad wouldn't talk about the *duinesidhe* if people who didn't know about them, such as my aunt, were there.

So as well as being anxious, I felt a little resentful—and ashamed of my selfishness—when Aunt Elizabeth, Nana, Sarah, Ryan and I filed into Dad's hospital room.

"Hey," he greeted us, smiling. The head of the hospital bed was raised so he lay on an angle. As we gathered around him, he turned off the portable stereo on the bedside table.

At the sight of him, my negative emotions blew away like morning fog. Forgetting my questions and the rest of my family, I ran across the room, throwing myself into his embrace. His warm arms wrapped around my shoulders as fiercely as mine did his. He didn't feel weak or tired at all.

Tears flowed from my eyes. I knuckled them away, suppressing a sob.

"It's good to see you too, pumpkin," he whispered in my ear. I looked up and saw wetness glittering in his eyes under the fluorescent lights.

They vanished, blinked away, when I scowled. "Don't ever do that again."

"I'll try not to," he said with a grin. "Although no one seems to be able to tell me what I did."

Sarah gave me a significant look. She was leaning against the windowsill, the same spot Jack had stood in the night before. I shook my head at her almost imperceptibly. Shoulders slumping, she turned to get me a tissue from the shelf beside the bed.

"Mum!" Dad exclaimed then, smiling at Nana. "Liz

told me you'd come across. I'm so glad to see you." But as he embraced her, I saw the deep pink of his aura flicker with amber for a moment. It reminded me of the orange lamp on a traffic light.

"How do you feel, David?" Aunt Elizabeth asked, leaning over the bed to give Dad a peck on his bristled cheek.

"Not too bad," Dad replied. "Tired; confused about how I got here. A bit like I reckon Sleeping Beauty felt after her curse was lifted."

I jumped at the word *curse*, covering my reaction by dabbing at my eyes with the tissue. Dad narrowed his gaze, but didn't say anything.

"Do you remember anything at all?" Ryan asked. "Did something hit you in the head?"

"Nothing I can remember. I was leaving the farm and got out of the ute to close the gate. I pulled a package from the mailbox. Then I woke up here."

"What was in the package?" This question was from Nana.

"I don't know. I never got a chance to open it."

"Mrs Wilson never mentioned finding a package," I murmured to my cousins.

"Maybe the old bat kept it," Ryan muttered back, earning himself a stern look from his mother. I agreed with her; Mrs Wilson was a busybody, not a thief.

"It might have fallen under the passenger seat in the ute or something," Sarah said, trying to keep the peace. "She could have missed it when she found the, ah…" She trailed off, blushing.

"The photos," I finished for her.

Dad gave me a long look. "You found them?"

"Mrs Wilson did. She gave them to me."

He opened his mouth and closed it without speaking. Suddenly he did look weary.

I tried to think of a way to change the subject, but Dad beat me to it. "So, what have I missed during my nap?"

I kept quiet, drinking in his animated expressions and his laughter as my grandmother, aunt and cousin— only one of them, because Ryan didn't talk much either— filled Dad in on the goings on of the past nine days. The truth was there wasn't a lot to tell; the biggest news was, of course, his illness ... and none of us wanted to burden him with the grief and worry we'd felt.

Although, Dad being Dad, he probably figured that out anyway.

Nana spent some time talking about her flight over and updating him on the status of the same relatives she'd told Aunt Elizabeth about in the car the day after she'd arrived. The most interesting bit of gossip was that two of Dad's cousins were grandparents already. Dad looked at me, seemingly horrified at the notion I might make him a grandfather sometime soon. I smiled back reassuringly. Life was complicated enough without little people running around.

When Nana was done, Sarah chattered on about our upcoming birthday party and how her friend's band was going to play—long past the point where I suspect Dad had lost interest.

Finally a nurse came in, a tall Scandinavian woman with sharp features and a prominent nose that reminded me of an eagle's beak. She took one look at Dad and ordered us to leave. Sarah looked crestfallen, cut off halfway through her description of the decorations.

"Come on, you lot." Aunt Elizabeth grimaced, mortified.

"We've overstayed our welcome." She stood to shoo us all from the room.

Dad caught my hand. "Stay a little?"

I hesitated, looking from the nurse to the rest of my family. The nurse scowled, about to say no, but Dad smiled at her and she softened. I saw the shift in her aura from harsh, bright colours to something mellower: pastel shades that moved more slowly. I rubbed my eyes. Colours whose names I knew swirled around everybody I saw, but their meaning was still a mystery. The distraction every time they shifted drew my attention from the conversation and made my temples ache. "Okay," the nurse nodded. Then she gave me a stern look. "But don't wear him out. I will be back soon to check on you."

"Here," Sarah said, handing me the keys to her car. I'd come to the hospital with Sarah and Ryan, while Aunt Elizabeth had brought her car with Nana. "We can catch a ride with Mum."

"Thank you." I gave her a hug. I knew she wanted to stay, not just out of curiosity but to provide moral support. Guilt sat like a stone in my stomach for ever wishing she hadn't come. "I'll talk to you later."

"You better," she replied, mock-fierce, and left Dad and me alone.

Nana looked unhappy as the door swung shut with her on the other side of it.

Silence fell, a merciful relief at first. I perched on the edge of Dad's bed, gazing at him, giddy with happiness that he was looking back at me.

Then the quiet began to feel a little uncomfortable.

"So," Dad said after a long moment. "I guess I owe you an explanation. About your mother." If he were standing, he would have shuffled his feet like a naughty child about to receive a scolding.

"Let me help you out a little," I said, twisting the edge of the blanket between my hands. "She was an *aosidhe* named Melpomene. She can manipulate emotions. And she's still alive."

He stared at me, mouth agape. His entire aura was suffused with electric purple, like the arcing plasma from a Tesla coil I'd seen at a science show: a more appropriate colour to depict shock I couldn't imagine. It was almost retina searing.

He closed his mouth with an audible click of his teeth. "You've been busy," he said, voice tight.

I nodded, reaching into my bag and bringing out the tattered envelope with the photos inside. "Here, these are yours."

He hesitated and then took the envelope, cradling it to his chest.

Despite everything, he still loved her.

"How did you meet?" I asked, my voice soft with sympathy.

"I'd just finished school. Some friends and I went on a backpacking holiday to Scotland." He cleared his throat, and his gaze drifted towards the window. "We were idiots. It was winter and cold. Really cold. We should have gone south, somewhere warmer. But we'd found cheap accommodation, a dingy hostel in Edinburgh. The others went to the pub. I was waiting for my socks to dry out a bit before I followed. I had them hung over this old bar heater and—"

He glanced at me, saw my nose was wrinkled up with disgust, and laughed a little. "Anyway, I followed them about half an hour later. It was after dark—in winter that far north the sun sets at four in the afternoon. I got a bit turned around. And then I found her.

"She was in an alleyway, and when I stepped closer her lower lip trembled. I asked her if she was okay, and she said someone was chasing her. She looked me in the eye and asked me to help her. And I loved her from that moment. I don't think I'd ever seen anyone as beautiful as her, and, when she needed my help—well, every young man wants to be a hero, don't they?" He laughed again, self-depreciatingly. "I didn't do a lot. I took her back to the hostel and we talked. She was pretty uncomfortable there, with the various steel fixtures and things, but it was safe for her. Her pursuer couldn't detect her through the steel."

I blinked, startled. "Wait a minute; you knew what she was?"

He nodded. "I was raised with tales of the fae. At that point she hadn't hidden the shape of her ears, and her sensitivity to the iron bed frame was another clue. Your nan knew a lot about them from when she was a girl. Liz was never that interested—she was always the sensible one. But I used to pester Mum for stories all the time."

"And you trusted her? Melpomene, I mean?" I couldn't bring myself to call her "mum".

"I shouldn't have," Dad said. "Not after everything your grandmother told us. But I made her promise not to hurt me, to swear. You understand about fae oaths?"

"A little."

"Well then. I knew I could trust her. She came back to London with me, and we got married and had you." He smiled, leaning forward to brush my hair away from my face.

I blinked at the story's abrupt ending. "I don't under-stand why she would do that," I said slowly. "From what Jack … that is, from what I was told, the *aosidhe* are pretty arrogant."

"Oh yes," he agreed. "And they can be cold. But she loved me too."

"Then why did she leave?" And there it was, the ques-tion that burned me the most. My throat tightened.

He sighed and looked out the window. "Because it was in her nature. Because, despite everything, she didn't belong in our world, and I didn't belong in hers. She gave me you, though."

We sat there in silence for a long while, Dad's gaze far away and wistful. He looked so happy, lost in his memo-ries. His hands ran over the faded ivory paper of the envelope containing the photos.

The photos and the wedding rings.

I remembered something then. One of the rings, the smaller one, had something engraved on the inside of it, and it had been scratched out. The thought nagged at me; I tried to dismiss it, but I couldn't.

My father had raised me to have an analytical mind.

"You're not telling me something."

A frown creased his forehead.

"It doesn't add up. Who defaced the engraving on her ring before she left? And why, if you both loved each other, did you flee to Australia and surround yourself with iron? Doing that pretty much guaranteed you'd never see her again."

He nodded, slowly. His expression was a curious mixture of consternation and pride.

"What was engraved on the ring, Dad?"

He spoke reluctantly. "It said 'true love.'"

"And who scratched it out?"

"She did."

"Why?"

"She was angry with me. Furious."

"Why?" I asked again. A suspicion was growing in my mind. When he didn't answer, I pressed him. "What did you *do*, Dad?"

"He made her swear an oath to love him," a voice said. We both jumped; we hadn't heard the door open. It was Nana.

"Mum!" Dad protested. My imagination flooded with images of my father using the same tone of voice with his mother when she'd embarrassed him as a teenager. But this was far more serious.

"It's true," she said, sweeping into the room past the other, empty bed. The door thudded closed behind her. "She needed your help to escape pursuit that day. In exchange for your help, you made her swear to love you and, because of the oath, she did. Because that's how *duinesidhe* oaths work. And you swore in turn to never let her be hurt."

I turned on Dad, a sick feeling in my gut. "Is it true?"

He nodded, miserable.

"You trapped her into loving you?"

"No, it wasn't like that." He sat upright in the bed, taking my hand. I pulled away, horrified.

"Then what was it like, Dad?"

"We really did love each other."

Nana spoke again then, standing at the foot of his bed with her hands on her hips. "Be truthful with the child, David," she scolded him. "She deserves to know what happened. Tell her about the day she was born."

"It…" He trailed off, took a breath, started again. "It broke the oath between us. That she would love me and I would protect her from hurt. Because, you see—"

"Childbirth hurts," I whispered. Dad nodded, miserable.

"That's why he came halfway around the world and took up ironwork," Nana said, relentless. "Because he knew she'd be angry. He knew she might seek revenge on both of you."

And there it was: the ugly truth. My mother hadn't loved me, hadn't wanted me. She'd gotten pregnant—the only *aosidhe* ever to become pregnant with a half-human—because she knew it would break their oath in a way that wouldn't cause her permanent harm. And that there was nothing Dad could do to prevent it.

I was a key. A tool. Nothing more.

I felt ill, as though I were in the presence of iron myself.

Nana opened her mouth to say something else, her expression reproachful. And in that moment I loathed her.

"Shut up!" I screamed at her. "Just shut up, you hateful old bat."

"Isla!" Dad protested from his bed.

Nana began to speak and I *pushed* her—not with my body but with my mind. All of the frustration, self-doubt and disgust I felt in that moment, I shoved into the mind of my elderly grandmother. If there was any thought at all in my head, it was to show her what she had done, to make her feel how I felt … but I acted more out of instinct and self-defence than anything else.

Her aura exploded with a confused riot of colour, a rainbow of static like the picture on an old analogue television when it lost the signal. She staggered back against the wall, hand to her chest, gasping for air like a landed fish.

"*Mum*? Are you alright?" Dad asked, swinging his legs around to climb out of the bed. "Isla, call a nurse. I think she's having a heart attack!"

I stepped back, staring at her in horror. What had I done?

I knew I had to undo it, but I wasn't sure how.

I tried to focus on the memory of draining the emotion from Jack and reached out, putting a hand on her shoulder, fingers resting on the base of her neck. Her skin felt hot; her pulse fluttered against my fingertips. I struggled to calm my thoughts, to visualise the violent burst of colour separating, draining, returning to a single dominant shade.

At first, nothing happened. I breathed deep.

I had done this. I *had* to fix it.

I recalled the touch of Jack's hand on mine when he helped me remove the elf shot. I used that memory as an anchor: the strong trunk of a tree that barely shifted, even as the branches were violently shaken, the leaves stripped bare.

It worked.

Slowly at first, and then in a rainbow flood, I drained the violent emotional assault from her into myself. The emotions returned to me in a skein, dulled after filtering through my grandmother's consciousness, diluted by a mix of her own feelings. Her lingering suspicions crawled along my skin. She believed my motives were impure, tainted by my half-fae blood. Her self-righteous anger at her older child for mixing with the fae after all her warnings warred with her deep concern that he'd made a devil's bargain, one that would cost him more dearly yet.

Underlying everything was her sadness that he'd pulled away from her and her disapproval, steadfast in his love for an *aosidhe*.

And, despite all this, the love for her son endured beneath the dull blue concern. A mother's love.

Or what a mother's love should be, if the mother weren't my own.

I picked that thread of love out of the tangle and fed it back to her, filling her aura with warmth for her son. The kernels of the other emotions were there—I was careful to strip nothing bare—but the brilliant rose of love washed over and overwhelmed them.

Behind me, the door to the room slammed open. I jumped back like a startled cat, wondering if I looked as guilty as I felt.

The stern Scandinavian nurse hurried into the room. Sarah slipped in behind her, biting her lip. "What is this racket? Why are you out of bed, Mr Blackman?" She saw my grandmother slumped against the wall and pushed me aside. "Are you okay, ma'am?"

"I'm quite fine, young lady," Nana said. "If you could…?" She held out her hand, allowing the nurse to pull her up. As soon as she was on her feet again, she turned and embraced my father.

Dad's eyes widened.

"I'm sorry, my boy," she said. Based on my few days with her, the loving tone was atypical. "I have been a—" she glanced at me and a little knot of suspicion flared slightly "—'hateful old bat', it's true."

"She's a sly old fox too," Sarah whispered beside me. "She said she needed to go to the bathroom and then slipped away. What happened?"

"I'll explain later," I whispered back.

Nana heard anyway. "No need to restrain yourself on my account. Why start now, after all?" she said. Her voice sounded strange—the words themselves were bitter but the tone was quite placid.

"Mum, please don't," Dad said, sounding resigned.

The nurse—her nametag said Helga—looked at all of us for a moment before shrugging. "Mr Blackman, I must insist you return to your bed at once. And your visitors must go. *All* of them." Her pointed look said she thought the fuss was my fault.

If only she knew.

Dad clambered back into the bed and Helga tucked him in firmly, as though by doing so she could stop him from escaping again. Nana stood beside the bed, running her fingers over Dad's arm in a familiar manner. He looked uncomfortable and alarmed by her sudden, affectionate behaviour.

Had I gone too far when I amplified her love for him? Made it too strong?

Only one way to find out.

"Come on, Nana," I said, reaching for her arm. She pulled away but, with the touch, I drained a little of the rose from her aura. The tiny kernels of her other emotions, less smothered, flickered brighter.

She relented and stepped away from the bed.

It was getting easier to manipulate emotions; I hadn't concentrated as hard, and it felt more natural. Energy fizzed through my veins, as though I could run a marathon or dance for hours. A healthy diet of others' emotions seemed to be all the food I needed.

The thought made me shiver.

Dad was looking between Nana and me, concerned there might be more yelling. "We're fine," I assured him, not sure it was true.

"Come back and visit me tomorrow?" he begged.

All three of us nodded.

"Out." Helga pointed at the door.

I grabbed my bag, leaving Dad with the envelope of photos.

Something about the whole incident made me uneasy, something beyond the increasing ease with which I'd changed my grandmother's demeanour. We were walking into the foyer, where my aunt and Ryan waited by a vending machine, when I figured out what it was.

The possessive, adoring way Nana had touched Dad's arm in the hospital room was the same way he'd run his fingers over the envelope full of photos of my mother.

I stopped in my tracks, startled into immobility.

Was it possible the reason Dad fell so desperately in love with my mother that day long ago was that she'd bewitched him with *duinesidhe* magic? What was it he'd said? That she'd looked him in the eye and he'd fallen instantly in love with her.

Of course it was possible.

In fact, the more I thought about it, it seemed not just possible but likely. Dad should have been wary of her. Nana had raised him to believe the worst of the *duinesidhe*, but he hadn't. He'd fallen in love.

The thought tempered my horror at what he'd done to her in return. He hadn't been himself.

Sarah tugged my hand, dragging me over to the rest of our family.

"You decided to come home after all, Isla?" Aunt Elizabeth

smiled, oblivious to the tension between us.

"The nurse chased us out," I said.

My aunt flicked a look at Nana, but relaxed when she saw the older woman's happy little smile. My grandmother didn't have that fixated, possessive look on her face anymore, but she still seemed a lot more relaxed than she had. Maybe I had found the correct balance this time. "Right, then," Aunt Elizabeth said. "Let's go home."

Sarah and I gave Ryan a lift to a friend's place and then the two of us drove back to our house. On the drive I recounted Dad's story and my theory that he'd been manipulated into an artificial love at first sight.

"They can do that?" Sarah asked, sounding awed.

"Um. Yes. But not all of them." I'd forgotten I hadn't explained that part of Jack's tale to her. "Apparently that's my mother's thing. Manipulating other people's emotions."

"Oh." She fell quiet for a moment, changing lanes to overtake a car towing a trailer.

"I should tell you," I added reluctantly, fidgeting with the strap on my bag. "It seems to be my thing too. Sort of."

"What do you mean?"

Shamefaced, I told her about the incident with Nana.

She stared at me, shocked, until I indicated the traffic in front of us with a jerk of my head. "Still driving!"

"Sorry," she muttered, swinging her head back to look at the road. "So you can change the way people feel about something?"

"Not very well, but yes. It seems so."

"And you can see how they are feeling?"

"I don't understand most of what I'm seeing. But yes." I grimaced. "I wish I couldn't."

"You're crazy," she said. "That would be so handy. Think of the possibilities."

"I am." My tone was sharp. "Like making someone fall so crazily in love with you that they go to the extreme of binding you with a magical oath so you have to stay with them until you can have a baby to escape."

She was quiet until we pulled up at a set of traffic lights; then she looked across the centre console at me, blue eyes brimming with sympathy. "I'm sorry."

"Me too," I apologised. "I shouldn't snap at you. It's not like this is your fault."

"Do you think you could do anything to remove the … spell she put on your Dad?"

I shrugged. "I don't know. I botched the thing with Nana. And my mother did what she did to Dad almost nineteen years ago. It's got to be pretty ingrained by now for him to still feel that way. Right?"

"Maybe Jack will know. You should ask him." She grinned. "And when you do, invite him to our party."

# CHAPTER SIXTEEN

*L*ater that afternoon, I was lying on my bed, brooding, when I got a text from Dominic.

*First Friday in December. Christmas tree lighting is tonight. Want to go?*

We'd been so preoccupied with Dad's illness that Christmas had crept up on us. Usually we put the tree up on the first day of December—as soon as Aunt Elizabeth would let us—but that had passed yesterday without comment.

The idea of throwing myself into the festivities lifted my heart. What else was I going to do? Lie here all night, thinking about how my mother never wanted me?

*Yes!* I replied, fingers flying over the phone's tiny keyboard. *Dad woke up last night and I want to celebrate.*

Dominic arrived twenty minutes later, a huge smile on his face and his aura a swirl of pink he'd never wear on a T-shirt. "I'm so glad about your dad," he said, kissing me hello.

"Me too!" I grinned, looping my arm through his as we walked to the car.

"Have they figured out what caused it?"

I hesitated. "No."

He rolled his eyes. "That's useful."

I grimaced but didn't say anything as we slid into the car. The hospital staff had given Dad the best care they could. There was no way they could've identified the cause of his illness, but how could I explain that without sounding like a crazy person?

Fortunately Dominic changed the subject once we hit the road, turning talk to the festivities. The Christmas tree was between the fountains on Civic Square, in front of the theatre and library. Tonight there would be kids' entertainment, carols and even a Santa, before the sun set at eight and the tree was lit. We didn't mind missing the preliminaries, so we ate at *Paddy's*, the pub that had offered Dominic a job—although he hadn't had his first shift yet.

The pub crowd disoriented my newly awakened ability; an overwhelming rainbow of emotions surrounded the other patrons. Some of the colours were blurry, as though I was looking through an unfocused pair of binoculars. Was that what drunk looked like? I kept my eyes fixed on either my food or Dominic.

But when we approached the square, my stomach swooped. I wasn't going to be able to join the crush immediately surrounding the tree. It rose twenty metres above them; unlit, the decorations blended into its green limbs. The people underneath, however, were a riot of colours. Children were predominantly violet, while the adults were every colour of the rainbow. Looking at them made my head spin, even from across the road. Gasping, I leaned into Dominic's chest, eyes squeezed shut. He put one arm around me, switching the picnic blanket to the other.

"What's the matter?"

"It's really crowded over there," I mumbled into his shirt. "Can we set up on this side?"

"Uh, sure." A few other couples had done the same, but there was still space for us on the grass under the leafy trees lining the pedestrian heart of the city. Even the trees were strung with pale blue fairy lights, giving them a magical glow, and the sound of carols carried over the intervening racket of cars and people.

"This is nice," I said, sighing and leaning against the trunk of the tree. Dominic sat beside me, long legs resting against my own. As long as I kept my eyes down, I could almost forget my new ability.

"It is," he murmured, wrapping one arm around my waist. His warm fingers curled against my hip. A moment later, his other hand brushed my cheek. "You look beautiful."

"Thanks," I said, feeling the heat of a blush burn the back of my neck. I forced my way past embarrassment and looked up, meeting his warm brown gaze. This close, his aura—which was shifting from pink to scarlet—was background noise. Ignorable. "You're not too bad yourself."

We leaned into each other as though acting on a single thought, our lips meeting in a gentle kiss. Dominic's hand stayed on my cheek, thumb stroking it even as his tongue flickered into my mouth. I forgot the hard trunk behind me, the cool grass beneath me, and lost myself in the moment—in him.

"Can I have a turn?"

A man loomed over us. Lime green and red blurred together in his aura, clashing in a way that hurt my eyes. Beneath his aura, his hands were on his hips. His eyes were bleary and his breath when he leaned over us reeked of beer.

"Go away, mate," Dominic said, pulling me closer.

"Make me," the drunk said.

Dominic's eyes narrowed. "You don't want that."

"Why? Are you a fag? You won't mind if I spend some time with your girl then." He grabbed for my arm, but missed.

Dominic's aura shifted even as he leapt to his feet, to the same red and black I'd seen in Nana's aura the night before. I gasped, scrambling to the side across crushed grass, as the drunk shoved him.

"Last warning," Dominic growled. The black grew in his aura as his eyes narrowed.

The drunk's aura shifted to a blurry copy of Dominic's. Neither of them was going to back down. Fingers shaking, I grabbed the drunk's hand and yanked out the red and black, spinning it into the sickly yellow of fear that Jack had shared with me the night before.

"Forget it," the drunk gasped, stumbling over his feet in his haste to disappear into the throng.

Dominic glared after him, swearing under his breath.

"Don't worry about it," I said, wriggling under his arm. "They're about to light the tree."

He hugged me back as the tree flared to festive life across the road. The crowd cheered.

Sarah and I returned to the hospital on our own the next morning. I was exhausted, so Sarah drove—and thankfully we didn't have the rest of the family for an entourage. Nana wanted to fetch a few things from the farm for Dad and, not willing to contend with Australian road rules, had asked Aunt Elizabeth to drive. Ryan begged off, sending his love. He had less than two days to finish his painting for Sarah—less again when you factored in the drying time—and wanted to take advantage of the quiet house to concentrate on the finishing touches.

The irate nurse from the day before was off shift, so we were able to walk into Dad's room without being intercepted.

"My favourite daughter! My favourite niece!" He beamed at us from his bed. We smiled at the old joke; we were his only daughter and niece. He was sitting upright, trying to read the local broadsheet. Pages were spread open on his little meal table and across his legs: organised chaos. "I'm trying to catch up on what I've missed," he explained.

"Not much," I said. "Politics, mostly. Boring."

"So it seems," he agreed. Then he looked at the door. "It's just you two this morning?"

"I expect Nana will be in later with some of your iron sculptures." I set my bag down on the other bed and slid into one of the chairs. Sarah leaned against the windowsill again.

"Oh." He hesitated, glancing at Sarah.

"It's okay, Dad. She knows."

"Right." He grinned, relieved. "I'm glad. It's nice to be

able to talk to people who know."

"You could have done that sooner if you'd fessed up," Sarah said. "And saved Isla a lot of stress."

"I realise that now." He reached out and took my hand. "I'm sorry, truly. I was trying to protect you."

"It's not like you knew all hell was going to break loose when I turned eighteen," I said. There was a tightening around his eyes, a flickering change in his aura. "*Did* you?"

"Not ... exactly."

"Dad!"

He folded up the newspaper pages and put them onto the meal table, taking the time to think about his answer. I tapped my foot, arms folded.

"When you were a baby," he began, "I was worried you might have inherited your mother's ... talents. And, more importantly, her vulnerabilities. I didn't have any iron around the house, for obvious reasons, but I noticed when I was out walking with you in the pram that you cried whenever we passed this house with a wrought iron fence." He met my gaze, looking solemn. "I wanted to protect you. So I found someone who could. It's hard to explain, but the way she told it to me, she bound the *duinesidhe* side of you."

"How?"

He shrugged. "I don't know."

"Was she *duinesidhe* too?" Sarah asked, stumbling a little over the pronunciation of the unfamiliar word.

"No. She was human. A witch."

We both stared at him for several heartbeats.

"Seriously?" Sarah said. Exactly what I was thinking.

He nodded. "The *duinesidhe* aren't the only beings out there with power. That's part of what I wanted to protect you from. But she told me I was only able to speak for you, to enter you into a contract with her, while I was your guardian. Once you became an adult in your own right, the spell would fail."

"So you knew it would happen when I turned eighteen?"

"I thought it would be when you turned twenty-one," he admitted, abashed. "At the time, that age was much more important as a rite of passage. It never occurred to me that as the 'coming of age' age—" he used air quotes, reminding me of Jack "—moved forward, that would change the end date of the spell."

"So you didn't give Isla the iron birthday present as a test?" Sarah asked, her eyes narrowed with suspicion. I gave her an admiring look; that hadn't even occurred to me.

"I always gave her an iron present." He laughed sheepishly.

"That's true, but you did bring it back to me later, after I forgot it at the restaurant," I pointed out.

"After your aunt told me Ryan had painted a picture of Melpomene... Well, I grew suspicious. And I was afraid for you. I would have wrapped you up in iron if I could, to protect you. Head to toe."

"Given what one little touch did, I'm sort of glad you didn't."

Silence fell. I nibbled my lip, turning what he'd said over in my mind. Dad had used magic to protect me until I was an adult. Had the ritual of the family dinner been some sort of trigger for the spell failing? Jack's theory that I'd been leaking energy like a sieve that night, accidentally turning Ryan into my *aislinge*, seemed to be true.

Although ... was the spell crumbling before that, given

the séance at Halloween attracted Jack's attention? That was also the same night I'd dreamt of my mother. Had she dreamed of me as well? Were my birthday and the events surrounding it what triggered Dad being attacked?

I wondered if the dominant colour in both Dad's and Sarah's auras—an unpleasant greenish yellow—was the colour of apprehension, because that was how I felt.

"I'm not protected anymore," I said slowly. "But neither are you, Dad."

"I never was, except by the iron. I'll be right."

"Dad, you got sick because you were elf shot. That's what caused the coma."

He paled, his tanned skin turning sickly. "I was?"

"I destroyed it," Sarah said, and then gave me a cheeky grin. "Isla helped."

"Do you know who sent it?" Dad's voice was casual but his aura was amber with warning.

"I was hoping you'd have a theory. Did you annoy any other *duinesidhe*? Besides my mother, I mean?"

"Not that I know of, but *duinesidhe* politics makes the stuff our political parties get into look tame." He rapped the newspaper with his knuckles. "And the *aosidhe* are worse. They can be vicious. It's possible the elf shot was sent by someone looking to gain an advantage over Melpomene."

I thought that was unlikely—although, given my father's steadfast love for my mother, I understood why he might like to believe it. But that sort of delusion could get him elf shot again. Or just plain killed.

"Melpomene. Not Melanie?" Sarah asked.

"No. She went with a more usual name with anyone who didn't know who and what she was," Dad said.

"Melpomene isn't Scottish."

"It's not. It's the name of one of the ancient Greek muses. She would have liked me to believe she was that old, but I think it was an affectation." He smiled fondly.

I made a mental note to ask Jack whether there was something I could do to reduce the adoring—artificial—love my father felt for my mother. It wasn't just out of concern for his safety, although that was part of it. Blind devotion was called "blind" for a reason. But my dad would never have a happily ever after with Melpomene, and the idea he would never have a normal relationship with someone saddened me.

"Melpomene was the muse of tragedy," Sarah said darkly, bringing my attention back to the conversation.

"That's a cheerful thought," I muttered. Then I took a breath. "Seriously, Dad. Whoever elf shot you, whether it was her or someone else, might try it again. You need to start protecting yourself. Carry a few lumps of iron in your pockets when you leave the farm or something."

He frowned. "But then you won't be able to come near me."

"Sure I can. It just means a bit of discomfort."

"And no hugging," Sarah put in.

"I'd prefer that to seeing you in another coma. Or worse. Promise me you will." He hesitated and I glared at him. "Promise."

"Okay, okay, you win," he agreed, throwing his hands in the air in surrender.

We stayed with Dad for the rest of the morning; when the nurse frowned and asked if he needed some rest, he charmed her with a smile and a joke about how he'd been asleep for days. After lunch, he managed to persuade her to let us take him for a walk around the hospital, him wearing long cotton pyjama pants, a T-shirt and a pair of ratty slippers Ryan had put into his overnight bag back when he was in the ICU. Sarah rolled her eyes at his outfit, but I couldn't stop grinning, almost giddy with relief. His reassuring company and—finally—honest answers to my questions were cold water on a scald: they took the heat from my wound, leaving it free to heal.

I even laughed at his terrible coma-patient jokes. If anyone had the right to, it was him. I did, however, wonder where he'd gotten them all from; was he surfing the net for material? And if so, how? He didn't have a smart phone.

The nurse insisted Dad have a nap after lunch, despite his protests that he felt fine. He tried to enlist our support but, unable to point out he was fine now the elf shot was gone, we weren't particularly persuasive.

I promised him I'd bring in a few books to help him pass the time.

"You'd better," he muttered as we picked up our bags to head for the door, where the nurse stood, supervising our departure with a gentle smile that belied her unyielding demeanour. "Either that or a jailbreak kit."

We headed home, grabbing kebabs and coffees from a Turkish restaurant on the way.

Nana and Aunt Elizabeth arrived home twenty minutes after we did, as we were finishing our lunch. My aunt bustled around in the kitchen, fixing a pot of tea and some sandwiches for herself and her mother.

Nana corralled Sarah and me in Sarah's bedroom.

She handed me a canvas shopping bag. I took it warily, even though I didn't sense the nauseating tang of iron. "I found that on the kitchen bench at your father's place," she whispered in a conspiratorial fashion.

Curious, but also cautious, I opened the bag and peeked inside. It was a mass of brown paper, stuck over with tape and wound around with string.

"What is it?" Sarah asked.

"Packing material," Nana said. "We had a coffee with that busybody neighbour of David's, Lily something, and she said she found it next to him when she discovered him unconscious. She was the one who left it on the bench."

The irony of my grandmother describing Mrs Wilson as a busybody wasn't lost on me, but I put it to one side. Why did Nana think the discarded wrapping from a parcel was significant? I picked it up by one corner, and lifted it out of the bag so Sarah and I could examine it.

The paper was only about the size of a letter, as though cut to wrap something small: about the size of the box my charm bracelet had come in.

Something small, like an arrowhead.

*Oh.*

I turned the paper around so I could read the address label. Written on a white sticker, partially obscured by a small tear, was Dad's address.

There was no return address. However, the postmark was from Edinburgh.

"I think this is the parcel the elf shot was mailed in," Nana whispered, stating aloud the conclusion I'd drawn.

"I thought it could fly," Sarah said.

"They do self-animate," Nana said. I stared at her, startled that she knew that much. Just how deeply had she been involved with the *duinesidhe*? "But they don't have enough energy to fly halfway around the world. Someone mailed the elf shot to him, and then when he took the parcel out of the mailbox…" She made a flying gesture with her hand for a moment before tapping Sarah in the chest with her fingers.

"Ow."

"That makes sense. The mailbox is at the gate, where he was found," I said.

"Precisely," she agreed.

"Mum," my aunt called from up the corridor. "Lunch is ready."

"Coming, dear," Nana called back. She turned to me again, blue eyes hard as ice. "Find out who sent that parcel. For your father's sake."

"How is she meant to do that?" Sarah protested.

"Ask Jack," I said.

Nana nodded sharply and left the room; we heard her talking to Aunt Elizabeth and the scrape of the dining chairs as they pulled them out to sit down.

"I thought she said Jack was dangerous," Sarah observed, closing her bedroom door.

"She did. But I guess she doesn't care if it means finding out who's after Dad." I thought about that for a moment. "I sort of agree with her."

"I never thought I'd see the day."

"It's shocking, but try to contain yourself."

"So when are you going to do it? Talk to Jack?"

"This afternoon, I guess, after they leave to go visit Dad."

"Don't forget to invite him to the party."

I rolled my eyes at her. "Nag."

I put the packing paper into a plastic sandwich bag, unsure what, if any, evidence Jack might be able to retrieve from it. Fingerprints, maybe? The thought of

Jack using modern policing techniques made me smile.

Although, given Nana, Dad, Mrs Wilson and I, and possibly Aunt Elizabeth, had handled the paper, it seemed like a long shot in any case.

Sarah didn't ask to come with me when I set out across the front lawn to the park. But, judging from the twitching curtains, I was pretty sure she was watching from the lounge room window.

The cooler weather lingered; usually mid-afternoons in early summer were scorching hot. But it was still pleasant. The sun beamed warmly down from a sky clear except for a couple of puffs of clouds drifting east. A faint breeze rustled the tops of the trees and stirred the long grass that fringed the edge of the park. The grass whisked against my calves as I strode over to the swing and sat, placing my bag between my feet.

I wondered with a half smile what Sarah was thinking, seeing me hang out in the park.

Jack took about ten minutes to arrive. He strode along the path that came from the shops, hands in his pockets. He was still wearing the red Canteen bandana, but this time he wore a navy blue tank top and black shorts. His sneakers looked brand new, gleaming white against the pavement. I stood to greet him.

"Another new outfit?" I raised an eyebrow. "Luxury."

He nodded. "I am glad to see you, Isla. How is your father?"

"Conscious," I grinned at him. "Talking, walking around and itching to get out of hospital as soon as he can."

He smiled back. "That is great news."

I couldn't remember whether I had expressed my gratitude, that day at the hospital. I'd been too distracted.

Dad would be ashamed. "Thank you, Jack. For every-thing. He wouldn't be awake now if it weren't for you."

To my surprise, he blushed, staring down at his feet. "My pleasure," he said after a long moment, peering at me through his eyelashes. "I like to help."

I remembered what Nana had said. "Is it because you're a hob?"

He frowned. "Where did you hear about that?"

"My grandmother flew in from England. She knows a bit about the *duinesidhe*, and she said there's a species that serves the *aosidhe*."

His jaw clenched. Had I offended him? "It is true that I am a hob," he admitted. "And it is true that the *aosidhe* have bound our race so we only truly thrive when we are serving one of them. They enslaved us." He spat out the words. "That is why I left the Old World and came here, why so many of us did. But Isla, I do not assist you because I have to. I do it because I want to."

He looked away, across the park to where a cat prowled through the grass, stalking a fluttering white cabbage moth. The cat's tail was a tortoiseshell mast on a grassy sea.

"Well, I'm grateful," I murmured. "Truly. And if you do get any personal benefit from helping me, that's the least I can do to repay you."

He took a deep breath, swallowing his anger, and nodded. I nodded back.

After a long moment, he changed the subject. "The elf shot is destroyed?"

"Yes. How did you know?"

"It created a bit of a fuss." He leaned against the ride-on frog, which rocked gently. Somehow he made it seem like the most comfortable pose in the world.

"Something I should be worried about?"

He shook his head. "I only heard it because I was close and listening for it—although its maker may know it was destroyed. I am uncertain. I was a little surprised you went ahead with destroying it without me."

I examined his expression and aura. Had I hurt his feelings again? Seriously, some days I shouldn't be allowed to leave the house. "I'm sorry. It seemed like a good idea to get rid of it straight away."

His mouth curved into a lopsided smile. "I am not offended. Being in the presence of iron is always uncomfortable, no matter the reason, so I am glad I did not need to attend." His gaze was untroubled, and there was no hint of distress in his aura. The brief moment of frustration was gone like it never happened.

I wished I could control my emotions as easily as Jack.

Getting off the swing, I reached into my bag and took out the plastic container with the elf shot in it. "Here it is."

He took it from me, turning the container over in his hands and looking at the fine powder from all sides. "It is dead. Safe. You can dispose of it as you wish."

"That's good to know."

He handed it back to me and I frowned. Should I throw it in the bin? Maybe Dad would want it as a keepsake from his hospital visit. Or was that a tad creepy, like keeping your appendix after it's removed?

I slipped it back into my bag, and my fingers brushed against the packaging Nana had found. I handed it to Jack, explaining my grandmother's theory about how the elf shot was delivered to my father. He listened, nodding, and examined the packaging without taking it out of the sandwich bag.

"I know I've asked a lot of you already, but is there anything you could do to find out who posted it?" I asked him, feeling sheepish.

Jack looked at me and shrugged. "I do not have a gift for that sort of thing, but I know others that do. I can ask them on your behalf." He hesitated and then added, "They may require payment for any information they can glean."

"If we can find out for sure who sent the elf shot, it'd be worth it."

"That would depend on what they ask in return, I would think," Jack said, a note of caution in his voice. He put the packaging into his pocket. "But I will see if there is anyone willing to help."

"It probably came from my mother," I told him. "You were right when you told me before that her motivations for seeking me might not be good."

"Oh?" He raised his eyebrows.

"Dad told me that, before I was born, he bound her with an oath." I didn't explain the details, still uncomfortable with the story. "She was apparently quite angry about it."

"An *aosidhe* bound by a human?" His sapphire eyes sparkled. "Oh yes, I can imagine she was."

"He still loves her, though," I sighed. "I think she manipulated his emotions the day they met, made him fall in love with her."

"And that is why he bound her? So she could not leave?" I nodded, and a wicked grin spread across his face. "It serves her right then, do you not think?"

Him binding her did have a certain amount of poetic

justice to it. Talk about being caught in your own trap. And it was a pointed example of why I needed to be careful myself. "Do you think there's a way to undo what she did to him? If she turned up intending to harm him, he'd walk straight into her arms. He's got no sense of caution when it comes to her."

"There might be." He shrugged. "Again, this is not something I can help you with myself."

"But you know others that can?" I asked wryly.

He smiled and nodded. "I told you that day at the hospital that I would speak to an acquaintance about your gift."

I remembered what he'd said and grinned. "My superpower, you mean."

He laughed. "Yes. Well, I have found a potential teacher for you—"

"That's great news."

"—but he is wary. He requires some persuading before he will consent to meet you."

"Payment, you mean?"

"We are not yet at the point of discussing payment, but still of convincing him to agree at all."

"Is it the fact that I'm a ... half-breed?" Was there was a social stigma attached to being only half *duinesidhe*?

His expression was solemn. "No, it is your *aosidhe* blood. Like I told you, there are many *duinesidhe* here that have fled *aosidhe* enslavement and mistreatment."

I was descended from a race of evil overlords. Great. "Well, I am happy to swear not to hurt him if that helps," I said. "At least, as long as he doesn't try and hurt me first."

"I will let him know. It may help." He looked over my shoulder and stiffened, standing up. A harried-looking woman headed towards the park from the street, two young children in tow. "I should probably go," he said as the older girl ran for the swings. I moved to the edge of the tanbarked area, out of the kids' way.

"Okay," I agreed. As he turned to go, I glanced back towards the house and saw Sarah's face peeking through the lounge room window. I'd almost forgotten—she would kill me! "Oh. Um, Jack?"

He turned back, a questioning expression on his face.

I spoke softly so the newcomers wouldn't overhear. "What with everything that's happened with Dad, I told my cousin Sarah about you. I hope that's all right?"

He hesitated. "Do you trust her discretion?"

"I do." Sarah could be a terrible gossip, but never when she'd promised to keep a secret—which was more than could be said for some of the other students at school.

"Then I shall do so as well."

"Thank you. The thing is, she is having a birthday party this weekend, and she, um, wanted me to invite you along."

Jack's blue eyes widened. "Why?"

"Curiosity, mostly," I admitted. "But she knows what you did for Dad as well, and that we're friends. So she said to ask you. She was quite insistent. I'm not sure she'll take no for an answer." I smiled ruefully.

His expression turned strange, and he blinked. "Friends?"

"Of course we are." I gulped. "Aren't we?" Did he think of me as an employer rather than a friend? Or as an annoying student ... or, worse, a charity case?

Awkward.

But a slow smile spread across his face, making his luminous eyes twinkle and his teeth flash white in the

bright sunlight. "I have never had a friend among the—"
He hesitated, glancing at the mother and her children.
The woman seemed preoccupied with her phone and the
older girl was trying to touch the sky with the heels of
her sandals, judging by the arc of her swing. But the
younger girl, a child of about four, watched us. "Among
your folk. Either of them," he finished instead. "Of course
I will come to your party."

"Great." I gave him a brief, tentative hug.

"Are you going to kiss?" the little girl asked loudly.

"Uh..." My cheeks flamed. Jack seemed unruffled.

"Isabelle," the mother protested, giving us an apologetic
look. "You wanted to go to the park, and now we're here.
Why don't you go play?"

The girl sighed and stomped over to the seesaw, walking along its length. When she reached the centre point
it tipped, the far side thudding to the tanbark; she walked
down the other side to the ground. Then she turned
around and headed back along it the other way ... but
she watched us from the corner of her eye as she did so.

"So. Um," I said to Jack, rendered awkward by the
child's gaze. "I'll see you on the weekend?"

"You will." He gave me a slight bow and then headed
back the way he came.

I gave a farewell wave to the woman before walking
back to our house and the third degree I knew I was
going to get from Sarah.

# CHAPTER SEVENTEEN

Sarah's birthday, which was also the day of the party, dawned bright and sunny. I went in to visit Dad at the hospital early, and on my own. Sarah was busy finishing off the decorations, and Ryan was doing something secret—and probably painting-related—in his room.

Dad was staging a breakout that day. The doctors were able to give no compelling reason why he needed to stay in hospital any longer, and he claimed his own home and bed would be far more restful than current arrangements.

In the face of Dad's rebellion, the only request his doctor made was that he not stay at the farm alone, in case he had another "episode". Dad had intended to ignore the doctor's advice, secure in the knowledge he was unlikely to get elf shot again any time soon. But the doctor was canny, repeating the request in front of Aunt Elizabeth and Nana the previous evening.

"Nana's going to *stay* with you?" I asked incredulously

when he told me.

Dad nodded so woefully I suppressed a grin. "She'll rearrange the kitchen. And mother me constantly. I know it."

"Well, she *is* your mother..."

He gave me a mock-sad look. "You're just glad because you'll get your room back."

"I hadn't even thought of that. No more sleeping on Sarah's floor!"

Dad looked thoughtful. "Maybe it won't be so bad. Mum staying with me for a bit, I mean. We had a serious falling out before you and I came to Australia, but she seems to have mellowed. It'll give us time to do some catching up."

I bit my tongue. It looked like I'd gotten Nana's emotional balance right the second time, which was great—especially for Dad, if he could use it to repair his relationship with her. But guilt was an ugly weight in my stomach. I'd manipulated her emotions. Sure, the outcome was favourable, but what was the cost? Wasn't changing the way she felt about something not far from taking away her free will altogether? How did my actions differ from what my mother had done to Dad all those years ago?

Because I'd emphasised an existing emotion, I told myself, whereas my mother had fabricated a new one.

I wasn't convinced by my own argument, though.

Dad was watching my face with a frown. "You look like you're pondering the fate of the world, kiddo."

"I am," I said quickly, forcing a smile. "But remember your promise to carry some iron with you whenever you leave the farm. Nana's pretty scary, but she can't protect you from everything."

He laughed.

I left shortly afterwards, taking with me his birthday wishes for Sarah, and a promise to buy her a present next week some time. "I know it will be late, but she'll have to forgive me. I overslept."

When I passed on the message to Sarah at home, she laughed. "At least if he buys me something I know it won't be some new iron sculpture."

"I expect his days of giving iron to the people who live in this house are over," I pointed out, glancing over my shoulder to make sure Aunt Elizabeth wasn't within hearing distance.

Her eyes widened in realisation and she nodded. "Even better."

We ate lunch as a family a couple of hours later; the only one missing was Dad, who hadn't managed to be discharged from hospital in time. Aunt Elizabeth made one of Sarah's favourite meals: a BLT chicken salad, with still-warm roasted chicken, dressed with mayonnaise and garnished with sliced avocado. For dessert, she served a rich chocolate mud cake served with double cream. And a candle.

After the cake, and a brief interlude for coffee while we recovered from death by chocolate, we gave Sarah our presents. She opened mine first, and, to my relief, was delighted with the wristwatch. It had a black leather wristband and a white analogue dial with gold hands. The dial was offset to the right of the watch's face. On the left was a miniature acoustic guitar charm, also painted gold. A couple of little gold notes were set either side of the guitar.

"Oh, look, the charm even looks like Amy," she enthused,

referring to her acoustic guitar. She held her arm out to admire the way the watch sat: it was chunky around her slender wrist, suiting her perfectly. "Thank you, Isla. It's brilliant."

Aunt Elizabeth handed her gift to Sarah with the glint of tears in her eyes. "This is for you," she said, a catch in her voice.

The small package contained a gift box covered in faded red velvet. Sarah's eyes widened with recognition. Inside was a yellow-gold ring with an understated cluster setting: a single ruby in the centre and six smaller diamonds around the outside, arranged like flower petals. "Mum, isn't this...?"

"My engagement ring from your father? Yes." Aunt Elizabeth reached across the table and brushed a strand of hair out of Sarah's eyes. "He would have wanted to give you something special the day you grew up, and this is the most special thing I have from him."

The expression on Sarah's face was torn; her aura spun. She loved the ring but felt guilty for accepting it. "I'm not sure I can take this."

"Of course you can," Aunt Elizabeth scolded with a gentle smile that gave lie to her tone. "I want you to have it as much as your father would have wanted to give it to you. I've been saving it for this day."

"Oh, Mum." Sarah gulped down her own tears and gave her mother a fierce hug. "Then thank you."

The ring fit her perfectly.

Not long ago I might have felt a moment of self-pity, witnessing such a beautiful mother-daughter moment, but the familiar twinge of jealousy didn't stir in my chest. I realised it was because I knew more about my mother, even though what I knew I didn't particularly like. The knowing meant I no longer imagined her to be the perfect mother figure no woman could be. And I'd come to appreciate how much I loved my father during his illness.

Also, it wasn't like I didn't have anything to remember her by: she'd given me an intolerance to iron and a superpower of dubious merit. The thought made me laugh behind my hand, earning me a raised eyebrow from Ryan and a suspicious look from Nana.

Nana's present was a designer handbag. Ryan looked across the table at me and mimed wiping sweat from his brow. I was glad I decided on the wristwatch after all.

Finally, he brought his present for Sarah out of his room, unveiling the canvas with a dramatic flourish.

"Oh!" Sarah exclaimed.

The painting he'd done of my mother was good, but this was his best painting yet. I'd seen the sketch, but that in no way prepared me for the completed artwork. He'd changed a few things, and added extra details; the electric guitar, for example, had *Amy II* stencilled in cursive writing along one edge. Sarah's hair still flared around her head, but he'd added a blond streak in the fringe. The leather bracelet around her wrist was now a watch.

The watch bore a startling resemblance to the one I'd given Sarah: black wristband, white-and-gold face. The angle prevented the viewer from seeing the details on the face, though, so I didn't know how far the similarity went.

Ryan knew I was getting Sarah a watch, but I'd never discussed the details with him. Did that mean this painting was an *aislinge* vision? I shivered, and the hair on the back of my neck stood on end.

"I call it *Rock Goddess*," Ryan told his sister, who

looked stunned and delighted.

"Well, you would, wouldn't you?" Aunt Elizabeth joked.

"It's very good," Nana observed, although her lips were pressed together with disapproval. Was it because of the short shorts Sarah wore in the painting, or the streak of blond in her hair? Probably both.

She wasn't going to be happy when she saw what we were wearing to the party that night.

Fortunately for both Nana and the two of us, Dad rang shortly afterwards to say he was being discharged from the hospital. My aunt bustled around, organising her keys and handbag, and Nana packed her suitcase, waving off our offers of help. Aunt Elizabeth was going to drive Nana and Dad back to his farm, and then come home afterwards. Given the length of the drive, Sarah suggested her mother stay the night at the farm, but Aunt Elizabeth gave us a long look and then shook her head. "I'd rather be in town tonight, in case you girls need me."

"We'll be fine, Mum. We're *super* responsible."

"I trust you girls, but what if you get gate-crashers at the party and need a hand? I'd rather be where you can reach me if something happens."

We were having our party at a scout hall. I privately thought gate-crashers might be an issue and was a little relieved at Aunt Elizabeth's offer—I'd heard some horror stories through the rumour mill at school, and we'd gone to great lengths to make sure the party hadn't been advertised on social media, to try and limit attendance. Sarah grumbled but agreed with her mother's logic.

After they'd left, we loaded up the last of the party decorations into Sarah's car and then drove to the hall to finish setting up.

The hall was bedecked in black and white, our theme colours. Helium balloons swayed near the open door, tethered in bunches. Streamers and party lights swooped from the ceiling. The various foods and drinks were spots of colour framed by white paper plates and black plastic cutlery. Even the tablecloths were white with black runners.

Kim and Natalie arrived as we were putting out the last of the food. Kim was wearing a gorgeous white *ao dai*: a tight-fitting silk tunic and long skirt embroidered with flowers. Her silky black hair was piled on top of her head and stabbed through with chopsticks. Natalie wore a suit and tie that, amazingly, fit her petite frame. The only hint of colour to either of them was Natalie's bright red lipstick and hint of blue eye shadow.

"Happy birthday." They greeted Sarah with enthusiastic hugs. "And happy belated birthday party," Kim added to me. "Need us to do anything?"

"We're all set up," Sarah said. "Could you hang around and let the band in when they arrive? We're going to zip home and get changed."

"I had noticed you were a little ... underdressed," Natalie remarked with a raised eyebrow, examining our dusty jeans and T-shirts with a critical eye. "Go. Hurry back."

After some consideration, we'd chosen matching outfits in reverse colours. We each wore a spaghetti-strapped top with a deep neckline and a ruffled skirt that reached the floor at the back, but at the front sat far enough above the knee I knew Dad—and Nana—wouldn't approve. Long necklaces of glass beads and matching earrings rounded out the ensemble. In Sarah's case, the top was white and the skirt and jewellery were black, and in mine it was reversed. We both wore black boots, though; neither of us was willing to spend money on white ones we probably wouldn't wear again.

"Lucky my new watch matches," Sarah admired it as I put the final touches on my makeup.

I smiled in agreement.

Ryan wasn't ready when we were, so we told him we'd meet him there and walked back, keys and phones in matching clutches. The hall was close and, now we didn't have party supplies to contend with, driving seemed like a waste of petrol.

Live music greeted us when we arrived at the scout hall; it was the same three-man band that played at the Halloween party. Sarah had befriended the mohawked guitarist and lead singer—his name was John. They were as loud as I remembered, but the volume wasn't quite as eardrum-rattling in the large hall as it was in a suburban lounge room.

A dozen guests beside Kim and Natalie had arrived, most of them people from school I hadn't seen since Dad fell ill. Sarah drifted towards the band, and I stood with Kim and Natalie, talking to others as they came up to say happy birthday and filling them in on the good news that Dad was being discharged from hospital. I also gave each person a helium balloon to tie around their wrist.

Sarah was eyeing John in a way that made me wonder whether there was something going on there. She hadn't mentioned anything, but I'd also been so preoccupied with my own troubles that she might not have. The thought gave me a pang, and I resolved to interrogate her about him the first moment we got.

Dominic arrived a few minutes later, pausing in the

doorway to let his eyes adjust to the relative dimness. I admired the view. He was dressed all in black: a cotton dress shirt with satin stripes running vertically down its length, neat slacks and polished leather shoes. When his gaze lit on mine, he smiled and hurried over, wrapping his hand around my waist. His lips touched my neck and he mumbled a breathy hello.

"You look dashing," I said, feeling my cheeks redden as Natalie and Kim nudged each other. I tied a balloon string around his wrist. A black balloon to go with his outfit, of course—the same colour as mine.

He bowed. "And you look good enough to eat." I sucked in a breath as Kim and Natalie burst into giggles. Thankfully Dominic changed the subject. "How's your dad?"

I glanced at my watch. "He should be halfway home by now."

"That's fantastic news."

"I know." I beamed.

"Did they ever find out what caused the coma?" Natalie asked.

I shook my head. It was technically true; the *doctors* had never figured it out.

Dominic pulled a card from his shirt pocket. "This is for Sarah. It's a movie voucher. I didn't know what else to get her."

"That's all right, she'll love it. Come on, let's give it to her."

Kim took the balloon strings from me with a wink. "We'll take over. Go have fun." His hand enveloped mine and we walked over to my cousin, who was dancing with a couple of other people in front of the speakers.

"Aunt Elizabeth would want me to tell you you're going to damage your ears," I shouted, leaning in close.

She poked her tongue out but moved back towards the door—where the music was loud rather than deafening—so she could say hello to Dominic.

She was halfway through opening his card when she stopped, looking towards the door with an open mouth. I turned to see who she was staring at.

Ryan entered, late as usual, dressed in black jeans and a tuxedo T-shirt. Why would Sarah care about that?

Jack followed behind him.

He was wearing a 1940s-era zoot suit: a long pinstripe black coat with wide lapels and padded shoulders over a crisp white shirt, black pinstripe trousers, and black-and-white pointy loafers. A watch chain looped from the belt to a little pocket. Pulled low on his head and covering the pointed tips of his ears was a black felt hat with a white band, a turned down brim and a pinched front crown.

"Who's the kid?" Dominic asked with a raised eyebrow. I glanced around the hall and saw incredulous looks on other people's faces too. The music hadn't quite jangled to a halt the way it would have done in a western, but the lack of conversation was uncomfortable enough.

"He's a friend of the family," Sarah said before I could think of how to respond. We should have planned our explanation earlier. Oops.

"His name's Jack," I added. "He's not as young as he looks."

"Poor guy if he's an adult already and that's as tall as he's going to get. He's your height, Isla."

"And Isla's not that tall," Sarah agreed, poking me in the ribs. "Jack's vertically challenged, that's all. We should go say hi." She took my arm and led me across the room. Dominic trailed after us.

"Glad you could come, Jack." I gave him a quick hug, conscious of all the curious gazes—especially Dominic's. Sarah gave him a hug too and whispered something in his ear.

"Sorry I am late. I would have been here sooner, but someone forgot to tell me it was black-and-white themed." He pulled a face at Sarah as though they had always known each other. She grinned back.

"Forgot?" Dominic looked incredulous. "You managed to rustle up that outfit at short notice?"

Jack glanced at me, a mischievous twinkle in his eye, and nodded. "I am very resourceful."

"No kidding." Dominic introduced himself and shook Jack's hand.

"What did you say to Jack?" I whispered to Sarah while the two guys were talking.

"To pretend we were old friends," she replied. "I thought, given I'd told your boyfriend I already knew him, he better not introduce himself to me."

"Oh. Good thinking."

"I know, right?"

A thought occurred to me. "Um, what are we going to do when people realise Ryan doesn't know him?"

"Crap," she muttered. "Let me get Ry out of here before they start talking." She hurried over to her brother, who was surveying the room for people he knew, and took his arm, leading him over to the drinks table and a couple of his mates.

And not too soon either. Kim and Natalie came over, ostensibly to give Jack his balloon, and started interrogating him with friendly smiles about where he was from, where he'd gone to school and how he knew us. He answered confidently, telling them he was from Sydney and that he'd known our family for years. Kim seemed enchanted with his bright blue eyes, golden hair and quick smile, and intrigued by his outfit. She kept touching his arm as she laughed at his jokes; her aura was a deep red.

Jealousy rose like bile in the back of my throat. I swallowed hard. Jack was neither my boyfriend nor my servant nor my possession. I had no right to feel anything when I saw him talk with girls my age.

Even if they were attractive girls.

No, especially then. My hot boyfriend stood at my side, batting my helium balloon out of his face. And Jack could look after himself.

"Let's dance." Dominic led me over to the spot by the speakers where Sarah and the others were. I threw myself into the music with a determined enthusiasm.

Sarah raised an eyebrow at me but said nothing.

I didn't keep an eye on Jack, exactly, but I couldn't help but notice he was the centre of an increasing flock of girls who were competing for his attention. Natalie and Kim were soon joined by Rebecca and Cathy, two girls who had graduated last year. Jack didn't seem uncomfortable with the attention, leaning against the scout hall's brick wall, but he did glance across at me occasionally. I couldn't read his expression, and from across the hall his emotions were lost amidst the swirl of other colours in the room.

But when a dark blond girl about the same age as us, with glasses and an upturned nose, joined them, I stopped dancing. It was Emma, the witch from the Halloween party who had conducted the séance.

"What's she doing here?" I demanded of Sarah, pulling her far enough away from the speakers that she could hear me.

"Who?" Sarah looked across the room and then shrugged. "I didn't invite her. I think she's uni friends with Cathy. She must have told her about the party."

I scowled, remembering how embarrassed and hurt I was after the Halloween party.

"Want me to ask her to leave?" Dominic offered.

I took a deep breath. Given everything I'd learned since, it was unfair of me to blame Emma for the way the séance had gone. I may not have liked what I'd heard, but that wasn't her fault. "No."

"You sure?"

"Yeah."

As though she sensed our eyes on her back—or maybe Rebecca or Kim, who were facing us, said something—Emma turned. When she met my gaze, she squared her shoulders and came across the hall, weaving her way through several groups of dancers.

"Hi, Isla," she said, looking uncomfortable. "Can I talk to you for a sec?"

"Sure."

"We'll be here if you need us," Sarah whispered in my ear before giving Emma a bright smile.

Emma led me out of the scout hall and into the evening air. The temperature dipped, offering much relief from the stuffy, still air in the hall.

"Look," she said when we were far enough away that we wouldn't be overheard—but still inside the circle of light spilling from the doorway. "I wanted to apologise for the way things went. With the séance. I heard you were upset afterwards."

"I was," I admitted, tipping my head to the side as I looked at her. Her apology seemed genuine; her aura was a charcoal grey I'd come to associate with regret.

"Anyway, I'm happy to leave if you want. I just wanted to come along and say I didn't mean to hurt your feelings."

I smiled, and she looked a little startled. "Don't worry about it. At the time I thought it was a hoax, that you did it deliberately. That's why I was mad. But I've learned some stuff since."

"Oh?" Her one word was full of curiosity.

"Well, let's say your ghosties were right. And I'm sorry too."

"Your mother...?"

I nodded and looked away for a moment, taking a breath. "Please don't be offended, but I don't want to talk about it."

"Fair enough," she said. "So we're good?"

"We're good." I hesitated before adding, "Just... Look, you might want to be careful with the séances. They can stir up all sorts of trouble."

She gave me another startled look and mumbled something about always being careful. It was pretty clear she wasn't going to heed my warning. But why would she? She didn't know what I was talking about, and I couldn't elaborate.

The loud rumble of a car engine drew our attention to the car park. A hatchback with glittering mag wheels and a too-large exhaust pipe crunched across the gravel, pulling to a stop in the middle of the lot and blocking in half a dozen other cars. Two men I didn't know got out; they were at least in their mid-twenties, tall and, judging by the way they stumbled and the odd blurring of their auras, already drunk.

"Uh oh," Emma said.

"You know them?" I murmured as the men headed towards us.

"Vaguely. Some meatheads from uni." She wrinkled her nose. "Professional gate-crashers."

"Nice balloons," one of them muttered to the other, who guffawed. My cheeks burned.

"Hey, ladies," the taller of them called. Eyes glittered in a small face dwarfed by a thick neck. "Is this a private party or can anyone join?"

"It's private." My arms wrapped my body, and I gripped my bare arms. Sarah handled confrontation better than me.

"Come on," the other, a blond, cajoled. He held up a six-pack of beer. "We brought our own drinks."

"I think you should go." I gasped with relief when Emma spoke up beside me.

They laughed loudly and with a hard edge that made my blood run cold. Emma glanced at me, a question in her eyes.

"You heard them," Jack said from behind us. "It is a private party."

I felt the change in the air. Their auras, still blurred, shifted towards an angry red. "Aww, look at the little fella in his fancy suit," said Thick Neck to his friend, cracking his knuckles. "Trying to be a big man for the ladies."

Out of the corner of my eye I saw Kim and Rebecca come out the door. Kim assessed the situation and disappeared back inside.

I hoped she was going to fetch help or at least a mobile

phone. I regretted not having a pocket for my phone; it was in my clutch, which was in a locked cupboard in the kitchen.

The pair reached the edge of the car park. They were only a couple of metres from us.

"I will not tell you again," Jack said, eyes narrowing.

The hair on the back of my neck stood up, and not because of the two drunken oafs. I didn't know what my *duinesidhe* friend was capable of. "Jack," I said, a warning in my voice.

He glanced at me and nodded.

"What are you going to do?" Thick Neck taunted.

Jack showed him.

Before any of us could react, he stepped past Emma and me, his balloon trailing behind him. He pushed Thick Neck hard enough that the taller man toppled over with a startled cry. His friend with the beer threw a punch at Jack's head. Jack ducked, grabbing the oncoming fist, and *squeezed*.

Swearing, the man swung the six-pack at Jack. The *duinesidhe* sidestepped, and the bottles crashed to the ground, three of them breaking. Glass and beer sprayed across the gravel, showering Thick Neck in fragments and amber liquid. Jack still gripped the blond's hand.

Thick Neck hauled himself to his feet, swearing when he cut his hand on a shard of glass. He launched himself at Jack.

Jack moved as fast as I'd ever seen a human move—and certainly faster than a drunk human could follow—stepping behind the blond and yanking his arm up behind him. Thick Neck barrelled straight into his friend, and the two fell to the ground in a tangle of limbs.

Jack stepped back, smiling fiercely. Freed from his

wrist by the violent commotion, Jack's helium balloon vanished up through the trees. But Jack's gaze was fixed on the two men, hands held at his sides as he waited for them to stand back up. His stance reminded me of the cat I'd seen stalking the moth in the park two days before: relaxed, focused ... and a deadly hunter. Jack's aura was violet and red, like a bloody bruise.

I had no doubt he was the most dangerous person here. My stomach swooped.

Behind us, I heard a few people cheer and a smattering of applause.

"I think it's time you left," Dominic said as the two drunks clambered to their feet. He stood beside me, putting a hand on my arm.

They looked from Jack to the growing crowd in the doorway of the hall. Thick Neck glared at Jack. "You wait, you goddamn midget. I'm gonna make you bleed."

"Promises, promises," Jack replied.

Growling and swearing, the pair strode back to their car and left with a screech of tyres. Gravel scattered in their wake.

"That was *amazing!*" Rebecca exclaimed, brushing past me and hurrying over to Jack. "Do you do martial arts?"

Jack blinked at her for a moment, like he was wondering who she was. Then he recalled himself. He nodded at her, straightening his jacket and checking that his hat was still in place.

"You must have a black belt or something," she said. "You could have really hurt them, couldn't you?"

He nodded again, looking at me solemnly.

"Thank you," I mouthed at him as Rebecca prattled on. For coming to our rescue, for not doing serious harm to the two idiots. I didn't say it aloud. I didn't need to. I knew he understood.

He nodded a third time, smiling at me. Then he gave Rebecca his full attention; she preened, and I suddenly didn't like her very much.

"Are you okay?" Dominic asked, leading me back inside.

"I am now." I told my hands to stop shaking or they'd make a liar of me. "I hope they don't come back."

"I doubt they will. That had to be pretty embarrassing."

Sarah hurried over from the dance floor; the band had stopped playing and the news of a fight was spreading through the hall like a grassfire. "What happened?"

I explained, and she pulled a face. "Lucky Jack was there."

"I only saw the end of the fight, but damn, that kid knows how to move," Dominic said, a peculiar catch in his voice. I looked at him sharply. Did the lime green pulsing in his aura denote jealousy?

"Are you okay?" I asked, before mentally kicking myself. Tactful much?

"I'm sorry that I wasn't there to..."

"Defend me?"

"I guess, yeah."

Sarah rolled her eyes. Dominic, who was facing me, didn't notice.

"Don't worry about it. Jack was near the door. It just worked out that way. It's not like you chose not to be there."

"The band's on a break," Sarah said loudly, changing the subject. I guess I wasn't the only one finding this conversation awkward. "Let's put some music on and try and get everyone back in the party mood, yeah?"

Sarah and I chose a hip-hop playlist from her music collection, and she put it on while I grabbed a drink. Dominic slinked off in the direction of the bathroom. Ryan's friends were still sitting near the drinks table, but his chair was occupied by Tyson, a computer genius from school who had thick-rimmed glasses and a prominent Adam's apple. Tyson was describing the fight, gesticulating wildly. His white balloon bobbed and swung around his head.

I watched Jack as I listened to Tyson. The hob was still near the door, talking to Rebecca, who'd been joined by Kim and Cathy. Jack nodded to whatever the girls said. The air of gleeful aggression had dissipated. He seemed harmless.

My grandmother's words sprung into my mind: fae were dangerous, not to be trusted.

Jack had never struck me as physically dangerous. Until now. It was clear—to me, at least—that he'd held himself back in the fight. He could have hurt or even killed those two idiots if he'd wanted to.

But he hadn't started the fight. And he was defending me. I couldn't help but be grateful even as it unnerved me.

"Boy, you've got it bad," Natalie remarked beside me. I jumped, whirling; I hadn't seen her approach.

"What are you talking about?" I spluttered.

"I can see the way you're looking at Jack." She took a sip of her drink. "Do you guys have a history?"

"No!" I yelped. Tyson and Ryan's friends looked over and I continued more quietly. "Not like you mean."

"You look at him like you do." Ah, Natalie. I didn't know anyone else as good at being as tactlessly blunt as she was.

"Shut up. I do not."

"If you say so," she replied. "But, if that's the case, you might want to tone it down a little when Dominic's around so he doesn't get the *wrong* idea."

I frowned, looking back at Jack. There was a history between us, sure, but not like Natalie was thinking.

Did I want there to be?

I liked Jack. I was grateful to Jack. Lord knows I owed him a lot. But I liked Dominic too. And he was the same species as me.

*You're a half-breed,* a traitorous voice whispered inside my head. *Jack's as much your species as Dominic is.*

*Oh, be quiet,* I told the voice.

"Yeah, that look? Stop it," Natalie murmured in my ear. "Here comes Dominic."

Feeling guilty, I whirled to see my boyfriend hurrying over. "Isla? Where's Sarah? Something's happened to Ryan."

# CHAPTER EIGHTEEN

Ryan was sitting on a low bench seat in the men's change room. He leaned forward, head in his hands. He was trembling.

I sat beside him. "Ryan? What's wrong?"

He didn't answer at first, and I looked up at Dominic, who hovered in the doorway. "Go find Sarah."

"I don't feel so good," Ryan murmured after a moment.

"Have you been drinking?"

"No."

"Drugs?"

He shook his head again, not looking up. His aura was a mottled, shifting pattern of greenish yellow, but it was shot through with golden flecks.

I took his wrists to move his hands away from his face. His fingertips were stained with lead from a pencil. That wasn't unusual for him, but he'd arrived with clean hands.

"Have you been drawing?" I asked, unable to keep the worry from my voice.

He looked up at the door to the toilet cubicle. "In there."

Sarah ran into the room with Dominic right behind her. I stepped back and let her take my place beside her brother, heading into the toilet cubicle with my heart in my throat.

At first I didn't see anything unusual; the walls were the same white-painted brick as the rest of the room. It wasn't till I looked behind the door that I saw Ryan's drawing. A huge monster with overly muscled arms, dressed in rags, glared at me. Its fists were clenched and it snarled, baring teeth like uneven stumps. Despite being rendered with hasty pencil strokes, it seemed real—like it could jump out of the door at any moment to throttle me with those huge hands.

And behind it, drawn in simple yet familiar lines, were several buildings I recognised. I'd grown up there, after all.

It was Dad's farm.

I rushed from the toilet, the door slamming shut behind me. "I need Jack," I gasped, pushing past the others and running out into the hall.

I barely made it a third of the way across the room before Jack noticed me; he excused himself from the conversation with Rebecca and the others and hurried over.

"What is the matter?" he asked.

"I think Ryan has drawn another true picture," I murmured, my voice tight in my throat. I wanted to yell the words at him, so strong was the sense of urgency. But there were watching eyes and curious ears all around me.

"Where?"

"On the back of the men's toilet door."

Dominic and Sarah frowned at us as we came back in; I stood near them with arms folded as Jack hurried into the toilet and, just as quickly, out again. He gave me a single, curt nod.

I ran to get my clutch and phone from the kitchen, trying Dad's mobile—no answer, which wasn't unusual as the reception at the farm wasn't good—and his house phone. I got an engaged signal. My stomach twisted.

"I have to go," I said to Sarah, wringing my hands.

"Why?" Ryan slumped at her side.

"I think Dad's in trouble." Again.

"You got that from the toilet?" Dominic's voice was incredulous.

"I know it's weird. But please, trust me."

Sarah nodded. She understood enough of what was going on to take the rest on faith. "I'll call Mum and she can come get Ryan."

I realised she intended to come with me. "You should stay with him."

"Like hell."

"It could be dangerous."

"That's why I should come," she insisted. "You're not going alone."

Jack stood forward. "No, she is not. I will look after her."

"I'll come too," Dominic said.

There was an awkward silence for a couple of heart-beats.

I glanced at Jack, who shrugged. This was up to me.

Dominic saw the exchange between us and bristled. "You didn't bring your car, Isla."

I wanted Dominic by my side. I did. His presence was reassuring; it warmed a cold place inside me. But he didn't know anything about the *duinesidhe* and, although he was fit, he wasn't a fighter. Jack was. It made my chest ache to think Dad was under some sort of attack. However, the idea of taking Dominic into a potentially deadly situation made the ache sharpen into a stabbing pain that burned the backs of my eyes and tightened my chest until I felt like I couldn't breathe.

I stepped forward and took his hands, my eyes pleading for understanding. "Can I borrow your keys?"

He looked down at me for a long moment while I wondered if my heart would break. Then he reached into his pocket and handed them to me without a word.

"Dominic, I..."

"Go."

We went.

As Jack and I left, all I could see was Natalie. She stood to one side of the scout hall door, shaking her head.

Dominic's car was a newer model than mine so, with the exception of the belt buckles, there was no exposed metal to trouble Jack on the drive to Dad's place. But tension thrummed through him as I drove, as though he was a clockwork toy that was overwound until the tiniest thing could set him off ... or break the spring. He sat with his shoulders hunched and his hands curled into balls on his thighs, and stared out the window with a fixed expression, as though he were concentrating on just breathing.

I gripped the steering wheel until my knuckles went white, and my stomach roiled with stress. Was Natalie right? Was Dominic going to take my choosing Jack's assistance over his as a fatal blow to our relationship? I hoped not, but a sick, leaden feeling in the pit of my stomach made me suspect otherwise.

So the two of us drove in silence for about twenty minutes, each of us preoccupied with our woes.

Jack relaxed minutely once we were out of Canberra and onto the winding bush roads leading to Dad's farm. Did being out of the city help him tolerate the steel better? Or maybe being that tense for that long had just worn him out.

"So what was the thing in Ryan's drawing?" Brooding over the probable imminent end to my relationship with Dominic wasn't going to get me anywhere, and I had other things to worry about.

"It is most commonly known as a *powrie*." Jack took his hat off and put it on the seat behind us, rubbing his ears as though they ached.

"A *powrie*?"

"They are also called redcaps, ogres or *dunters*. They are tall, fast and incredibly strong. But not bright. The *aosidhe* use them as enforcers. If there is one at your father's farm, it is probably working for the same *aosidhe* that sent the elf shot."

"Great," I muttered. "How do we fight one?"

"*We* do not," he corrected me. "*You* should stay in the car. The presence of this much steel should deter it from striking you."

Part of me would have liked nothing better than to stay in the car and let someone else make my problems go away—the memory of that fiercely scowling creature in the drawing turned my knees to jelly. But... "The *powrie* are enforcers and the hobs are servants, right?"

"Yes. So?"

"So although you're pretty good in a fight—" I swallowed "—this *powrie* is probably better."

"I am faster than a *powrie*," he said.

"But not stronger?"

He shook his head reluctantly. "No. Not stronger."

"Then let me help you."

"How?"

"You said it's not smart. We'll think of something." But my voice shook with uncertainty.

We stopped a couple of kilometres from Dad's farm so I could get Dominic's chrome-plated wheel wrench out of the boot. The heavy weight of it across my lap was reassuring as we turned off the road and onto the track leading to Dad's gate. When I pulled over I kept the engine running, looking around to see whether anything was approaching us.

"It's probably closer to the house," I said. "That's where Dad set up the iron all around the fence line. This far out, it would be easy for it to get in."

He nodded, scanning the moonlit paddocks with narrowed eyes.

When there were no signs of movement around the car, I got out, wrench in hand, and crept over to the gate. The bare skin of my arms and between my shoulder blades prickled with the faint hint of a breeze, leaving me feeling exposed.

I stared in consternation at the twist of iron that bound the gate to a ring in the fencepost.

Crap.

I gave the ring an exploratory poke with the wrench to see how firmly it was fixed into the post. It didn't budge. Dad had screwed it in with a typical—but in this instance inconvenient—thoroughness.

Leaning the wrench against the fencepost within arm's reach, I wrapped my hands in the long hem at the back of my skirt, took a deep breath, and began to untwist the wire.

The iron was hot at first, as if I was holding a simmering saucepan with a too-thin oven mitt. The skirt fabric tangled around my fingers made gripping it awkward. By the time the wire fell to the track at my feet, my fingertips burned. I let go of the hem with a whimper and examined my fingers in the glow of the car's headlights. They were red with inflammation.

"You should have let me do that," I jumped at the sound of Jack's voice. He was right behind me.

"Don't be silly," I replied. "Iron burns you more than me. You would've been more badly hurt than this."

I bent to pick up the wrench, but he grabbed my wrist first, lifting it towards his mouth. "At least let me heal them for you."

I was tempted—my fingers were throbbing now—but shook my head. "If there's going to be a fight, you're more likely to need your hands than I am." He scowled, and I relented a little, "You can do it afterwards. Let's make sure Dad is safe first, okay?"

He nodded reluctantly. I opened the gate and we got back in the car.

"Should I drive all the way up to the farmhouse or should we walk the last little way so we can sneak up on it?"

"Drive," Jack said. "It has probably already heard the engine by now anyway."

"Right." I put the car into gear, holding the steering

wheel gingerly. "You know, I'm going to feel like an idiot if they're both fine."

"The drawing was a true one."

"Yeah, but what if it's about something that's going to happen tomorrow, not today? I ought to train Ryan to paint every image holding a current newspaper or something."

He laughed softly.

As it turns out, they were not fine.

As we rounded the final, low hill, the headlights illuminated the silhouette of a figure. It stood in front of the farmyard gate, the black shape of the darkened house a shadow behind it. For a second I thought it was Dad, but my father was neither that tall—the creature was approaching seven feet in height—nor that bulky.

Also, even on his scruffiest days, Dad didn't wear rags the colour of blood.

The *powrie* snarled at us, shielding his—I assumed it was male, although I couldn't be sure—beady, red-hued eyes against the glare of the headlights with one hand.

Behind him, on the other side of the farmyard fence, was my father. He was holding a long piece of iron out in front of him and squinting into the headlights as well.

It gave me an idea.

"Follow my lead," I murmured, killing the engine but leaving the keys in the ignition. Silence filled the cabin, broken only by the nearby, panicked bleating of my father's sheep and the *powrie's* noisy breathing. I took a breath, flicked the headlights onto high beam and slid out of the car, concealing the wrench behind my back with one hand.

The *powrie's* aura was the same, arterial-blood red as his clothes: the colour of violence and rage. I walked around the front of the car, back ramrod straight and head high, as though I owned the place.

The way I imagined an arrogant *aosidhe* would walk.

As I came to stand between the headlights, Jack falling in beside me, I tried to fill the *powrie*'s aura with the sickly yellow of fear. I certainly had a ready supply of it available to use. But I'd never tried projecting an emotion onto someone without touching them first; it wasn't as effective as with physical contact. The emotion ate around the edges of the sea of red, curling and spreading within it like a splash of dye in a bucket of water.

The *powrie* shook his head like a dog trying to dislodge an insect from its ear.

"Get out of here," I commanded, stepping towards him. Amazingly, my voice contained no hint of the terror that clawed at my ribs, trying to escape. The breeze carried his stink towards me: rank, unwashed flesh and the iron tang of blood.

His eyes widened and he lowered his hand. There was a jagged scar along his jaw, as though someone had tried to tear out his throat and missed. "I know you." His voice was gravely and deep. "Melpomene!"

"Yes," I lied, hoping it wasn't her who had sent the *powrie*. If it were, the lie wouldn't last a second. Behind him, my father raised his head, looking hopeful. My heart ached, but I couldn't say anything to show him the truth. Not right now. "This place is under my protection. Leave now or face my wrath."

I was laying it on thick, but the *powrie* looked over his shoulder at my father and hesitated. "Can I take him?"

"No. The humans of this place are under my protection too." Gosh, he was thick. Best to be sure. "Everything is."

"Oh."

"Swear you will never return here and I will let you leave unharmed."

He hesitated. I could almost see the thoughts slogging their way through his mind. For a moment I thought my gambit might work. Hope unfurled within me.

I hadn't banked on the *powrie* not being alone.

"What are you doing?" a Scottish-accented voice demanded from off to our right. A figure walked into the headlights. It was a hob. He was slightly taller than Jack, with the same golden hair and the smooth skin that indicated he was in the service of an *aosidhe*. But his eyes had an unnerving violet tinge.

Trailing behind him was a huge black dog. It stood almost four feet tall at the shoulder and its jaws were red with blood. A tuft of fleece clung to its teeth.

The poor sheep.

"Melpomene." The *powrie* pointed at me with a shaking finger tipped with a chewed and filthy fingernail.

The hob sniffed the air, and then snorted. "You idiot. That is a human. Grab her."

The *powrie* hesitated for a moment longer. When he lumbered towards me, it was like watching an old loco-motive lurching into motion. I stepped to the side and wildly swung the wrench, but the huge fae blocked my blow with one meaty arm and grabbed my wrists, shak-ing them until I dropped my improvised weapon from limp fingers. I struggled to pull free, but my hands were caught in a vice. He transferred both my wrists to one huge hand. It encircled them without difficulty.

The ease with which he'd captured me was galling.

Jack lunged at the *powrie*, but the black dog darted

forward and knocked him back against the car. There was a sizzle as the back of his legs struck the painted metal of the bonnet, and he screamed.

"Well, what have we here?" The strange hob stalked forward. "It is the notorious Jack, and looking surprisingly healthy too, given his much-vaunted vow to never serve again. Who is your new master, Jack?"

Jack glared at him, gritting his teeth against the pain in his legs. The black dog snarled at him, bloodstained saliva dripping from its jaws.

"And who is the girl?" The strange hob peered into my face, his nose inches from my own. "She *looks* like Melpomene, but she is not." He sniffed me again, his nose pressing against my cheek. His hot breath puffed against my skin. Repulsed, I pulled my head back as far as it would go.

But it was too late. He smiled. His canine teeth were filed to points, like those of a movie vampire. "She smells of human *and aosidhe*. Could it be that the rumours are true? Did Melpomene whelp a bairn to a human male?" He laughed. "How embarrassing for her."

He turned to my father. "Is this your daughter, David Blackman?"

Dad stood beside the farmyard's fence now; he peered into the headlights, unable to see properly, but there was a sick look of realisation on his face.

Of course it was me.

The hob read his expression as easily as I did. "How charming this is." He smiled at me. "I am pleased to meet you, half-breed. What is your name?"

I didn't answer. The hob snaked his hand behind my head and grabbed a fistful of hair, pulling my head backwards. Pain knifed through my skull. "Answer me, or I will tell my friends here they can play with you for a bit. You will not like that, I assure you."

"Isla," I hissed, almost drowned out by Jack's cry of protest.

"Pretty," the hob said, stepping back and bowing. "Jack has not introduced me, but perhaps he does not know who I am. I am not as famous as him and only arrived in your country this morning. Let me remedy the situation. I am Moray."

"Who do you work for?" Jack growled from between clenched teeth.

"You will find out soon enough, Jack." Moray ran a gentle hand down the side of my face. "And so will you, Isla, child of Melpomene. My master will be interested in meeting a half-breed *aosidhe*. Especially since you are presumably the one who removed the elf shot. I was quite surprised to find your father on his feet and being troublesome."

"Let them go," Dad yelled.

Moray looked over his shoulder at my father, who paced with agitation behind the protection of the fence. "And what will you give me if I do, human?"

"You can take me instead. That's why you came, isn't it?"

Moray smirked. "Done."

"Dad," I gasped, kicking at the *powrie's* shins. He grunted and held me at arm's length. My feet barely touched the ground and my arms ached, stretched above my head.

"Swear it." Dad gripped the fencepost, his knuckles white.

"I swear to you that if you hand yourself over to us,

we will let these two go." Moray spoke carefully, and I felt a faint tremble in the air as the oath settled on him, a shimmering mantle.

Shoulders slumped with defeat, Dad dropped the iron bar into the dirt and let himself out of the farmyard gate, latching it behind him.

With quick efficiency, Moray bound my father's hands behind his back with a short length of rope. Dad winced as the rough braid cut into his wrists.

The hob nodded to his companions. "Let them go."

I stumbled when the *powrie* released me but still managed to catch Jack, who fell forward. I couldn't see his legs, but the pain in his eyes made it clear the steel had burned him badly.

"Okay, now recapture them," Moray said.

His eyes never leaving the *powrie*, Jack grabbed my wrist and pulled me down along the side of the fence.

Cursing, Dad glared at the violet-eyed hob. "You promised!"

"Do not blame me for your lack of specifics," Moray shrugged. He glowered at the other *duinesidhe*. "What are you waiting for?"

"You only pay us to capture one human. This cost extra," the *powrie* grated.

"Fine, fine," Moray said, waving his hand. "I will double the payment. Kill Jack if you must, but the girl will be valuable to my master. Now do it."

"No!" My father ran at the hob. Moray kicked his legs out from under him with a satisfied smile. Dad fell, his breath exploding from his lungs in a wheezing gasp. The hob ground his face into the dirt with his heel.

The *powrie* and the black dog charged towards us.

"Run, Isla!" Jack threw himself between me and the two onrushing creatures. They slammed into him, the dog grabbing his jacket in its teeth and attempting to pull him to the ground. I kicked it in the head; it yelped but didn't let go. The jacket fabric ripped.

The *powrie* snatched at me, catching my arm in its fist. It smiled at me with broken teeth; its breath was a sewer.

With a power born of terror, I placed my hands on its dirty skin and *shoved* my blind panic into its aura, fuelling the curling twist I had placed there earlier until it flared bright, filling the creature's heart with the panic that clutched at my own.

It released me with a terrified bellow.

And there was another cry, from within the safety of the fence.

"Oh no, you don't."

It was Nana, dressed in a floral nightgown and too-large gumboots. She bore down on Moray, who stood over Dad, leering at him.

With a pitch a cricketer would have been proud of, she threw a pebble-sized *something* at the hob.

The object flew over the fence and struck the Moray in the temple. There was a thud and a hiss as it burned through his scalp as though he was made of butter, not flesh and bone.

Moray dropped to the ground, falling on top of Dad. His aura winked out as though someone had blown out a candle.

Nana lofted another piece of iron; this one was a large nail. "He can't pay you now." She smiled grimly at our other two attackers. "Time to go."

The *powrie* was the first to flee, bolting into the night with a wordless howl. The dog hesitated a moment, calculating the odds in its head. Then it fled too, its tail between its legs.

Slowly the normal sounds of a summer evening in the bush resumed, broken only by my panting breath.

"Are you okay?" I gasped at Jack. "Did it bite you?"

"No, just my suit." He ran one hand down the front of his jacket, fingers brushing the tear

"Are you hurt though?"

"I am just burned from the car." His gaze was fixed on Nana, who stared back with open hostility.

Her aggressive pose hadn't changed.

"Stop it, Nana. He's on our side."

"So you say. But you're wrong to trust him. You don't know who he serves."

Jack took a step forward, hands held open at his sides. "I swear to you, lady, that I only serve your granddaughter." Again I felt the unnerving shimmer of an oath settling.

Nana's eyes widened and she lowered her hand. But she didn't drop the iron.

"A little help here?" Dad asked. He was still lying on the ground, Moray's body draped across him.

I hurried over, kneeling at his side. Jack limped after me, but Nana raised her hand again. "That's close enough."

He stopped.

"Isla?" Dad's voice was tight with stress from under his grim blanket. Not that I blamed him. After a moment's hesitation, I took Moray's limp shoulder in my hands and rolled him into the dirt.

The hob was dead, his eyes glazed, staring dully at

the stars. The iron sizzled inside his skull, and I swallowed against a sudden wave of nausea.

Except for the eye colour, it could have been Jack lying there.

Dad struggled to sit with his hands bound behind him. "Are you okay, pumpkin?"

"Yes." I swallowed hard. "I'm glad you're okay." I shuffled behind him to pick at the knotted rope. "Do you think they'll come back?"

Jack and my father both shook their heads. "They were probably locals, being paid by the hob on behalf of an *aosidhe*," Jack explained. "They have no reason to continue the hob's work now he cannot pay." He glanced again at Nana, who watched us with narrowed eyes.

Despite her bravado, she hadn't come out of the protection of the fenced yard.

"Did you know them? The locals?"

Jack shook his head again. "I meant local as in not recently from the Old World. They were not from the nearest *sidhe*, where I live."

"Do you know who he was working for?" Dad asked Jack, indicating Moray with a jerk of his chin.

"No. But it was the same *aosidhe* who sent the elf shot. They were expecting you to still be under its effects."

"Lucky for me Isla was there to save me." My father smiled at me. "Then and again tonight. Thank you, pumpkin."

"Jack helped," I pointed out, giving Nana a significant look. She looked abashed, finally dropping the nail into a lacy pocket.

"How did you know I needed saving?"

"I'll tell you later." I bit my lip, not wanting to explain

about Ryan in front of my grandmother. "Just try not to need saving again any time soon, okay?" He laughed rue-fully. "I tried to call you. Why didn't you answer the phone?"

"They cut the power. I was on my way out to the shed to start the generator when they started attacking the sheep. I think they were trying to draw me out."

The rope finally began to loosen beneath my worrying fingers. "We don't know who sent them, but we did learn one thing from all of this," I murmured, pulling the rope from around Dad's wrist and throwing it to the dirt. His skin was raw. "It wasn't her. My mother."

My father turned, his eyes bright with faith in, and love for, a woman I'd never met. He'd never believed for a minute Melpomene was his attacker.

It filled me with a confusion of wistful sadness, caution ... and hope.

# THE END

# ISLA'S OATH
## BOOK TWO

*Australia is a long way from the Old World and its fae denizens ... but not far enough.*

Isla is determined to understand her heritage and control her new abilities, but concealing them from those close to her proves difficult. Convincing the local fae that she isn't a threat despite her mixed blood is harder still. When the dazzling Everest arrives with a retinue of servants, Isla gets her first glimpse of why her mother's people are hated ... and feared.

But Isla isn't the only one with something to hide. Someone she trusts is concealing a dangerous secret. She must seek the truth and stop Everest from killing to get what he wants: Isla's oath.

**Read on for an excerpt of *Isla's Oath*.**

# ISLA'S OATH

"**R**eady?" Jack asked, standing beside me. He was wearing board shorts and a tank top, his feet bare on the sandy path. Blond hair stirred in the evening breeze, brushing his shoulders. He looked like any Australian male on holiday at the beach.

Except your average male didn't have long ears protruding from sun-bleached hair, each easily four inches long from scalp to tip.

"I guess." I took a deep breath, savouring the briny smell that evoked memories of summer vacations with my father. I picked my way down the path to the beach, thongs clicking against my heels as I stepped between the weathered log retainers. Jack followed. The plastic bag he was holding rustled faintly.

When we reached the beach I shook off my shoes and picked them up, hooking them over one finger. The sand was cool under my feet; the radiant heat of the hot summer day had almost faded. "Where to?"

Jack pointed towards the worn, even stones scattered at the feet of the towering headland. The water pounded, working patiently to undermine the rocky bluff and send it crashing into the sea. A deep rock pool shimmered in the moonlight, connected to the ocean by a winding channel that surged and retracted with the tide.

We picked our way across the stones to the empty pool. I glanced at Jack. "This is the place," he assured me.

I nodded, trying not to feel nervous. Jack seemed calm—his aura was a uniform light blue, like a winter sky—and I resolved to try and emulate him.

I could have taken a sample of that light blue calm to help me relax, but I didn't know how to do it without damaging him. That was why I was lurking on a south coast beach in the middle of the night in the first place.

One of the shadowy rocks in the pool moved, floating towards us. I jumped, staring. The shape drifted from the shadows into the moonlight, revealing that it wasn't a rock but a head, hairless and with tiny, round ears. Two solid black eyes opened wide, examining us for a long moment before their owner stood.

Water streamed off its—his?—naked body, splashing into the pool. His skin gleamed silvery blue and his chest was broad and flat, tapering to a narrow waist. He didn't have a bellybutton. Mercifully, the water was opaque and reached the middle of his taut belly, so I didn't have to avert my gaze from an ironclad confirmation of his sex.

"So this is your half-breed master?" The creature spoke to Jack with a watery hiss, slow and deliberate.

Jack bristled. I stepped forward. "I'm Isla."

"The half-breed *aosidhe*," the creature insisted, narrowing his eyes.

I shrugged. His tone was insulting but the words were true. My mother was an *aosidhe*, a noble faerie, and my father was a human. "If you say so."

"I do." He smiled, showing two rows of serrated white teeth, like a shark's jaw they'd shown us in science last year. What would it be like to be torn at by such a set of teeth? The worrying thought was more insistent now than it was in school, because the jaw was still attached to its owner.

The creature chortled, enjoying my reaction to his appearance. Irritation surged, making me scowl. "And you are?"

"I am Mako. A full-breed siren."

I ignored the jab. "Jack says you've agreed to teach me how to manipulate emotions."

"I agreed to talk to you," Mako corrected, waggling a fine-boned finger at me. "I need a couple of things from you before I agree to be your teacher."

"We have the meat." Jack reached into the plastic bag and pulled out a tray of pork chops. He held it up so Mako could inspect the contents.

The siren ran a blue-grey tongue over his teeth. "Oh yes. It's been a long time since I've had land-meat. Very good."

"Here." I pierced the transparent wrap with my finger and pulled a chop out, tossing it to the creature in the pool. He caught it dextrously, tearing a piece of raw flesh free and chewing it with disturbing enthusiasm. I was glad the poor light bleached the colours from the world, so I wouldn't have to see the red-brown of the blood that trickled down his chin.

"Another?" Mako asked when he finished the first chop. There were two more in the packet.

"You can have one more halfway through the lesson, and the last at the end," I said, handing the tray to Jack. I rinsed my fingers, which were faintly sticky from handling the raw meat, in a rivulet of seawater that ran past my feet.

Mako stared at me. Worry knotted in my stomach—would he refuse? But after several heartbeats he smiled that toothy smile. "Very well, half-breed. I will be your teacher. But you must swear me an oath first. That you will not harm me."

"Will you swear the same oath to me?" I asked, mindful of the speed with which he'd devoured the raw pork chop.

The siren stiffened, glaring at me with outrage. "Do you mock?"

I glanced at Jack, who shook his head. "The sirens swore an oath generations ago not to harm any living thing not born in the sea," he murmured. "He cannot harm you, even if he wishes to."

"I'm sorry," I said to Mako. "I didn't know."

This mollified him. He gazed at the tray of meat, and I felt sorry for him ... until he spoke. "We used to be able to hunt our own land-meat, but now we only get to eat it if it falls into the water, already dead."

I knew what he meant. Drowning victims. Dumped animal carcasses. I shuddered before biting my lip, steeling myself. This was the only teacher Jack had been able to find me. I had to be polite.

I recited the words Jack and I had agreed on beforehand. "I, Isla Blackman, swear not to harm you, Mako, in exchange for you teaching me how to control my ability to see and manipulate emotions."

Mako nodded, considering, his thin lips pursed. "Agreed,"

he said finally.

I felt the oath settle over the two of us, shivering against my skin as it bound me to uphold my word.

And so my lessons began.

# ACKNOWLEDGEMENTS

*F*or an occupation that is seen as a solo endeavour, writing sure involves a lot of people. If it weren't for the following, *Isla's Inheritance* wouldn't be in your hand— or on your e-reader—today.

To Peter, alpha reader and friend, thank you for your initial feedback, moral support and those invaluable brainstorming sessions. I couldn't have done it without you. To my beta readers, Mikey, Chynna-Blue and Ali, you're the best. I owe you all chocolate. To my parents, Lorraine and Fred, thank you for not trying to talk me out of studying writing at university (even though you probably should have!). And finally a big thanks to the rest of my support team: Craig, Karen, Kristy, the Aussie Owned and Read girls—especially Stacey, Lauren and Kim—and the BC09 crew.

Thank you also to the amazing Jennifer Anderson, my editor at Turquoise Morning Press. First you believed in my book enough to champion it, and then you helped me level up my writing. Thanks also to the rest of the team at TMP; I'm so grateful for the experience I gained from publishing this series through you.

The cover and internal design are brought to you by the aforementioned Kim from KILA Designs, who constantly amazes me with her talent and ability to translate my vague design ideas into something breathtaking.

And finally, thanks to all the readers and book bloggers who have supported the *Isla's Inheritance* trilogy, both back when it was at TMP and now that it is flying solo. You're basically the best thing ever. Don't you forget it.

# ABOUT THE AUTHOR

**C**assandra Page is a mother, author, editor and geek. She lives in Canberra, Australia's bush capital, with her son and two Cairn Terriers. She has a serious coffee addiction and a tattoo of a cat—which is ironic given her cat allergy. When she's not reading or writing, she engages in geekery, from Doctor Who to AD&D. Because who said you need to grow up?

www.cassandrapage.com